Saul wasn't looking forward to what he had to do,

and Olivia's uninhibited pleasure at seeing him made him feel even worse.

He waited until she had made them both a drink before starting to speak.

"Livvy, there isn't any easy way to do this," he began quietly, whilst Olivia's heart turned over at the ominous tone of his voice.

"What is it? What's happened? Caspar…" she demanded and then stopped, her face flushing as she realized from Saul's surprised expression just how wrong and revealing her reaction was.

"No. This doesn't have anything to do with Caspar," Saul said.

He took a deep breath.

"It's David…"

Dear Reader,

Penny Jordan's favorite reading is sagas, and when she became a writer, her dream was to create her own series of connected novels, following the dramatic lives and loves of one particular family across the generations. Now, with the Crightons, she has succeeded in her lifelong dream!

Nothing is as idyllic as it first appears in the privileged Crighton family home. Illicit passion, rivalry and seething ambition lie just beneath the surface of their charmed lives. Each story will draw you deeper into their fascinating world.

The saga was launched with *A Perfect Family* and continues now in *Starting Over*.

All the novels featuring the Crighton family can be read in isolation, as each tells its own compelling story, but if you wish to read the whole collection, then these are the novels to look for:

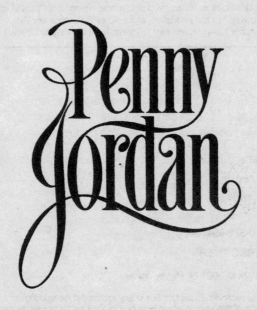

STARTING OVER

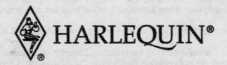

HARLEQUIN®

TORONTO • NEW YORK • LONDON
AMSTERDAM • PARIS • SYDNEY • HAMBURG
STOCKHOLM • ATHENS • TOKYO • MILAN • MADRID
PRAGUE • WARSAW • BUDAPEST • AUCKLAND

ISBN 0-373-83473-X

STARTING OVER

Copyright © 2001 by Penny Jordan.

This edition published by arrangement with Harlequin Books S.A.

® and TM are trademarks of the publisher. Trademarks indicated with ® are registered in the United States Patent and Trademark Office, the Canadian Trade Marks Office and in other countries.

Visit us at www.eHarlequin.com

Printed in U.S.A.

The Crighton Family

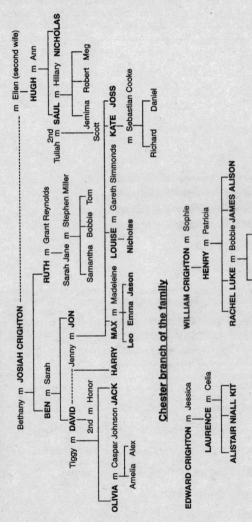

Haslewich branch of the family

Bethany m **JOSIAH CRIGHTON** ------------------- m Ellen (second wife)

BEN m Sarah — **RUTH** m Grant Reynolds — **HUGH** m Ann — **NICHOLAS**

Jenny m **JON**

Tiggy m **DAVID** ------------------ m Honor
2nd

Sarah Jane m Stephen Miller

HARRY — **MAX** m Madeleine — **LOUISE** m Gareth Simmonds

OLIVIA m Caspar Johnson **JACK**

Amelia   Alex

Leo   Emma   Jason

Samantha   Bobbie   Tom

Nicholas

Jemima   Robert   Meg

SAUL m Hillary
Scott

Tullah m 2nd

KATE   **JOSS**

m Sebastian Cooke

Richard   Daniel

Chester branch of the family

EDWARD CRIGHTON m Jessica

LAURENCE m Celia

ALISTAIR   NIALL   KIT

WILLIAM CRIGHTON m Sophie

HENRY m Patricia

RACHEL   LUKE m Bobbie   **JAMES   ALISON**

Francesca   Mark

CHAPTER ONE

'HAVE YOU ANY idea just how long it is since we last had sex?' Caspar knew the moment the words were spoken that they were the wrong ones, not just for Olivia's own mood but as an expression of what he himself was truly feeling, but it was too late to recall them. He could see that from Olivia's expression.

'Sex! Sex! Is that all you can think about?' she demanded furiously.

'We're married. We're supposed to have sex,' Caspar told her recklessly, his own anger and sense of ill-usage picking up from hers as he compounded his original folly.

'We're supposed to do an awful lot of things,' Olivia couldn't resist pointing out sharply. 'Yesterday for instance you were supposed to take the girls out to the park, but instead you went playing golf with your brother.'

'Oh, I see, so that's what all this is about is it?' Caspar challenged her. 'No sex, because yesterday I was out having a bit of R and R with my brother.'

'Your half-brother actually,' Olivia corrected him coldly.

Her heart was thudding frantically fast, trying to

push its way through her ribs, her skin. She felt sick, breathless, overwhelmed by the sheer intensity of her own emotions and the effort it was taking for her to control them.

Any minute now she would start breaking out in a sweat and then...then... But no she wasn't going to allow herself to *feel* sick never mind *be* sick; doing that brought her far too close to the shadow of her own mother and the neuroses that drove her. The perpetual cycle of binging and then purging which had dominated her life and the lives of those around her.

They had been in the States for a number of weeks, initially to attend the wedding of one of Caspar's half-brothers, but also so that Caspar could spend some time with his large and extended family and introduce his English wife and their daughters to them.

Olivia had never wanted to attend the wedding in the first place; right now she was so busy at work that taking a few days off never mind a few weeks made her feel sick with anxiety, and she and Caspar had quarreled bitterly over her refusal.

The fact that she had at the very last minute changed her mind, was not out of a desire to please Caspar, but because of her point-blank refusal to join the rest of her family in welcoming her father, David, back to his home town. Her total boycott of the family celebration, not just of his return, but also of his marriage to Honor, had caused the existing rift between Caspar and herself to deepen into a very dangerous hostile resentment.

Why had she ever deceived herself into thinking that Caspar was different, she asked herself bitterly now. That he would put her first? He was just like all the others, just like everyone else in her life. Oh, they might pretend they loved her; that she mattered to them, but the truth was…the truth was…

She closed her eyes shivering despite the warmth of their hotel room. The pressure inside her skull increased as she fought not to remember the expression in her uncle Jon's eyes when he had talked about his twin brother…*her* father… How could he possibly still love him like that after what her father had done?

Some days ago Jon had telephoned her urging her to return home so that she could attend the party being thrown at Fitzburgh Place to celebrate her father's marriage to Lord Astlegh's cousin Honor, but Olivia had refused.

Olivia couldn't explain to herself or even begin to unravel the complex twisting and contorting of emotions which were causing the increasingly hard to control surges of panic she was experiencing. The knife-sharp fear. The horrifying sense of dislocation, of distance from the rest of the human race.

Caspar was getting out of the bed now, his face tight with anger. Had she really once believed she loved him? It seemed extraordinary to her that she could have done. Blank numbness filled her now whenever she tried to recall the feelings she had once had.

'Danny has invited us to join his family at the cabin in Colorado. We can ski and—'

'No,' Olivia refused without allowing Caspar to finish.

As she watched her husband Olivia was filled with a sense of despair and hopelessness. The love which had once tied them together and created their two daughters had gone. They were strangers to one another now. So much strangers that Caspar couldn't even seem to appreciate the kind of back-log of work she was going to have to face once they returned, as it was.

The tension in her head reached a screaming crescendo. All her life she had had to fight against the opposition of her grandfather to her desire to follow in the family tradition and qualify as a solicitor. How he would enjoy crowing over her now if she failed.

'I have to go home. My work...'

'Your *work*. What about our *marriage?*'

Their marriage. Distantly Olivia looked at him.

'We don't have a marriage any more, Caspar,' she told him. The sense of relief that filled her as she spoke was so intoxicating that it was almost as heady as drinking champagne. She could feel her spirits lightening, the tension leaving her body.

'What...what the hell are you *saying?*' she could hear Caspar demanding but she was already turning away from him, her decision made.

'I think we should separate,' she heard herself telling him.

'Separate...?'

She discovered she was holding her breath as she

detected the shock in his voice as though she were waiting...but waiting for what?

'Yes,' she continued calmly. 'We will have to do everything properly, of course...legally...'

'Of course that *would* be the first thing *you* would think about—as a Crighton,' Caspar told her bitterly.

Olivia looked away from him.

'You've always resented that, haven't you?' she demanded quietly.

'What I've resented, Livvy, is the fact that this marriage of ours has never contained just the two of us.'

'You wanted children as much as I did,' Olivia retorted, stung by the unfairness of his accusation.

'It isn't the girls I'm talking about,' Caspar snapped. 'It's your damned family. You're like a little girl, Livvy, living in the past, clinging to it.'

'That's not true.' Her face had gone paper-white. 'Who's the one who's supported us...who's—'

'I'm tired of having to carry the can for other people's imagined sins against you, Livvy. I'm tired of being held responsible for them just because I'm a man like your father and your grandfather and Max. I'm tired of having to carry all that emotional baggage you insist on dragging around...that ''I'm a victim'' attitude of yours.'

'How dare you say that?'

'I dare because it's true,' Caspar told her coldly. 'But as of now I'm through with playing surrogate grandfather, father and cousin to you, Livvy...and I'm sure as hell tired of playing surrogate punch ball. It's time *I* got a little something out of life, wrote that book I've been promising myself, got that Harley and rode around this country…chilled out and lived…'

Olivia stared at him as though he were a stranger. This wasn't the Caspar she thought she had known so well, this selfish insensitive stranger with his adolescent fantasies and his total lack of regard for the needs of either his children or her.

'I can't imagine why I ever thought I loved you, Caspar,' she told him, her throat raw. 'Or why I married you,' she added as she wondered if he could hear the sound of her dreams, her ideals, her love, splintering around them into a million tiny painful shards.

'No? Then you've got one hell of a short memory. You married me because you wanted to escape from your childhood,' Caspar told her.

Her childhood. As he strode out of the room Olivia closed her eyes, her body tight with tension.

There was a bitter taste in her mouth. She had never really *had* a childhood. Sometimes she felt she had almost been born knowing that she wasn't the child—the son—her father, and more importantly her grandfather, had wanted.

Because of them Olivia had grown up determined to prove herself, to prove her worth…her value. Because of them she had pushed herself these last months to meet self-imposed work targets that increasingly made her feel as though she were walking a tightrope stretched across a sickeningly deep chasm. All it would take to send her crashing down would be one wrong step…one missed breath…but she had had to do it. Not just for her own sake but even more importantly for her daughters. There was no way she was going to have *them* growing up under the burden, the taint of being her father's grandchildren. Ever since David had disappeared and the truth about him had come to light, Olivia had been haunted by what he had done, haunted by it…shamed by it…tormented by it.

And now he was back and instead of being shunned as he rightly deserved he was being feted, lauded, whilst *she*…

The pain inside her head intensified and with it her panic and despair.

She would be better once she was back home she promised herself, once she was back at work. Back in control….

CHAPTER TWO

HASLEWICH.

Sara Lanyon *still* didn't know what she was doing here. She had certainly not intended to turn off the motorway *en route* home to Brighton from her visit to her old university friend, so some unknown power must surely be responsible for her being here.

Haslewich…Crighton land…

Crighton land. Her mouth with its deliciously full upper lip curled into a line of angry contempt.

She had heard all about the Crightons from her step-grandmamma, poor Tania.

She had been so very damaged and fragile when her grandfather had rescued her, gently building up her confidence and her life for her.

'There are always two sides to a situation like this, Sara,' her father had cautioned her when once she had exploded with anger against the Crightons for what they had done to Tania.

'But, Dad, she's so vulnerable, so helpless…there can't be *any* excuse for the way they abandoned her. It was heartless…cruel….'

Her dark-green eyes had filled with tears and her father had shaken his head ruefully.

She had been eighteen at the time then and perhaps a little inclined to judge everything in black or white. She was older now and more able to apply a little of Richard Lanyon's admirable dispassion to her judgements, but deep down inside she still was reluctant to give up her antipathy towards the Crightons. Overemotional of her—illogical. She shook her head. No, they were plainly an insensitive brutish lot, motivated only by preserving their own interests and sticking together in a clannish fashion.

'The Crightons practically *are* Haslewich,' Tania had once told her in her soft pretty girlish voice. 'Locally everyone admires them and looks up to them, but...' She had stopped and shivered. 'They used to make me feel so...so intimidated and...and unwanted. Even my own children...'

As her eyes had filled with tears so had Sara's and now, here she was, her car parked just off the town's main square as she walked curiously across it.

It was almost lunch time and she was hungry—very hungry. She looked uncertainly round the square and then decided to investigate the possibility of a narrow, interesting-looking lane that ran off it.

A signpost at the top of the street read To the River.

The river. Sara loved water. Her father was a keen sailor and Sara had crewed for him as a girl.

She was halfway down the street when she saw the restaurant. A quick glance inside showed that it was busy and the smells wafting from the kitchen were certainly enticing.

Making up her mind Sara pushed open the door and then stopped in bemusement as a harassed-looking middle-aged woman pounced on her asking anxiously, 'Sara...?'

'Er, yes,' she replied automatically, frantically wondering how on earth the woman could possibly know her.

'Oh, thank goodness for that,' the older woman exclaimed. 'The agency have let us down so many times but they promised me this time... It's this way,' she added beckoning to Sara to follow her as she wound her way through the busy tables.

Feeling rather as though she had stepped straight into a page from *Alice Through the Looking Glass,* Sara followed in her wake.

Once they had reached the rear of the restaurant the woman pushed open the door telling Sara as she indicated for her to precede her into the room it led into, 'I must apologise for the mess. We've been so hectic. I've tried to keep up to date with the paperwork, but it just hasn't been possible. Still, now that you're here... Oh, and the computer's working again, thank goodness. I think the news that we'd got our Michelin threw it into as much of a state of excitement as it did us. Of course, now we're being inundated with requests for tables which is marvellous. Or at least it would be if we weren't committed for the next three Saturdays to weddings. Not that we don't want them, we do...but...' As she paused for breath Sara looked round the small cluttered office.

Rather oddly it had French windows that gave onto an attractive little town garden and when the woman saw her looking at it she smiled.

'We only moved into these premises a little while ago. It was originally a café and we bought the house next door. The office was the house's back parlour and we decided we'd leave the French windows....'

'It's very pretty.' Sara smiled.

'Well, yes, and hopefully next summer we shall be able to make better use of it. I'm Frances Sorter, by the way,' she introduced herself. 'I expect the agency will have told you that my husband and I own the restaurant. Our chef is so keen on organic produce my husband grows as much as he can himself.

'Now, I don't know whether or not the agency discussed terms with you.'

'Er, no, they haven't,' Sara replied truthfully.

Now was the time to tell Frances Sorter that there had been a mistake and that she wasn't the person the woman thought she was but for some reason Sara discovered instead that she was actually listening whilst she was told the surprisingly generous terms of her 'employment.'

'It will only be for a few months, of course,' she was told a shade anxiously. 'You do know that, don't you? Only Mary, our regular office manageress, is having a baby and she says she will want to come back, but...'

A few months... Sara started to frown. She had decided to move on from the school where she had been

working as a supply teacher at the end of the previous
school year. She had several options she was consid-
ering, including working abroad and her father had
even suggested she could have her old university holiday job back with him working as his assistant if she
wished. There was really no earthly reason why she
should want to come and work here in 'Crightonville.'
In fact, there was every reason why she shouldn't. So
why was she nodding her head and assuring Frances
Sorter that yes, the salary they were paying was fine?

She had always been inclined to be impulsive, a trait
which had got her into plenty of trouble as a girl but
even she was surprised to hear herself accepting the
job whilst saying, 'There's one problem though.
I…er…don't actually have anywhere to live locally as
yet and—'

'Oh, *that's* no problem.' Frances Sorter beamed.
'There's a flat upstairs that you could have rent free.
In fact, if you did you would be solving another of
our problems. The insurance company are insisting
that the flat is tenanted. Apparently they consider that
an empty property is more at risk from thieves and
vandals. It's only small but the previous owners had
it completely refurbished since they lived "over the
shop" and, well, let me take you up and you can see
for yourself.'

Well, Sara reflected ruefully half an hour after she
said goodbye to Frances. This morning as she left her
friend the last thing on her mind had been coming to
Haslewich, never mind accepting a job here, and yet

here she was... Sara was a firm believer in fate and in taking the kind of chances other people more cautious and less imaginative would give very wary distance to. Life was an adventure—or at least it should be. Her eyes began to sparkle. Who knew, she might even get the opportunity to even the score a bit for her sweet vulnerable little stepgrandmamma and put some of those powerful lordly Crightons in their place. Now *that* was a challenge she would accept with relish!

NICK CRIGHTON stifled a small sigh. It had been very kind of his brother Saul and his wife Tullah to offer him a room in their home to recuperate in following the injuries he had sustained whilst visiting one of his clients who was incarcerated in a Thai jail.

Another inmate had attacked Nick's client in a drug-crazed frenzy and when Nick had gone to help him, he had ended up being knifed.

Luckily the knife had missed all his major internal organs, even if his recovery was taking longer than expected thanks to an infection that had developed in the site of the wound. That had cleared up now but he had been told by his doctor to take things easy until the wound had completely healed.

Yes, it was kind of Saul and Tullah to insist that he stay with them, but the truth was that he was beginning to get rather bored by all the cosseting he was receiving.

He was a grown man, after all, a man used to spending his spare time on the outdoor pursuits he enjoyed:

rock climbing and sailing, white water rafting...
anything with just that little touch of exhilaration and
excitement about it—not that he ever took foolhardy
or dangerous risks.... Well, not often!

The last time he had had a medical check-up he had
tried to persuade his doctor that he was well enough
to return to work. After all, as a lawyer he was hardly
likely to be overtaxing himself physically he had suggested slyly to his GP.

'Mmm...I take your point,' the other man had
agreed. 'Sitting at an office desk or even standing in
court certainly aren't going to do you too much harm
now that the wound has actually started to heal....'

'Great! So I can go back to work then?' he had
pounced eagerly.

'Don't be so ridiculous, Nick,' the doctor had refused affably. 'You *may* be a lawyer but I happen to
know that your job is very much a hands-on affair.
You run a business that involves taking the kinds of
risks that no sane man with a healthy respect for his
own physical safety would ever take.'

Nick had shrugged, knowing that there was nothing
he could say. His work as a negotiator for people
caught up in the legal systems of other countries often
took him into situations that were physically dangerous. It hadn't been unknown for him when dealing
with a particularly corrupt government to bribe his
'client' out of gaol and then have to make a quick and
sometimes dangerous getaway over the border with
him or her.

As a newly qualified solicitor he had volunteered to help the parents of a university friend to make an application to a far Eastern government for their daughter to be released from prison where she was being held on drug smuggling charges.

After he had successfully won the case he had been besieged by other parents requesting his help with similar cases.

It appalled Nick that even now when surely the most naive of travellers must be aware of the dangers, young people, especially young girls, fell into the trap of allowing themselves to be used—sometimes knowingly but more often than not as mules—by drug traffickers.

He did other work, of course, as a locum which allowed him plenty of time to travel. Work to Nick was a means to an end, not an end in itself.

'I've booked us a table at the Sorters' new restaurant for tonight,' Tullah had announced this morning over breakfast. 'They've got their Michelin now and I must say I'm looking forward to sampling their latest menu. You'll enjoy it, Nick.'

Well, yes, he would enjoy it, but...but what he was hankering after right now was something a little bit more adventurous than domesticity of the type enjoyed by his brother Saul and his wife and family. It was all very well...all very cosy, but it was not for him...not yet. This mating, nesting instinct that seemed to have affected so many members of his generation of Crighton males was not one he shared. Not that he was against commitment or marriage per se…he wasn't; he just didn't want it for himself—not now—not ever! He valued and needed his freedom far too much.

'DO YOU THINK he'll like it?' David asked his wife as they stood arm in arm studying the just finished small suite of rooms they had had converted from a loft over what had once been stables but which were now a garage.

'He'll love it,' Honor assured him with a smile, her breath racing in her lungs as he turned to kiss her.

'You two!' the elder of her daughters from her first marriage had complained the last time she had visited them. 'I've never known a couple so besotted with one another.'

'Mmm—are you besotted with me?' David had asked her whimsically after Abigail had gone back to London.

'Certainly not,' Honor had denied sternly, her voice softening as she added, 'Only just totally crazily head over heels in love with you—that's all!'

'I wonder when he's going to arrive?'

They had been married a few short weeks ago and had known one another less than a year but Honor had never for one moment doubted that she was doing the right thing. She knew the story of David's past with its shadows and secrets, its shame, and she knew too of his glorious resurrection, his rebirth from the shell of his own past. Now she was looking forward to welcoming into their home the man who had played such a large part in that rebirth—Father Ignatius—the Irish priest turned missionary who was presently in Ireland on a visit. David and Honor were pleased that they had managed to persuade him to leave Jamaica and make his home permanently with them.

'He's due to fly to Manchester from Dublin tomorrow,' David said with concern. 'I wanted to meet him off the plane but he wouldn't let me. He said there were things he had to do.'

'Yes, I know,' Honor agreed patiently as though she hadn't heard all of this a dozen or more times already.

'And then he said that he wanted to make his own way here and not have me drive over to Dublin to collect him.'

Honor smiled soothingly again.

'I just hope he's going to be happy here with us.'

'He will be,' Honor told him positively, adding softly as she leaned close to him, 'It's you he's coming here for, David…you he wants to be with….'

Honor had met the priest briefly when she and David had married in Jamaica and she had discovered that he was everything David had told her he was and more. They shared an understanding, a belief in the dignity of nature and a respect for the world.

A rueful smile lit David's eyes and he laughed. 'All right, so I'm fussing,' he agreed.

There were still days when he had to pinch himself to make sure that he was really awake and not merely dreaming. It humbled him unbearably to reflect on how lucky he was—and how undeserving. He had said as much to Jon, but his brother had shaken his head in denial of his claim.

David had been given so many precious gifts in this fifth decade of his life. His friendship with the priest. The love he shared with Honor, his acceptance back into the hearts and lives of his family. David's eyes became slightly shadowed because, of course, there was one member of his family who had *not* accepted him back, Olivia, his daughter. She had every reason not to do so. David understood that. He had not been a good father to her and she had been forced at a very young age to take charge not just of her own life but those of her younger brother and their mother as well. When you allied to that his own father's dismissive attitude towards her whilst Jon's son Max was praised, it was no wonder that she should feel so hostile towards the father who had failed to take her part.

But the pain he felt at their continued estrangement was not just for himself, it was for her as well. He was a different David from the one who had simply walked out of his old life because he wasn't able to face up to what he had done. Now he knew and understood the power negative emotions had to hurt their owner even more than those they were directed against. And Olivia was hurting—David knew that.

'Give her time,' Jon had counselled him.

There was David's son as well, but Jack had had the benefit of getting the parenting from Jon and Jenny that David and his ex-wife Tania had not been there to give him. Jack, unlike Olivia, was secure in himself…happy in himself. Jack might watch him with a certain wariness…waiting, judging…but there was none of the fury or the fear in Jack's reaction to his return that there had been in Olivia's.

Her point-blank refusal to see him or speak to him was perhaps understandable. Her father's return had come as a shock to her—he knew that and he knew, too, that he had hardly given her any reason to either love or respect him; but he had hoped that she would mellow a little towards him and at least attend the wedding party he and Honor had given at Fitzburgh Place. He was desperate to make some kind of reparation to her, to talk to her, to explain…apologise.

He had no right to expect her love; he acknowledged that. But it was her pain that made him hurt more than his own…her pain, his blame.

Every time he looked at Max and saw what Jon's son had become he reminded himself that Max had the very best parents any child could possibly have had, just as whenever he thought of Olivia he knew that she had not and that he and his selfishness were to blame for that.

As Honor saw the sadness in his eyes she guessed what had put it there—Olivia… She couldn't imagine how she would feel if one of her daughters were to reject her…to feel so hurt by her and detached from her that they refused to let her into their lives; or rather she could, and it was so untenable that it made her shiver.

Honor was a good listener and she had heard a lot

about Olivia from other members of the family, not because they had gossiped about her or criticised her. No, the Crightons if they were nothing else, were fiercely loyal to each other. No. What she had learned was how very concerned in their different ways all her relatives were for her.

'She was so happy when she and Caspar married,' Jenny had said. 'And when the girls arrived...'

And her inference had been that the happiness had gone.

'She works too hard,' someone else had said and there had been other comments, all made with loving anxious concern which Honor had correctly interpreted as meaning that Olivia's life was shadowed and unhappy.

'Sometimes she seems almost...afraid to let herself relax and have fun....' had been the most telling statement of all made by Tullah, Saul's wife, her magnificent eyes darkening as she spoke. There had been, Honor guessed, enough damage done to Olivia as a child for her to feel a need to take refuge in controlling and pushing herself to reach self-imposed targets. And to have a very fragile sense of self worth.

Leaning over to nibble on David's ear Honor whispered enticingly, 'Let's go to bed.'

'What!' David pretended to be shocked. 'It's still afternoon....'

'Mmm...siesta time.' Honor smiled seductively.

Arm in arm they made their way across the gravelled space that separated the house proper from the outbuildings.

Honor was looking forward to the arrival of David's old friend and mentor and as she walked past the lavender she paused to brush her free hand against its leaves and breathed in the scent she had released.

It was her plan to grow a wide variety of herbs here and to make her own herbals and potions from them.

Olivia reminded her a little of her lavender... outwardly sturdy and tough but inwardly so sensitive that the merest touch could bruise and damage.

CHAPTER THREE

BOBBIE, Luke Crighton's wife, was the first member of the family to hear Olivia's news. She had called at the house knowing that Olivia, Caspar and the girls would have arrived home, eager to learn all about their trip and to see if there was any shopping she could get for Olivia whilst she did her own.

'Mummy's upstairs,' Amelia informed Bobbie as she knocked on the open kitchen door and then walked in.

'Yes, she's packing Daddy's things,' Alex added innocently.

'Dad's staying in Philly...in America....' Amelia supplied and both of them stood and looked at her with such grave-eyed sadness that Bobbie ached to sweep them up into her arms and hold them tight.

'Olivia,' she called out from the bottom of the stairs, 'It's me—Bobbie. Can I come up?'

When Olivia appeared on the landing Bobbie saw from her expression that she hadn't been able to conceal the shock the sight of Olivia had caused her. She had lost weight and her skin looked grey, lifeless, like her eyes. She looked...she looked...Bobbie swallowed painfully. Now it was *Olivia* herself she wanted to hold and comfort.

'The girls have told you, have they?' Olivia guessed tiredly.

'They said something about Caspar staying on in Philadelphia,' Bobbie agreed awkwardly.

'You'd better come up,' Olivia said. 'Caspar and I are separating,' she informed her when Bobbie got to the top of the stairs. 'It's for the best, for *all* of us. Things haven't been good between us for a long time and...he isn't the man I married, Bobbie...and I...' Olivia's voice thickened and Bobbie could see the tears standing out in her eyes as sharp as broken glass.

'No,' Olivia denied as Bobbie reached out towards her. 'No. Don't sympathise with me...I don't need it...I'm not sorry. I'm glad. Our marriage just wasn't working,' she told the other woman tensely. 'I think once he got over his initial shock of hearing that I wanted to end it, Caspar was actually relieved.'

As she heard the pain in her own voice Olivia started to frown. Why *should* she feel pain? She didn't love Caspar any more. It was a relief not to have him standing at her shoulder complaining that she spent far too much time at work and far too little with him and the girls. It was a relief, too, to only have her relationship with them to worry about. Now that her father had come back people would be watching her even more closely, waiting to see her fail...fall...

'I know sometimes things happen between a couple

that can seem to be very aggravating, small issues really but like a stone in a shoe they can—' Bobbie was saying quietly.

'*Small* issues?' Olivia interrupted her with a bitter laugh. 'This isn't about *small* issues, Bobbie. The last time Caspar and I had sex was months ago....'

For a moment Bobbie thought that Olivia was complaining that Caspar would not have sex with *her* but then when Olivia continued angrily, 'I just didn't...I just couldn't...' Bobbie realised her mistake.

'Caspar seemed to think I was just being bloody minded...just withholding myself from him to score points. That's how far apart we've grown,' Olivia burst out. She had started to tremble visibly, her hands moving in quick agitation. 'We had the most awful rows about it. It was so destructive and damaging for the girls. I tried but Caspar...'

'Did you think of trying counselling?' Bobbie asked her softly.

Olivia's pain and despair were almost a visible physical presence in the room with them. She was normally such a calm, contained sort of person, so controlled that Bobbie was shocked by the change in her.

'Counselling!' Olivia gave a mirthless bitter laugh. 'You mean like my *mother* ought to have had? I'm sorry,' she apologised to Bobbie. 'I know...' She stopped speaking, pressing her hand against her mouth as though she were trying to silence herself, Bobbie recognised compassionately.

'It's too late for that now,' Olivia told her. 'Our marriage is over.'

'What will Caspar do?' Bobbie asked her.

'He's taking a sabbatical. He's had it approved by the university that he can take time out from lecturing. He says he's going to ride around America on a bike, a Harley-Davidson,' Olivia told her derisively. 'It's something he's wanted to do since he was a boy.'

To her own shock she suddenly discovered that she was crying without knowing why.

'Oh, Livvy, Livvy,' she heard Bobbie saying emotionally; but as Bobbie stepped towards her holding out her arms, Olivia backed away shaking her head.

There was so much she needed to do, so many arrangements she needed to make. She wanted to be in her office before eight when she started work on Monday. That would give her an extra hour to start going through the post that would be waiting for her and then, if she brought the rest of it home with her on Monday night, she could read it whilst the girls were in bed. At least now that she didn't have Caspar to consider she would have more time in the evenings to work.

'SOMETHING'S WRONG,' Bobbie told Luke that evening after she had broken the news about Olivia to him.

'Of course something's wrong,' he agreed dryly. 'She's left Caspar.'

'No, I mean apart from that…something's wrong *with* Livvy,' Bobbie persisted. 'She was…different somehow….'

'She's upset. That's only natural.'

Bobbie sighed under her breath. Much as she loved her husband there were times when they just weren't on the same wavelength. Another woman would have understood immediately what she meant.

'I wonder if Jenny knows yet?' Bobbie said. 'She must do, surely. She and Olivia have always been so close.'

Jenny was Jon's wife and she had acted as surrogate mother for Olivia through all her difficult childhood. Olivia was now a partner in the family legal practice of which Jon was the head.

Quickly Bobbie reached for the phone and dialled Jenny's number.

'What is it? What's wrong?' Jon asked Jenny when she walked into the study looking worried.

'Bobbie's just been on the phone. She went over to see Livvy this afternoon. *I* would have gone myself but I had a Mums and Babes committee meeting. Livvy and Caspar have separated. Livvy's come home without him.'

'What!'

Jon's reaction mirrored Jenny's own shock. He started to shake his head.

'I thought they were so happy.'

'They were,' Jenny agreed, 'until David came

home....' Try as she might she could not keep the accusatory note out of her voice.

She could see from Jon's face that her words had upset him and she knew, too, that they were unjustified and unfair but she couldn't make herself call them back.

Jon had changed since his brother's return. He seemed almost to live, breathe and think *David* these days. So much so that *she* felt that she was being shut out, excluded almost from his life, which was ridiculous, of course. They had been married for over thirty years and these last years of their marriage had brought them very close, brought a new depth to their marriage...their love.... These last years...the years without David.

But now David was back and Jon wasn't exclusively hers any longer. It was David this and David that. Jenny could see his love for his brother in his eyes, hear it in his voice, every time he spoke his name.

'David isn't responsible for the breakdown of Livvy's marriage. He can't possibly be,' Jon objected.

'Maybe not,' Jenny was forced to concede. 'But he *is* responsible for what Livvy is, Jon...you've said so yourself often enough.'

'Livvy didn't have a very happy childhood,' Jon agreed. 'But that wasn't just down to David....'

Jenny gave a small impatient sigh.

'Before David came home you said yourself that

you were concerned about her, that you felt she was working too hard.'

'Yes. She was…is,' Jon acknowledged.

It had disturbed him to discover in her absence just how much extra work Olivia had taken on and quite unnecessarily. Had she said that she needed help, Jon would have seen to it she got some. But she had insisted that she did not, becoming almost angrily defensive. With that kind of workload it was no wonder her marriage was under stress. The locum he had hired to cover the period she was away had not come anywhere near being able to cope and Jon had had to take on some of the extra workload himself and share the rest between Tullah who worked part-time and his daughter Katie who was also part of the family practice.

As Jenny walked past the back of his head without bothering to stop and kiss the top of it as she normally did he hesitated, wanting to reach for her but before he could do so she had gone.

Since David had come back Jon was so involved with him that he hardly seemed to notice she existed, Jenny reflected crossly as he let her walk out of the study without sliding his arm around her waist to give her his usual hug.

She knew how much he loved his elder brother. Did he perhaps envy him a little as well? Did he compare their own staid comfortable marriage with the excitement of David's obviously passionate relationship with his new wife Honor? Honor who was so much more glamorous and exciting than she was herself.

Stop that, Jenny warned herself as she walked into the kitchen. She might have felt inferior to David's first wife, nicknamed Tiggy, the glamorous model, but there was no way she was going to allow history to repeat itself.

The large kitchen seemed so empty now that their family had virtually all grown up.

Of their four children only Joss, the youngest, still lived at home, although soon he would be following Jack to university.

Of course Maddy and the children, her grandchildren, were regular visitors—there was scarcely a day when she didn't see them, but...

Empty nest syndrome they called it, didn't they, when a woman began to suffer the pangs of missing her grown-up children.

Firmly Jenny reminded herself of how fortunate she was—unlike her niece-in-law.

Poor Livvy. Jenny's heart ached for her.

'MADDY. Are you all right?' Max queried anxiously as he caught her indrawn breath and saw the way her hand lifted to the pregnant mound of her belly.

'It's nothing,' Maddy assured him. 'I just felt a bit nauseous.'

'Come and sit down,' Max instructed her, shaking his head when she insisted that she was all right.

This fourth pregnancy which they had both greeted
with such joy was tiring her far more than Max remembered the previous three doing and he cursed himself for allowing her to become pregnant again when
she already had three children to look after plus his
elderly grandfather.

He would have a quiet word with his mother and
ask her to keep an eye on Maddy for him, make sure
she wasn't overdoing things.

'Livvy was due home today,' Maddy commented.
The sickness had subsided now, thank goodness. The
last thing she wanted was for Max to start worrying,
fussing.

'I know they've only been away for a matter of
weeks but so much has happened that it feels as
though it's been much longer,' Maddy continued.

'Mmm…'

'I wonder how she's going to cope with having her
father back? Honor says that David is desperate to heal
the breach between them but that he feels he owes it
to Livvy not to force anything on her.'

'Give it time,' Max counselled her. 'David's return
has been a shock for all of us but especially so for
Olivia.'

Maddy was just about to remark that her concern
for Olivia, his cousin, wasn't limited to her troubled
relationship with her father. She was also uncomfortably aware of the sentiments and grievances about his
marriage that Caspar had once revealed to her—but

just as she was about to speak a fresh sickening wave of nausea struck her.

It was probably nothing, she assured herself. She was due to visit the antenatal clinic—an overdue visit, in fact, since she had had to miss her last appointment because Ben had not been feeling well. Her swollen ankles and the fact that she felt so nauseous and tired were nothing to worry about. Why should they be? She had not experienced any problems with her other three pregnancies.

'YOU'VE DONE *WHAT?*' Sara's father laughed as she held the telephone receiver closer to her ear and explained to him just what had happened.

'...and you'll never guess what,' she continued. 'Some of the Crighton clan are booked in for dinner tonight so I shall get a first-hand view of the "enemy."'

'I've told you before, you've only heard one side of the story,' her father reminded her forthrightly.

'I don't care. If only half what Grandmamma Tania has told me is true then they treated her abominably.'

On the other end of the telephone line Richard Lanyon suppressed a rueful sigh. His daughter was very much inclined to champion lost causes and underdogs and he just hoped that life wouldn't strip her of too many of her ideals and illusions.

Privately he considered his father's second wife to be an almost naively childlike but totally selfish woman. His father adored her and protected her but he sometimes found her irritating and exasperating.

'Well, I'd caution you against trying to slay too many dragons,' he warned Sara drolly now.

'I won't,' she agreed. 'But it's time someone took the Crightons down a peg or two. Enjoy your holiday,' she added warmly.

Her father was an architect and he and her mother owned a villa on a luxury complex in the Caribbean which he had helped to design. Sara knew she could have gone with them and enjoyed a long holiday at their expense but she had too much pride and independence to do so. She had chosen teaching as her career because she wanted to help others and in her book the gift of education was one of the most precious that could be given; but the realities of modern day teaching were eroding her ideals and dreams.

Now, she was dauntingly aware that she was having second thoughts about her professional future. A short spell of working here in Haslewich would give her time to think through her options—as well as taking up cudgels on behalf of Grandmamma Tania?

Sara wasn't going to deny that she felt that the Crightons had treated Tania badly despite what her father had said.

Having put away her few belongings in the pleasant accommodation Frances Sorter had shown her, Sara made her way back to the restaurant where Frances greeted her arrival with a warm smile.

'We wouldn't normally expect you to work in the evening,' Frances told her, 'but if you *were* prepared to make a start now...'

'I'd be glad to,' Sara told her and meant it, grimacing as her stomach suddenly gave an embarrassingly loud rumble.

'Oh, good heavens, you must be starving,' Frances exclaimed. 'Normally staff meals are eaten when we've finished serving but I can arrange for something to be sent into the office for you.'

'A sandwich would be fine,' Sara told her.

'A *sandwich!*' Frances looked horrified. 'This is an award-winning restaurant,' she told Sara mock primly, an amused smile tugging at the corners of her mouth. 'How do you feel about chargrilled vegetables and wild salmon?'

'I'm in love with it already,' Sara told her solemnly, her eyes full of laughter. She was going to enjoy working here. Frances had a good sense of humour even if she was slightly frazzled at the moment.

Nearly an hour later Sara grimaced as she took her eyes off the computer screen to take a final mouthful of the delicious meal she had been served. She had become so engrossed in what she was doing her food had gone cold—not that she was still hungry! The more than generous portion she had been served would easily have satisfied two people.

She frowned as the computer refused to give her the information she needed to complete the task she was working on. She would need to have a word with Frances about this.

Getting up she opened the office door and walked down the short corridor that separated it from the restaurant, hesitantly going inside.

Frances had told her that she was 'fronting' the restaurant tonight but Sara couldn't see her anywhere. The restaurant was very busy, every table taken.

'BOBBIE RANG me earlier,' Tullah told Saul as the waiter filled their wine glasses.

'Livvy's back but Caspar hasn't come with her. He's staying on in America and according to Livvy the marriage is over.'

Tullah frowned a little. At one time Saul and Livvy had been very close and Saul himself had admitted to her that he had been very attracted to his second cousin, but that was all in the past now. She was Saul's wife.

'It's the girls I feel sorry for,' she continued.

'It's so hard for children when their parents split up.'

Saul had three children from his first marriage and Tullah could still remember how fragile and lost they had seemed when she had first met him and them.

Saul's first wife had abandoned not only her husband but her three children as well, claiming that there was no place for her son and daughters in her second marriage to a man who was not family oriented.

It had not been easy for any of them when she and Saul had first fallen in love and married, Tullah acknowledged, even though now the children totally accepted her. A child of their own had completed their family but Tullah knew she felt a fierce extra protective love for Saul's eldest three children, especially his daughter Meg, and her heart went out to Amelia and Alex.

'If you ask me, men and women should be kept strictly apart except for purposes which are purely recreational,' Nick told them both tongue-in-cheek, his eyes dancing with wicked amusement.

Like all the Crighton men he was outstandingly good-looking, but Nick had an added air of excitement and danger, an added aura, a certain very challenging maleness about him Tullah recognised as she gave a small admonishing shake of her head and told him, 'You're incorrigible, Nick, you really are.'

'Nope, I'm just determined never to fall into the trap of allowing my emotions to ruin my life,' Nick told her firmly.

Saul said nothing. He was thoroughly familiar with his younger brother's antipathy towards marriage and commitment.

'One day you'll change your mind,' Tullah warned him. 'You'll see someone and fall in love with her....'

'What is it?' she asked anxiously as Nick suddenly yelped in pain. A girl was standing next to his chair, her face flushed and pink as she started to apologise.

She had obviously bumped into him accidentally as she crossed the dimly lit room. She was extremely pretty, Tullah recognised, amused to realise that Nick was receiving her apology with something less than his normal savoir faire. He might spurn marriage and commitment but that did not mean that her brother-in-law was averse to female company—far from it. Although to be fair to him, so far as Tullah knew his 'relationships' were limited to women who shared his views on the advantages of their short shelf life.

Her face crimson with mortification, Sara stammered an apology to the man she had inadvertently bumped into, but her embarrassment was replaced by indignation as he gave her a look of biting scorn instead of accepting her apology in the spirit in which she had given it.

She was still trying to find Frances and having seen her on the other side of the room had been attempting to make her way through the packed restaurant, her eyes on her quarry instead of what was in front of her.

Was it really her fault anyway, she asked herself indignantly as she returned Nick's angry glare with one of her own. *He* had been sitting at the table at an odd angle with the chair pulled out more than was surely necessary.

'You look cross. Is everything all right?' Frances asked in concern when Sara eventually caught up with her.

'I've just had a bit of a run-in with one of your

diners,' Sara admitted ruefully. 'I bumped into him but when I tried to apologise—'

'Which one?' Frances interrupted her.

'That table over there,' Sara replied, showing her.

'Oh, Tullah and Saul Crighton's table.'

Crightons!

Immediately Sara twisted round to stare at the trio. As luck would have it the couple, obviously Tullah and Saul, were seated with their backs towards her. But the man she'd bumped into...

Sara's breath rattled in her throat as he lifted his head and glared at her.

'Oh, poor Nick,' Frances was saying. 'He's not been very well.'

'You mean like a bear with a sore head not well,' Sara responded pseudo sweetly.

Frances's eyebrows rose.

'Oh, dear, he really *has* upset you, hasn't he?' she sympathised before continuing briskly, 'No, actually he was involved in a very unpleasant incident. Like nearly all the Crightons he's a qualified solicitor but the work he does is extremely specialised and often rather dangerous. Although in this case...' Quickly she explained just how Nick had come to be hurt, but stubbornly Sara refused to be impressed.

'Perhaps it might help if he carried a sign warning people not to get too close to him,' she suggested through gritted teeth.

Frances forbore to comment. Sara was a gorgeous-looking girl and Nick was a singularly handsome man. Therefore, it seemed logical to Frances that the two of them should be attracted to one another. As the mother of young adults she was also well aware that sometimes such attraction presented itself disguised as hostility.

'It's nine o'clock. You've been working all evening,' she told Sara with a smile. 'Why don't you call it a day.'

'Not yet,' Sara refused determinedly. Armed with the information Frances had given her she was sure she could solve her problem with the recalcitrant computer.

Frances smiled ruefully as she watched Sara walk away, this time giving the Crighton table a wide berth.

She had liked Sara on sight, sensing within her a gutsy determination allied to a warm sense of humour. Her stunning good looks would cause havoc, of course!

'NICK,' Tullah expostulated as she saw the grim way her brother-in-law was watching the woman's determined circumnavigation of their table.

'Little madam,' Nick seethed without taking his eyes off her departing back. 'Did you *see* the look she gave me?'

'Well, I certainly saw the one *you* gave her,' Tullah told him dryly.

'Yes,' Saul corroborated. 'You were hardly your

normal charming smooth self with her, Nick,' he pointed out. 'Pretty girl,' he added appreciatively, laughing when Tullah gave him a mock glare whilst saying with wifely warning, 'Saul...'

'Very pretty,' Nick agreed sourly. He wasn't even sure himself just why he had reacted so badly to her. Common sense told him that the painful jolt she had given his still aching wound had been completely accidental and he knew that normally he would not only have accepted her embarrassed apology gracefully but that he would probably have done everything he could to create a good impression and set her at her ease.

So why hadn't he?

Not surely because of that sharp little jolt of male sensual electricity, that more than a mere frisson of sensation that had seized him at their accidental bodily contact. After all, he had experienced physical desire for plenty of other women before her.

Physical desire, yes, but not that swift pang of dangerous knowledge, that unwanted awareness, that instinct that...that what?

That *nothing,* he told himself firmly.

'You're right,' he announced, even though neither Saul nor Tullah had said anything. 'I behaved very boorishly...and by rights I should apologise. I wonder where she's gone.'

'Frances will probably know,' Tullah informed him. 'She was talking to her.'

Ruefully Nick pushed back his chair and got up.

'Sara?' Frances responded in answer to his question. 'Oh, she'll be in the office. She's standing in for our office manager....'

Thoughtfully she watched as Nick made his way through the tables.

SARA GAVE a small crow of satisfaction as she finally got the computer to do as she wished. Nick heard it as he pushed open the door of the office. Sara was standing looking at the computer screen, her eyes alight with triumph and pleasure. She was more than just *pretty* Nick acknowledged as he felt his heart jolt fiercely against his ribs.

Sensing someone's presence Sara turned her head away from the screen, the breath rushing out of her lungs on a shocked whoosh as she realised who the intruder was.

'Frances said I'd find you in here,' Nick told her. Her body had stiffened and the look in her eyes was both wary and hostile.

Immediately his own body—and emotions—re-acted.

'I owe you an apology,' he began tersely.

'Yes, you do,' Sara agreed spiritedly, 'But you're a Crighton and of course Crightons never apologise, especially to women....'

Nick stared at her. Her reaction was so unexpected and so extraordinary that it had taken him completely by surprise.

'What on earth…' he began, but to his fury he saw that Sara was ignoring him, concentrating instead on the screen in front of her, blanking him so totally and completely that he might just as well not have existed. Women *never* blanked Nick. *Never!* Whilst a part of him was distantly relishing his shock the rest of him was sharply and furiously angry that she could dare to both speak and act as she had.

'Now look here,' he said grimly, 'there's no way you can make *that* kind of statement without explaining just what it's supposed to mean.'

As he spoke he moved closer to the desk, so close in fact that Sara could feel the angry heat coming off his body. This close he was overpoweringly male. Tall, broad, his eyes so dark that they could almost have been black, not the navy-blue she knew they were. Excitement and fear raced through her veins like rocket fuel. Caution told her that she had gone too far, but the voice of caution wasn't one Sara wanted to listen to. No, she would much rather listen to the siren lure of the exultation egging her on, telling her she was giving Nick what he deserved.

Ignoring him she continued to work.

Nick had had enough. Irritably he reached out towards her, merely intending to cover her hand to stop her working the keyboard, but the moment his fingers brushed her skin a surge of such powerful sexual immediacy coursed through his veins that the original cause of his physical contact with her was forgotten.

'Just let go of me,' Sara snapped at him, her face as white now as it had been flushed when she had bumped into him earlier in the restaurant, her eyes brilliant with the intensity of what she was feeling. And what she was feeling was… Instinctively Nick knew that she was as aware of the sexual chemistry between them as he was himself.

For a man who was used to being totally in control of himself and his emotions, what he was experiencing was totally unwanted, so incomprehensible.

'I came in here to apologise,' he reminded Sara sharply.

Angrily Sara raised her head to look at him but the sarcastic response she had been about to make died on her lips unspoken, as for some inconceivable reason her gaze was drawn to his mouth and then his eyes and then back to his mouth again.

Almost as though he were standing outside of himself watching what he was doing Nick was aware of his own actions and his inability to stop them. It seemed to take an aeon of time for him to lean forward closing the gap between Sara and himself and then to cover her mouth with his, but in reality he knew it could only have been seconds. Her mouth tasted velvety warm, sweet salt sexy and the pressure of his own against it intensified.

Beneath the hot crushing sexuality of Nick's kiss Sara's senses reeled. This was the kind of kiss she had dreamed of as a young awkward girl…the kind of man…the kind of sensual immediacy that could not be contained or controlled. Instinctively her mouth softened beneath Nick's and then outside in the corridor she heard someone laughing.

Immediately reality intruded, breaking the spell she was under. In the same second that she pulled back from him Nick released her. Wordlessly they glared at one another. Two pairs of eyes both reflecting the same furious resentment, both reflecting the same hot aching desire.

'EVERYTHING all right now?' Tullah asked Nick when he rejoined them. Saul had gone to pay the bill so only she was there to see the shattered, shocked expression in Nick's eyes.

'Everything's fine,' he lied as he guided her towards the exit where Saul was waiting for them both.

Crighton men! Sara seethed, her emotions in chaotic turmoil, her body equally disturbed. Tania had been *so* right about them.

CHAPTER FOUR

'GOOD LORD, is that really the time?' Frederick de Voysey exclaimed as he glanced at his watch. 'I had no idea. Can't remember when I last enjoyed m'self so much...excellent dinner, m'dear,' he praised Honor.

'I'll drive you back to Fitzburgh Place.' David smiled. He had deliberately not had any wine with his meal, knowing that he would be driving Honor's cousin home afterwards.

He had been a little bit uncertain about the wisdom of inviting Freddy round for dinner the same day that the priest was arriving, but as always Honor's judgement had proved better than his and the two men both in their seventies had got on famously together. So much so that Lord Astlegh had already invited the priest to join him in a game of chess later in the week.

'In terms of religion they may be poles apart,' Honor had agreed when David had raised that issue. 'But in terms of their desire to help their fellow man they are very similar and surely that matters more.'

And so it had proved to be. From the tone of Freddy's conversation David suspected that it wouldn't be too long before the priest found himself involved in one or other of the peer's 'good works,' but right now he could see that the older man was looking tired. He had, after all, only arrived from Ireland a few hours earlier.

'I think I'm ready to call it a night as well,' Father Ignatius agreed.

At the front door Honor kissed her elderly cousin fondly.

'I've had the plans back for the orangery,' he reminded her. 'You'd better come up and see them.'

'I shall,' Honor assured him affectionately.

Closing the front door behind him she smiled at the priest. 'Would you like to wait here until David comes back or would you prefer to go straight to your bed?'

'Straight to bed if you don't mind,' he confirmed.

It had been a tiring journey from Ireland but it was a peaceful kind of tiredness. He had gone there for a purpose, back to the place where his ministry had begun. Now he could settle to a life in the Cheshire countryside. Father Ignatius was at the place that he knew would be his final home on earth.

He allowed Honor to walk with him to the small self-contained apartment they had prepared for him. Its rooms had a stark almost cell-like bareness that he knew was deliberate. David's decision or Honor's? It didn't really matter. He felt comfortable here. At home…and was appreciative of whichever of them it was that had had the sensitivity to know that this would be what he wanted.

The books on the simple bookshelves were David's

choice—he knew that—and would have known it even
if Honor had not whispered to him that David had
spent days combing antiquarian booksellers lists for
them.

They were books they had talked of in Jamaica. He
reached for one, smoothing the aged leather cover,
opening it and breathing in the familiar smell of its
pages. There had been books like this at the Jesuit
college where he had been educated. How long ago
that seemed now.

'DO YOU THINK Father Ignatius is all right?' David
asked Honor an hour later. They were in bed lovingly
curled up together like two spoons. Whilst he waited
for her response David started to nibble tenderly at the
exposed curve of Honor's neck. There was something
uniquely adorable and almost absurdly youthful about
the back of her neck. Closing his eyes he breathed in
the unmatchable Honor scent of her. He was lucky, so
undeservably blessed.

'He's tired after his journey, that's all,' Honor reassured him. 'He certainly enjoyed Freddy's company.'

'Okay, I concede, you were right about them getting
on well together,' David laughed.

'Olivia and Caspar were due back today, weren't
they?' Honor said quietly.

'Yes,' David agreed. There was no laughter in his
voice now.

Immediately Honor turned round to look at him.

'Give her time, David,' she counselled him. 'I know
how much you want to show her what she means to
you, but—'

'She hates me, Honor,' David interrupted her sadly.
'I can feel it....'

'No, it isn't you she hates,' Honor told him wisely.
'It's herself. Poor Olivia...'

'It's my fault that she is suffering so much,' David
told her.

'In part, yes,' Honor agreed steadily.

'I was a bad father,' he said heavily.

'Yes,' Honor acknowledged. 'You *were* a bad father, David,' she told him truthfully.

'I just want to make it up to her but she won't let
me get near her....'

'Give her time,' Honor repeated.

She could hear the pain and frustration in his voice
and see it in his eyes.

'Somehow it's easier with Jack,' David continued.
'He's—'

'...male?' Honor supplied.

'No,' David denied immediately.

Honor shook her head and told him truthfully,
'That's what *Olivia's* going to think, David. The
blame doesn't all lie with you, though. Your father...'
She stopped.

'Olivia is my daughter. I should have protected her
from my father's prejudices.' David closed his eyes.
'I shouldn't burden you with all this.'

'Of course you should,' Honor told him immediately. 'That's part of what loving someone is all about…sharing…the bad as well as the good.'

Smiling she reached out and cupped his face and then very gently and slowly started to kiss him.

'Mmm…more,' David coaxed hopefully as he gathered her into his arms and started to kiss her back.

JENNY FROWNED over her shopping list. It seemed pathetically brief, but now, after all, she was only shopping for two. Joss had flown out to America to visit Jon's aunt Ruth who was living there with her American husband, his last chance to do so before he started focussing on his school exams.

Joss and Ruth had always been particularly close and Jenny smiled as she thought about her aunt-in-law and her youngest son. Both of them were blessed with a special temperament, a serenity and wisdom that had a gentling effect on everyone they came in contact with.

The telephone started to ring and she went to answer it.

'Jen, it's me,' she heard Jon saying. 'Look, don't wait for me for dinner tonight. David's asked me to go up to Fitzburgh Place to see Lord Freddy. He's got some business he wants to discuss with me.'

'Is David going to be there as well?' Jenny couldn't stop herself from asking tersely.

'David?' She could hear the confusion in Jon's voice. 'I don't know. He could be. Why?'

'Nothing,' Jenny fibbed. She could imagine how

Jon was likely to react if she gave in to the childish desire to complain that just lately he seemed to be spending more time with his brother than he was with her. He had gone out earlier to play golf and she had been expecting him to return within the hour.

On her way back from her shopping she would call and see Olivia, she decided, to see if there was anything she could do to help.

'MUMEE…Mumee… Wake up. I'm hungry.'

Olivia opened her eyes as she heard Alex's voice, her heart pounding as she saw the time. Ten o'clock. She was *always* up at six. She could feel the now familiar ice-cold nausea rising up inside her as fear flooded her veins. Her skin felt clammy but icy cold.

More than anything else she wanted to stay where she was, here in bed, to pull the duvet over her head and shut out the world and her problems but she couldn't. She had responsibilities…duties…two children…a job…. Mentally she started to list the day's tasks. There was the washing, the girls' school uniforms for tomorrow, her own case notes to read…food to buy…meals to cook…the house needed cleaning. Her heart was thudding even more frantically now as anxiety-induced adrenaline shot through her veins.

'Mummee…' Alex persisted. 'I'm hungry…I'm *starving*.'

Olivia could feel the scream building up inside her but she knew she must not give voice to it. It wasn't Alex's fault she was feeling like this. She had no *right* to be feeling like this. She was a woman…a mother…a wife… No, not a wife any more…not now…

Caspar… Suddenly her whole body started to tremble.

'Mummy,' Alex had started to cry and Olivia could see the fear in her eyes. More than anything else children needed security and love. No one knew that better than Olivia herself.

'It's all right darling,' she reassured her. 'I'm going to get up now. You go downstairs and wait for me.'

Caspar…Caspar… *Why* hadn't he understood…? Why hadn't he *helped* her…? Why hadn't he *loved* her…? No one had ever loved her….

As she walked into her bathroom Olivia raised an unsteady hand to her face to wipe away her tears. *Her—crying?* But she never *cried*…

IT WAS five o'clock in the morning and still dark outside. Caspar lifted his head from his pillow. Next to him lay a small toy, one of Alex's. He had found it after she had gone. Gently he touched it with his fingertips. He ached with the pain of missing his daughters—and his wife? His mouth compressed grimly. Olivia might be his wife but she wasn't the woman he had married, the woman he had fallen in love with and who he had believed loved him.

Ultimately they were going to have to sit down and talk. There was no way he intended to be merely a weekend father to his kids, but right now…right now, locked up in the garage of his half-brother's house where he was spending the night was the gleaming Harley-Davidson motorbike he had bought the previous day and tomorrow he was going to start out on the journey he had first promised himself he would make when he was still in high school, right across America from coast to coast.

'You're going to do what?' his father had asked in disbelief, adding, 'Hell, Caspar, a man of your age can't ride something like that. It's for kids.'

He shifted uncomfortably in the too soft, too big bed that felt even bigger and emptier without Olivia's presence at his side, her body tucked close to his.

Tucked *close* to his. It was one hell of a long time since they had shared *that* kind of night-time intimacy.

Closing his eyes he tried to think back to exactly when it had been, certainly before Alex's birth. She had been a colicky, light-sleeping baby causing Olivia to get up so many times during the night to her in the first weeks after her birth that eventually Olivia had started sleeping in the nursery with her. They had both agreed that it would be unfair to Amelia to bring Alex's cot into *their* room. And after that? After that Olivia had spent so much time working that when she did go to bed it was purely and simply to sleep.

Was that when sex had ceased to become a shared pleasure between them, turning instead into a reluctant exchange on Olivia's part which he had had to barter for?

Caspar started to frown. Loving someone wasn't

just about sex. But Olivia didn't want his love any
more than she wanted his body. Bleakly he closed his
eyes.

'JON...'

Jon smiled as he saw his twin waiting for him when
he got out of his car at Fitzburgh Place.

'I had to come up to collect some plants from the
greenhouses for Honor so I thought I might as well
hang around and wait for you,' David explained as
they exchanged affectionate hugs.

'Olivia and Caspar were due back yesterday,
weren't they?' David asked with such deliberate studied carelessness that Jon's heart went out to him. 'I
expect she's already been round to see Jenny to tell
her all about their trip....'

Jon frowned.

'No...she hasn't.' There was no easy way for him
to tell David what had happened.

'*Livvy's* come back David, but *Caspar* hasn't.
They've separated,' he told his twin bluntly.

'What...?'

Jon could see the shocked disbelief in David's eyes.
'But I thought they were so happy together.'

'They were,' Jon agreed heavily, 'But...look, I
don't know the full details.'

'I'm going to go and see her,' David announced
starkly, 'She's my daughter...I'm...' He stopped, his
face twisting with unhappiness. 'I was going to say

that I'm her father but of course, I don't deserve to be considered fitting for that role—not really.'

'Look, I know how you must feel,' Jon tried to comfort him. 'But why don't you wait until Jenny's been to see her?'

'Has she brought the girls back with her, do you know?' David asked him.

'Yes,' Jon confirmed.

David let out his breath in a leaky sigh. He ached to get closer to his granddaughters, to be for them all that he had not been able to be for their mother. Just watching Jon with Max and Maddy's children brought out such a yearning in him to hold his own granddaughters in his arms that it was almost a physical pain. Right now he felt that same urge, that same need, to hold Olivia—adult though she was.

'Oh, by the way, I ought to warn you that Dad isn't too pleased about the fact that you've invited Father Ignatius to live with you,' Jon told him ruefully.

'I know, he told me,' David acknowledged without adding that Ben had actually hinted to David that if he and Honor were to move into Queensmead with him he would make the house over to him.

'Queensmead! You've already promised *Queensmead* to Max,' David had reminded his father grimly. 'Maddy has spent a fortune of time and effort on the place and—'

'More fool her. I never asked her to,' Ben had returned surlily.

Honor had been both shocked and angry when David had told her what Ben had said.

'When I think of the way Maddy has looked after him,' she had exclaimed. 'He really is the most thoughtless, chauvinistic man....'

'All that and more,' David had agreed wryly. He was working himself up into a real royal fury. 'What's wrong?' he had questioned when Honor had started to frown.

'Well, although for his age he's relatively healthy, he *does* have a heart condition. He told me and I checked with Maddy,' Honor informed him.

'Just how serious is it?' David had asked her.

'Well, it isn't going to do him any good if he over-does things and that includes working himself up into a furious temper. He's well into his eighties, David,' she had added gently.

'I understand what you're saying,' David had agreed, 'But just because he's got a heart condition that doesn't mean he can be allowed to get away with hurting other people, especially someone like Maddy.'

'He *can't* hurt Maddy,' Honor had assured him gently. 'She's far too well protected by Max's love.'

No, he couldn't hurt Maddy but he had hurt Olivia. Olivia who should have had his, her father's love, to protect her.

'I won't come up to the house with you if you don't mind,' David told Jon abruptly.

Jon shook his head guessing that David wanted to

talk over what he had told him about Olivia with Honor.

DAVID FOUND Honor in the kitchen with Father Ignatius who was peeling the potatoes for their meal.

'I went to early communion this morning,' the priest told him. 'I like your church.'

David waited for him to finish before turning to Honor to tell her, 'I've just seen Jon up at Fitzburgh Place. Olivia and Caspar have separated.'

'Oh, David!' Honor exclaimed, coming over to him.

'I want to go and see her, Honor…talk to her…help her…'

'Oh, David,' Honor protested in a different tone. 'I don't think…'

'She won't want me. Jon's already told me that,' David agreed flatly.

'Perhaps I could go and see her,' the priest suggested gently.

David laughed mirthlessly and shook his head.

'She'd be as reluctant to see you as she would me. You're tainted by association,' he told him. 'Your association with me. I'm sorry,' he apologised to them both. 'I know I'm over-reacting.'

'Give her time,' Honor had counselled him earlier, but suddenly as she listened to him Honor sensed intuitively that Olivia no longer had that time.

Her heart ached for the woman who was now her stepdaughter and she longed to be able to help her for Olivia's own sake just as much as David's.

Like the priest, she too had a need; a *mission* to heal and repair the damage that life could inflict on her fellow men and women, but she suspected that Olivia was dangerously close to shutting herself away from anyone's help.

CHAPTER FIVE

'But I can't stay in hospital, I've got a family, three children, a husband and my father-in-law....'

Maddy's shocked outburst broke the silence of the small consulting room.

'I'm afraid there is no other option—not at this stage,' the obstetrician told her gently. 'Your blood pressure is high and there is protein already showing in the tests we've done.'

He and the nurse exchanged glances.

'It's a pity you weren't able to make your last appointment. Had we discovered what was happening then...'

Maddy bit her lip. She could hardly take in what she had been told. Of course she had been aware that she was putting on more weight with this pregnancy than she had with her others and that she was suffering badly with swollen ankles and legs, but this...the appalling news the doctor had just given her that she was exhibiting all the classic early signs of pre-eclampsia and that for her own and the baby's sake she would have to stay in hospital whilst they brought her blood pressure back down to normal had shocked her rigid.

'Why don't you ring your husband?' the nurse suggested gently.

MAX WAS IN the middle of a conference meeting with a client's solicitor when Maddy's call came through.

As she tried to tell him what had happened he could hear in her voice her fear and distress. He felt as though a knife were being turned in his heart. Maddy was ill…his Maddy, and she was frightened as well.

'I'm sorry,' he told the solicitor swiftly. 'But I'm afraid I'm going to have to leave. My wife isn't well.'

The solicitor, a sophisticatedly elegant thirty-something with a high-profile reputation and a prestigious client list, thinned her carefully made up mouth. She had travelled up especially from London for this meeting and she was not accustomed to dealing with Counsel who put their wives before their clients.

At the back of her mind was something a little more than professional irritation. Max was stunningly attractive and even more stunningly male. She was certainly not the sort to indulge in seedy one-night stands with good-looking business associates but the thought of suggesting to Max that they share dinner together after their meeting *had* crossed her mind. As had her mentally wondering if she possibly had the time to pay a visit to that very chic designer store she had just happened to notice as she walked through Chester this morning before her appointment with Max. Now, though, she wouldn't need to pick up something alluring to wear this evening.

IT TOOK MAX twenty minutes to reach the hospital. He found Maddy sitting anxiously on her bed in a small private room off the main ward.

As he crossed the room and took her in his arms she burst into tears.

'What is it? What's happened? What's wrong?' Max asked her anxiously as he smoothed her hair back off her face and cupped it, his gaze searching hers as his heart hammered against his ribs.

She was so precious to him, so very much beloved, the bedrock on which his life was now built.

Whilst Maddy tried haltingly to explain the situation Max tried and failed to comprehend how he could possibly endure his own life if he were to lose her. All the sins of his own past came back to him; this was his deepest and most secret dread; this fear that somehow the same fate which had given him so much, forgiven him so much, should choose with savage and inescapable malignancy to punish not him but those he loved most; and of all those that he did love, Maddy was his most beloved.

In his more logical moments he knew his fears were unfounded and illogical, but the same change of heart which had shown him the error of his old ways and opened the locked door in his heart to show him the true meaning of love, had also opened that same door to show him fear; fear, not for himself but for those he loved.

He could hear Maddy telling him something.

Above the fierce pounding of his own heartbeat he

could hear Maddy's voice. Determinedly he focused on it and on what she was saying.

The obstetrician had told her that she was suffering from pre-eclampsia, a condition which could, if left untreated, threaten the life of both her and her baby. In order for them to treat it she would have to stay in hospital where her progress could be monitored and she would not be allowed to return home until they were satisfied that she was well enough to do so.

A nurse appeared in the room giving Max a frowning look as she reminded Maddy that she must try to keep calm.

'Can I see Mr Lewis?' Max asked her.

She pursed her lips.

'He's with another patient at the moment and I don't know how long he will be.'

'I'll wait,' Max told her in a tone of voice that said he wasn't going anywhere until he had spoken to the consultant.

'Oh, Max, I'm so afraid,' Maddy confessed. 'And I feel so guilty. If I hadn't missed my last antenatal appointment they would have found out then what was happening but Ben wasn't well and—'

His grandfather! Max closed his eyes and willed himself not to over-react.

'You're going to be fine,' he tried to reassure Maddy as he held her tightly, 'Both you and the baby.'

Ten minutes later, having told her that she wasn't to worry about anything and having promised that, yes, he would get in touch with Jenny and, yes, he would pick the children up from school and bring a bag of things into the hospital for her, Max kissed his wife and followed the nurse who had come to tell him that the consultant was ready to see him.

'…and there's nothing you can do?'

'In the sense of making the condition completely disappear, no,' the man agreed. 'But in the sense of getting it under control, yes. Our first priority is to bring your wife's blood pressure down and for that we need to keep her here in hospital. Once we are satisfied that it is safely under control then she will be allowed to return home but only on the understanding that she does not overdo things.'

'And if you can't bring her blood pressure down?' Max pressed.

The consultant stood up and walked over to the tiny window of his office, keeping his back towards Max as he said quietly, 'That shouldn't happen.…'

'But if it does?' Max persisted.

There was a long pause before the consultant replied.

'If the condition runs its course unchecked in the final three months of pregnancy it can lead to the mother suffering from fits and to the deterioration of the placenta which obviously affects the baby. Ultimately—'' he paused and looked at Max ''—when this happens the mother can suffer from convulsions which in a worst-case scenario causes brain damage for mother and child and potentially death.'

Max stared at him in white-faced disbelief, and

sensing his feelings the other man assured him, 'These days the risk of that happening is minimal. As I've explained, now that we've detected the problem we should be able to bring your wife's blood pressure back to normal and keep it there.'

'You say should,' Max interrupted him grimly. 'What if you can't?' he demanded, his heart hammering against his ribs.

There was a long pause before the doctor told him carefully, 'If we were to consider that there was any threat to your wife's life then we should need to discuss with her terminating her pregnancy.'

'Have you told Maddy any of this?' Max asked him grimly.

The consultant shook his head.

'At this stage I do not believe it is either necessary or constructive to add to your wife's anxiety. And I must reiterate to you that we are talking about a worst-case scenario.'

'There is no way I would ever countenance anything that would put Maddy's life at risk,' Max started to tell him. 'Even if that meant that…the baby…that a termination…'

The consultant looked at him with sympathy. 'We'll advise you and your wife of the best course of action as her pregnancy progresses.'

Max closed his eyes in mute despair. He knew full well just how Maddy would react. She was the kind of person who would always put the needs of others before her own, all the more so when that other was their unborn child.

Behind his closed eyelids Max cursed himself for the fact that she was pregnant. They already had a family, three children. He found himself wishing passionately that the coming baby had never been conceived, hating it almost for the danger it represented to Maddy, and hating himself even more for what he was feeling. Surely the best thing that could happen now for all their sakes would be for this pregnancy to end.

Couldn't nature step in on Maddy's behalf and remove from her the danger to her life?

Guilt burned like bitter gall in Max's throat and belly as he acknowledged the grim horror of what he was thinking. The death of his own child before it had even known life.

'Surely if Maddy's life was at risk you could just act,' he began, but the consultant was shaking his head.

'We would strongly recommend a termination if your wife's life were in jeopardy, but we would need to consult with her first,' he told Max sternly.

He felt sorry for Max, but the needs of his patient were his prime concern. His patients, in this case—both Maddy and her unborn child. And there was another problem that he still had to raise with Max.

A little brusquely he did so. 'Your wife is eighteen weeks pregnant,' the consultant reminded Max steepling his fingertips together. 'Twenty weeks is the latest time I personally would want to perform a termination. After that...'

'After that, what?' Max could hear the raw fear in his own voice, taste it in his mouth. 'That only leaves two weeks to bring Maddy's blood pressure down.'

'I'm aware of that,' the obstetrician conceded quietly. 'It is unfortunate that your wife missed her earlier antenatal appointments. Had she not done so we could have picked up the problems that much earlier.' He glanced away from Max before looking back at him to tell him bluntly, 'I do understand how you must be feeling, but I've had prem babies under my care who have survived birth at twenty-three weeks. To abort—' He stopped compassionately as he saw the emotion Max was struggling to keep under control.

'Maddy will never agree to sacrifice her baby,' Max told him. 'She'd sacrifice herself first.' When the consultant said nothing, Max protested furiously, 'For God's sake, in all humanity you can't expect...I should be the one to make the decision, to take responsibility. She's my wife. We already have three children.'

Max could feel the burn of his own emotions stinging the backs of his eyes. Was this then fate's punishment for him? That in celebrating their love, in his reaffirmation of his vows to love her, he had quite literally sowed the seed of Maddy's death?

'We're talking about a situation that may never occur,' the consultant reminded Max firmly. 'If your wife responds well and quickly to treatment, then all

will be well. It is, of course, essential at the moment
that she is not subjected to any kind of...upset
or...pressure.' He gave Max a long look. 'I hope I
make myself clear.'

Max made a terse nod of his head. He knew that
the obstetrician was warning him not to discuss the
situation with Maddy or allow her to see his own distress. 'I understand,' he confirmed. 'I have to go home
now...to collect our children from school, but I'd like
your permission to bring them in to see her.'

He paused and waited.

'Yes, I can agree to that,' the doctor told him.

'...and for me to be able to stay the night here with
her,' Max continued swiftly.

With a small sigh the consultant nodded his head.

'But I must warn you, any sign that your wife is
being upset or distressed in any way by either the presence of her children or her husband and I shall have
to ask you to leave.'

Grimly Max inclined his head.

JENNY'S MOBILE rang just as she was about to leave
the supermarket and drive to Olivia's. When she answered it she heard Max's voice.

'Mum...'

'Max.' She could detect the tension in his one word.

'I'm at the hospital.'

'The hospital?' Jenny gripped the mobile. 'What's
wrong...Ben?'

'No, it isn't Ben, it's Maddy,' Max told her tersely.

'She's suffering from pre-eclampsia. I don't know what's going to happen yet,' he continued, overriding Jenny's anxious questions, 'but they're keeping her in. That's one of the reasons why I'm ringing you. Could you go over to Queensmead and check up on Ben and—Mum—we're going to need your help not just with Ben but with the kids as well.'

'Don't worry,' Jenny reassured him. 'You know I'll do whatever you need me to do.'

'I'm on my way to collect them from school now. I'm taking them straight to the hospital to see Maddy, but if you could come and take them home, I'm going to stay overnight at the General with her but the kids need...'

'Of course,' Jenny agreed immediately. 'I'll drive over to Queensmead now and check on Ben.'

She could hear the relief in Max's voice as he thanked her. When she started the car her hands were shaking. They all took Maddy so much for granted, her sunny nature, her calm gentleness, her ability to find room in her generous heart for even someone as irascible and difficult as Ben.

Virtually singlehandedly she had turned Queensmead from a cold unwelcoming barn of a house that no one had ever liked to visit into a warm welcoming haven which increasingly had become the hub of Crighton family life. The work she did for the Mums and Babes charity was of incalculable value. She had surprised everyone, including herself, not just with her administrative talents but even more so with her flair for fund raising. No matter how busy she was she still always found time for those who asked for it.

Max adored her and if anything were to happen to her... Jenny knew how potentially serious her condition was—how dangerous.

Her hands tightened on the steering wheel of the car. The first thing she did when she reached Queensmead was ring Jon but all she could reach was his message service. Her mouth compressing, Jenny dropped the phone into her handbag without bothering to leave any message.

Ben was asleep in his arm chair when she walked into the library. Gently she woke him up.

'Where's Maddy?' he demanded irritably. 'I'm hungry. Gone off gadding somewhere with Max, I suppose. She's supposed to be here looking after me. Acting like this house is their own. Huh...we shall see about that....'

Squashing her irritation, Jenny explained what had happened. The whole family made allowances for the often irascible Ben who had never reconciled himself to the death of his twin brother. But, increasingly, he was making challenging and hurtful comments about both Maddy and Max and about their future tenure of the house.

Jenny knew that Max felt concerned enough to have bought a large piece of land on the other side of town on which he hoped he would be able to build a new house for himself, Maddy and the children if Ben ever did carry out his threat to disinherit him.

'David has promised that if Dad *should* leave Queensmead to him he will immediately hand it over to you,' Jon had tried to reassure Max.

When Jenny reached the hospital, Max and the children were in the waiting room. Max hurried towards her and she could tell from his expression just how anxious he was about Maddy.

'Can I see her?' she asked him once she had hugged and kissed the children.

Shaking his head Max told her, 'She's asleep at the moment. This is all my fault,' he added emotionally. The bleakness in his eyes tore at Jenny's heart. Silently she hugged him, trying to offer him some comfort but inwardly she was as frightened for Maddy as she could see he was.

'They can do so much these days,' she tried to reassure him.

'I should have guessed—seen—I know she hasn't been feeling well.' His voice was torn with pain. 'Where's Dad?' he asked abruptly. 'I thought he would come with you.'

'He's up at Fitzburgh Place. Apparently David rang him whilst he was playing golf to tell him that Lord Astlegh wanted to see him.'

She gave Max a forced smile. With all that he had to worry about the last thing she wanted to do was to have him guess how she was feeling.

'I'll take the children home with me now and don't worry about having to get home tonight, Max. I'll stay at Queensmead with them and make sure they get to school in the morning.'

FROM THE SMALL ROOM at home she used as an office Olivia could see Amelia and Alex playing in the garden. At the moment they seemed happy to accept that Caspar had stayed behind in America whilst they had come home but soon she knew they would start to miss their father and ask questions. They would be upset she knew. They both adored Caspar. But surely they were better off living with her in a loving happy atmosphere than enduring the kind of misery *she* had known as a child knowing that her parents were not happy together. Her agitation increased, her heart starting to pound with a now familiar sickening speed and intensity. She hated the fear she felt threatening to flood over her, hated the sense of loss of self-control it brought.

Pushing her hands into her hair she tried to massage the tight band of pain out of her skull. She had just spent the last hour reading through the work notes she had made before leaving for America but instead of calming her, easing her anxiety, they had only served to *increase* it.

She thought of Jenny and looked anxiously towards her silent telephone. Her aunt hadn't even rung to welcome her home. But then why should she? Olivia was only a niece to her. Jenny had sons and daughters of her own who were far more important to her than Olivia ever could be and Jenny had grandchildren, too.... Far more loved by her than Olivia's children could be. Fiercely Olivia swallowed against the tight ball of angry pain stuck in her throat.

Tania, her own mother, had never even seen her grandchildren.

'Darling, I'd love to see the new baby,' she had announced over the telephone after Amelia had been born, 'But there's just no way I could ever come back to Haslewich....' Olivia had been able to visualise the shudder which would have run through her mother's fragile body as she listened to her. 'And even if I could, I know that my darling Tom would never allow me to do so. He can't believe how cruel your father was to me. And I'm afraid we couldn't invite you to come down here. We just don't have the room....'

And of course her mother didn't want to make room. Olivia had known that, but to offset that pain there had been Jenny. Jenny ready to open her arms to Olivia and her new baby and to become the loving wise surrogate grandmother Olivia had ached for them to have.

But then, one after the other, Jenny's own children had married and produced grandchildren for her, and Olivia had started to distance herself from Jenny a little, out of a fierce maternal desire to protect her own daughters from being hurt as she had been.

Everywhere she turned it seemed to Olivia that she was not as valued as other people were. Neither of her own parents had *truly* loved her—she knew *that*—and as for Ben, her grandfather, he had made his preference for *Max* as plain as his contempt for her.

At work she had tried to prove that she could work as hard, do as much, as any man. Even Caspar, who she had thought loved her, had chosen his family over her.

Outside the sun was shining brightly but all Olivia could see was the bleak future that stretched ahead of her.

JON FROWNED as he let himself into the unlit empty house. Where was Jenny? He knew she had planned to visit Olivia but he had expected her to be back at home. No familiar Sunday dinner smells were wafting appetisingly from the large family kitchen, empty now like the rest of the house of the busy noisiness of their growing children and their friends. Ruefully he remembered how often once they were teenagers, he had looked forward to quieter times. Times when he and Jenny would be able to have moments to themselves. Now that they had... He frowned. If the early years of their marriage had been difficult, these latter few years had more than compensated for that with the happiness and love they had brought him. The discovery that Jenny, who he had married believing she could never love him, had in fact done so right from the start, had brought a sensual late blooming to their relationship which he had quite frankly relished.

Now, though, Jenny seemed not to want him sexually any more. He appreciated that life had become increasingly busy for her. She might have sold her half share in her antique shop to her partner Guy Cooke, but she now played an increasingly demanding role in the Mums and Babes charity his aunt Ruth had established as well as being very involved with their local community and the lives of their children and grandchildren.

Still frowning he dialled the number of her mobile phone. It was out of character for her to go out without leaving any indication of where she was or when she would be back.

'Jenny?'

Answering her mobile, Jenny quickly scanned Queensmead's kitchen table, making sure that her grandchildren were eating the meal she had prepared for them.

'Where are you?' she heard Jon demanding.

'I'm at Queensmead,' she told him.

'Oh… When will you be back?'

Quickly she explained to him what had happened, adding, 'I shall have to stay here until Maddy is well enough to come home, and even then…'

She could tell from the sound of his voice how shocked he was by the news she had given him.

'I'll come over,' he was telling her, adding, 'Why on earth didn't you ring me straight away?'

'I tried to,' Jenny informed him crisply, 'but you didn't pick up. I dare say the business David had arranged for you to discuss with Lord Astlegh was too important to be interrupted.'

As he heard the sharp note in her voice Jon sighed. He hated there being any kind of disharmony between them and it hurt him that Jenny, whom he loved so very much, could not be as pleased by David's return as he was himself.

'Yes, I'm sorry, I did switch it off,' he acknowledged. 'Freddy loathes them according to David.'

Jenny tensed. Here it was, even now, with Maddy so poorly, Jon was *still* thinking about putting David first...

'I've got to go,' she fibbed, quickly ending the call before Jon could object.

'MUMMY, *this* isn't the way to school,' Amelia protested.

'No darling, I know it isn't,' Olivia agreed as she checked the traffic. 'I want to call and see Auntie Jenny before I take you to school.' She wanted to see Jenny to ask if she would pick up the girls from school for her and to see if it was possible for her to have them until she, Olivia, got home from work. Ultimately she was going to have to make proper childcare arrangements but that would take time and until then she would desperately need Jenny's help.

Frantically she tried to run through everything she had to do. The school would have to be told that Jenny would be picking the girls up, of course. It ran an after-school crèche which she could book them into if necessary and until she had sorted out a reliable nanny perhaps Jon would agree to her doing her paper work from home.

It would mean rearranging her appointments. Some of her clients weren't always free to see her until after they themselves had finished work which was one of the reasons she was home so late so many evenings.

Jon would have to be told about her and Caspar's separation, if he didn't already know about it, which Olivia suspected he must. She could well imagine how it would be received by certain members of the family. No doubt Ben would once again compare her with Max—to *her* detriment! Max, of course, had the perfect marriage, just as he had the perfect everything else.

'Mummy,' Amelia cried out in alarm and just in time Olivia saw the cyclist she had previously been oblivious to, swerving out to avoid him.

'Wait in the car for me,' she instructed the girls when she pulled up on the forecourt to Jon and Jenny's home.

Running as quickly as she could over the gravel, which wasn't an easy feat in her office court shoes and straight-skirted business suit, she pushed open the kitchen door calling out, 'Jenny, it's me, Olivia.'

'Livvy!'

Olivia frowned as she saw not Jenny come hurrying into the kitchen but Jon.

'I—I'm just on my way to work,' Olivia told him defensively, 'I wanted to see Jenny to ask if she could pick the girls up for me this afternoon.'

'Oh dear, I'm afraid she's at Queensmead,' Jon told her.

Queensmead. Olivia's heart sank. It would take her a good ten minutes to drive to the other house. But she *had* to see Jenny. Without giving Jon time to say any more she hurried back to her car.

Jon grimaced as Olivia left. He'd had no chance to explain to her what had happened. He was already late for a very early client meeting. He had missed Jenny's familiar presence in their bed last night and hadn't slept well.

ANGRILY Olivia stabbed her foot on the car's accelerator. She was going to be late for the office, a fact which Jon would have already noted. That was a great start to her new life as a single parent she reflected bitterly.

Her awareness of her own exposure, her vulnerability, increased her defensive anger. By the time she had negotiated the fast-building traffic and was turning into Queensmead's drive she had worked herself up into a state of furious anxiety.

Stopping her car she got out and hurried towards Queensmead's back door and opened it.

In Maddy's kitchen Jenny was trying to answer her grandchildren's increasingly anxious questions about their mother's absence.

'Livvy,' she exclaimed guiltily as Olivia walked in, her heart sinking as she realised that in her panic over

Maddy she had not found time to get in touch with her niece.

To Livvy's eyes the orderly scene in Maddy's kitchen where Maddy's children were being given their breakfast by their doting grandmother was one that made her sharply aware of the difference in these children's circumstances and her own.

'I'm sorry I haven't been in touch,' Jenny began to apologise, 'But as you can see—' She stopped as they both heard Maddy's youngest child crying for her grandmother from upstairs.

Olivia could practically feel Jenny's desire for her to leave. Distraught, with no one to turn to and overwhelmed by a fierce surge of protective maternal love for her own children, Olivia lost her temper and interrupted Jenny angrily.

'Yes I *can* see that you're very busy Aunt Jenny…far too busy obviously to have time for *me!*'

The strength of her feelings was making her shake.

'I'm sorry to have bothered you. Of course, I should have realised that you've got far more important things to do than help *me*….' Without giving Jenny the chance to say anything to her Olivia stormed out of the kitchen, slamming the kitchen door behind her as she left.

Helplessly Jenny watched her, torn between going after her and responding to the increasingly voluble cries from upstairs. But Olivia was already opening her car door and getting in.

As she started her car Olivia was shaking with anger

and distress. She had been relying on Jenny, not just for practical help but as someone she could unburden herself to…someone she could confide in, but Jenny didn't have *time* to listen to her…. Her feelings were threatening to overwhelm her but she *had* to get the girls to school and then she had to go to work. What had she expected Jenny to do, anyway—throw her arms around her and tell her that everything was going to be all right?

A tear trickled down her face. Bitterly she brushed it away. Nothing had ever been all right in her life and nothing was *ever* going to be!

At the school, whilst the girls went up to join their friends, she went in search of the head teacher to ask if she could enrol them both for the after-school crèche.

It was almost nine o'clock and normally she was at her desk far earlier. The now all too familiar sensation of her own anxiety tensed the whole of her body.

'LIVVY, my dear…'

Jon frowned as Livvy turned away from him as she said curtly, 'I'm sorry I'm so late. I had to drop the girls off at school.'

'Good heavens, Livvy, I was expecting you wouldn't come in at all today…. We've heard about Caspar…I'm so sorry.'

'Why?' she questioned sharply. 'The marriage wasn't working…it's a mutual decision.'

Jon's frown deepened. She looked far too thin, her

face pinched and pale but it was her *attitude* that was giving him the most cause for concern. He had expected her to be upset. He knew how hard she strived for perfection in every aspect of her life, how sensitive she was; but this edginess, this angry aggression almost was so unlike what he knew of her and it disturbed him.

When Olivia walked into the office several minutes later the phone had already started to ring. Quickly she answered it. One of her clients was on the other end of the line wanting to make an urgent appointment. Tensely she reached for her diary.

Shaking his head Jon made his way to his own office. Normally the first thing he would have done right now would have been to ring Jenny so that he could discuss what had happened and the best way to help Livvy, but of course Jenny was at Queensmead and he didn't want to add to her problems.

The look of haunted bitterness in Olivia's eyes had shocked him, though. It was almost as though she thought he was her enemy. He was imagining it, he told himself firmly. Naturally she was not herself. How *could* she be? Her marriage had broken up compounding the distress she had already suffered with David's return.

It was such a pity that she was so antagonistic towards her father. Jon could understand her point of view, of course, but things were different now. *David* was different and Jon knew how much he longed to make reparation to her. But he still could not shake off the feeling that Livvy had erected a barrier between them.

His phone rang just as his secretary brought in his post and morning coffee.

'David!' he exclaimed with genuine pleasure as he heard his twin's voice on the other end of the line.

'We've just heard about Maddy,' David told him. Then he asked gravely, 'How is she?'

'We don't know—as yet—but they're going to keep her in for the time being. Jenny's staying at Queensmead to look after the children and Ben.'

'Well, that answers my next question. Honor wanted to know if there was anything *she* could do to help.'

'Well perhaps a magic potion to keep Dad quiet might be a good idea,' Jon suggested wryly.

There was a brief pause before David asked hesitantly, 'And Livvy…she's…she's all right?' David questioned him.

Jon's heart sank. He knew he couldn't lie to him.

'She's…she's going through a very difficult time and obviously it's bound to be affecting her,' was all he felt he could say.

IT WAS LUNCH TIME before Jon saw Livvy again, their paths crossing in the reception area of the practice.

'Oh, Livvy, I forgot to say this morning,' Jon told her, 'obviously you're going to need to spend more time at home at the moment. I'll have a word with the agency and see if Mark, our locum, can stay on for a few more weeks to give you a bit of breathing space.

If you do have to see any clients you could schedule those appointments during school hours which will leave you free to arrive later in the morning and go home midafternoon...'

Olivia stiffened. It didn't matter that what Jon was suggesting was exactly what she had known she would have to do. She sensed a cautious air about him. Did he doubt her ability to cope? Where had the old closeness between them gone?

'That won't be necessary,' she told him sharply. 'I've already made arrangements for the girls.'

It wasn't entirely true of course, but with all the professional agencies that were in existence surely it wouldn't take her too long to find the right person to look after them when she couldn't be there.

'The assizes are coming up,' Jon reminded her gently, 'and if any of your cases run over you could find yourself having to stay over in Chester....'

'Chester is hardly the other end of the universe,' Livvy snapped. Worriedly Jon watched her walk away. He hated seeing her like this, so prickly and defensive. She had been such a loving little girl. Shy and reluctant to put herself forward. That was Ben's doing, of course, and her parents'. But once she had been coaxed out of her shell she had been a joy and Jenny, he knew, had a special place in her heart for her.

'LIVVY...how are you...?'

From the concern she could hear in Tullah's voice,

Olivia knew immediately that Tullah had heard about her separation from Caspar. Normally she would have been happy to see the other woman, but right now all she could think of was how lucky Tullah was to be married to a man like Saul who loved and supported and valued her.

'I'm fine,' Livvy responded dismissively and untruthfully, starting to turn away and then stopping as Tullah asked tentatively, 'Have you spoken to Jenny today?'

'Only briefly,' Livvy responded, once again making to leave the practice's reception area and head for her own office, but before she could do so Tullah was continuing anxiously, 'Did she say anything about Maddy...or how long they're going to keep her in hospital? Max must be going out of his mind....'

'Maddy's in hospital?' Olivia couldn't keep the shock out of her voice, the work waiting for her on her desk forgotten.

'Yes, she is. Didn't you know?' Tullah looked confused. 'Oh, well, when she went to hospital for her normal check-up they told her that she would have to stay in because she's suffering from pre-eclampsia,' she started to explain. 'Saul had to ring Max about something, that's how *we* know. *I* tried to ring Jenny earlier but I couldn't get through and I thought...'

Olivia wasn't concentrating fully on what Tullah was saying. In her confusion, she was too busy dealing with the sickening sense of disbelief and guilt that was filling her. Jenny had been looking after her grand-

children because Maddy was in hospital seriously ill—
and *she* had said… The burning sensation, a combi-
nation of guilt, shock and anxiety which had stormed
her face before spreading to the backs of her eyes now
ached emotionally in her throat, shocking her out of
the black misery of her own despair.

'I—I didn't know,' she acknowledged shakily.
'What has the hospital said? How long…'

'I don't know any of the details,' Tullah interrupted
her as they shared eloquent looks, both of them united
as women and as mothers in their shared feelings for
Maddy herself as an individual, a friend and a relative
whom they both loved.

'I tried to catch Jon earlier before he left,' Tullah
confided, 'But I missed him and I knew you would
have seen Jenny….' Her voice tailed away.

'It was just a quick call…this morning…on my way
here,' Olivia responded uncomfortably.

She looked so shocked and anguished that Tullah
felt guilty for having raised the subject.

During the afternoon when Olivia should have been
concentrating on her work she was desperately wondering what she should do—what she could do to put
things right. She knew what she wanted to do. She
wanted to go straight round to Queensmead and throw
herself on Jenny's mercy, to beg her for her forgive-
ness, her understanding. But what if Jenny refused to
listen to her? What if she was so disgusted, so *appalled* by Olivia's selfish behaviour that she refused
to accept her apology and explanation and refused to

have anything further to do with her? She would be perfectly within her rights to do so; Livvy knew that she had been unpardonably selfish and rude.

Olivia's face went grey-white with guilt as she recalled her own sharply accusing bitter words.

And what about Maddy? How must *she* be feeling? Olivia looked at the telephone on her desk.

Before she could change her mind she reached for it. Less than two minutes later she was through to the hospital.

'We are unable to put you through to Mrs Madeleine Crighton,' the anonymous voice on the other end of the line announced, enquiring politely, 'Are you a close relative?'

'No…not really,' Olivia responded. 'I'm her cousin by marriage… Is she…' As her anxiety started to overwhelm her, her voice began to tremble.

'She's resting at the moment,' she was told calmly. 'But if you want us to pass a message to her…'

'Just tell her that I'm thinking of her, please,' Olivia responded having given her name.

Would it help Maddy to know that she was being thought about or would it only add to her distress and fear?

As she replaced the telephone receiver Olivia ached to be able to talk to Jenny. Taking a deep breath she quickly punched into the keypad Queensmead's number.

'Jenny is staying at Queensmead to look after the children,' Tullah had said.

When only the answering machine responded to her call Olivia put down the receiver in silence.

Bad as her own problems were they were *nothing* compared to what she knew Maddy and those closest to her must be going through.

NICK SIGHED as he drove into Haslewich. Much as he appreciated the company and the hospitality of Saul and Tullah he was itching to return to his own life…his own home.

'No way, little brother.' Saul had shaken his head when Nick had suggested doing so. 'I *know* you, with Mum and Dad away at the moment once you get back to that remote den of yours you'll be back at work, taking heaven alone knows what kind of risks and if anything should happen there's no one there.…'

'Okay…okay,' Nick had given in.

His Welsh farmhouse was remote, two miles down a narrow track with no neighbours nearby. Saul was right, within days if not hours of returning he would be back at work.

He had been approached to take a potentially fascinating case just before his accident. A young woman was threatening to sue her family for snatching her away from the cult with which she had become involved. Nick had been approached by a friend of the family for his advice.

But it wasn't his work that was on his mind right now. It was Sara!

He was fully aware that his behaviour in the restaurant and more specifically in the restaurant *office* had been far from exemplary or *gentlemanly*. It didn't matter that he had been provoked. He still should not have allowed things, matters, to get so out of hand. An apology was quite plainly in order, or so he had reasoned.

IT WAS EARLY afternoon and Frances was just seeing the last lunch-time diner off the premises when he walked in.

'I wonder if I could have a word with Sara?' Nick asked once they had exchanged greetings.

'Oh, I'm sorry, she isn't here at the moment,' Frances told him. 'She's taking a late lunch hour. I insisted that she ought to get out and enjoy this unseasonal sunshine we're having whilst she could. Do you want me to pass on a message?'

Shaking his head Nick left the restaurant. It was true that the weather was mild, sunny and warm. From where he stood he could see the bright light glinting on the river. He paused to study it. Nick had always loved water. His farmhouse was on a hill overlooking the sea off the Pembrokeshire coast.

He didn't own a boat himself but he sometimes crewed for a friend who did. Automatically he started to head for the river.

Sara paused to laugh at the antics of some ducks as they dived into the water for unseen food. Further downstream she had seen some swans, their stately elegant progress so at odds with the frantic paddling that must be going on beneath their gently floating bodies. Like galleons in full sail they seemed to glide effortlessly over the water. Hers was the only human presence here on the river path and Frances had urged her not to rush back.

'I can't believe how much work you've done already. You really are a marvel…I'm so grateful to you,' she had praised Sara. Sara reflected on the telephone call she had taken earlier from the frantically apologetic employment agency explaining they had been let down by the girl they had intended to send to the restaurant. It didn't matter now Sara had told them—the job had been filled. Why had she decided to stay on? She liked Frances yes, but… Unbidden a mental picture of Nick Crighton came into her head. She was not staying because of him! She loathed him. He was arrogant, humourless, contemptible—and worse! Angrily she sucked in her breath.

NICK SAW SARA before she saw him. She had her head thrown back as she laughed at the ducks she was watching and her hair was ruffled by the breeze, the sunlight burnishing its rich warmth. She was wearing a soft woollen jumper which the wind had flattened lovingly against the curves of her breasts and Nick felt the immediate primaeval reaction of his body to her femaleness.

She had seen him now, her body stiffening defensively, her expression hostile.

As he reached her she moved to one side of the

path, deliberately leaving as much space as she could between them before starting to walk past him.

'Sara...'

As she heard Nick say her name Sara tensed. She wasn't idiotic enough to pretend that she was in shock because a man had kissed her and neither was she going to throw a histrionic fit about it, but she knew that her reaction to him, her *awareness* of him, was far stronger than anything she had experienced before. She had guessed from putting two and two together from Frances's comments about him that even by male Crighton standards Nick was something of a rogue card in the family pack. Sara had made no comment when Frances had said that for all that Nick prized his freedom and avoided any kind of permanent involvement, once he fell in love all that would change.

'The Crightons are one-woman men,' she had informed Sara, grinning when the younger woman raised a doubting eyebrow and adding, 'Well, at least they are once they've found the right woman....'

'But they enjoy trying out several wrong ones before they do find her,' Sara suggested cynically.

She considered that her own sexual experience was about average for a woman of her age and her background but she was forced to admit that what she had felt when Nick had kissed her was something way outside that experience. It was also something that made her feel extremely wary about allowing it to happen again.

Nick was 'man trouble' with a capital *T*, and man

trouble was the last thing she wanted in her life. She was enjoying her freedom and enjoying, too, the limitless possibilities that lay ahead of her. She did not want to become involved with any man, but most especially a Crighton man.

'Sara...wait!' Nick insisted.

Warily Sara did so.

'I feel I owe you an apology....'

'Another one?' Sara queried coolly.

Immediately she realised that she had said the wrong thing. The dark tide of colour beneath his skin wasn't embarrassment; it was anger she recognised.

'Oh, for God's sake,' he ground out. 'This is ridiculous. Look, let's not beat about the bush, shall we? Both of us are adults, both of us know what's happening...what's happened, but right now, right now I'm not in the market for a relationship—of any kind.'

Sara stared at him. His directness stunned her and for a minute she was tempted to retreat into convention and pretend that she didn't know what he meant. But she was too busy trying to ignore that small sharp stab of disappointment his words had brought her.

To counteract it she took a deep breath and told him quickly, 'Well, that's just as well because *I'm* not in a position to *have* one,' she lied. 'In fact...' She looked expressively at her ring finger whilst a part of her brain looked on in shocked disapproval at what she was doing and saying. Recklessly she ignored it; the fierce flood of danger and excitement pouring through her veins was fuelling an unfamiliar rebellion.

'You're *married*,' Nick demanded, obviously shocked.

'No…' Sara admitted. 'Not yet…'

What on earth was she doing? But it was too late to recall her words. Nick was already insisting, 'But there *is* someone…'

'Yes,' she fibbed, crossing her fingers superstitiously behind her back.

'I see.' Furiously Nick fought against his own feelings. The anger, the sharp sense of possessiveness, the desire to remove whatever man there was already in her life with force if necessary. His feelings were totally ridiculous, he knew, totally irrational.

He paused and then frowned, remembering something.

'Tell me, what did you mean by that remark you made about Crighton men never apologising?'

Sara shrugged. There was no point in lying or concealing the truth. Why should she?

'My grandfather is married to the ex-wife of David Crighton.'

'What?' Nick looked puzzled for a moment but then his frown lifted.

'You mean Olivia and Jack's mother…Tiggy… Tania…' He groped for the vaguely remembered name.

'Tania. That's right,' Sara confirmed coolly.

'But she…' Nick began, remembering what he had heard on the family grapevine.

'She what?' Sara demanded sharply.

Nick shook his head. He had no way of knowing just how much Sara knew about Tania's past.

When she realised that he wasn't going to say any more Sara started to walk away from him. She had only taken a couple of steps when she heard him saying from behind her, 'What's his name?'

'Whose name?' she asked in bewilderment, turning round.

'The man,' Nick told her softly.

'The *man?*' The penny dropped and frantically Sara searched for a suitably impressive macho type male name whilst Nick watched her. A sudden suspicion had come to him.

'There isn't any man, is there?' he challenged her softly.

Sara stared at him for once lost for words. She could feel the hot betraying colour staining her skin.

'Why did you lie about him, Sara?' Nick asked her even more softly.

Sara shook her head. His perception had totally unnerved her.

'I—I don't know....'

'Oh, yes, you do,' Nick corrected her. 'It was because of *this,* wasn't it?'

Before she could stop him he had taken her in his arms and was kissing her with the same relentless sensuality she had felt before.

She fought not to react to him but every tissue in her body was swamped with the intensity of her response. She could feel his arousal against her body and knew that her own flesh was just as sexually eager as his. It was as though he held an awesome fascination for her which she had no way of controlling or resisting.

Her body burned with heat and excitement and a wild reckless urgency that was totally unfamiliar and totally insane. Without the control of her mind she knew her body would have been perfectly willing for Nick to lie her down right here where they were and complete what he had started in the most intimate and intense way there was.

There was an ache within her that shocked her almost as much as Nick's kiss had done. Behind her closed eyelids images of their naked bodies tormented her. She could see just how he would look, how he would feel, how he would taste. Oh yes…yes…she wanted that…wanted *him* so much.

The words screamed silently through her head as Nick withdrew his mouth from hers. They were both breathing heavily she noticed, just as she noticed how immediately and shamelessly her gaze went to his crotch and then to his face.

'This isn't going to happen,' she told him shakily.

Nick's face looked oddly pale beneath his tan, the bones standing out sharply.

'It already *has,*' he told her rawly.

'God help us both,' Sara thought she heard him saying as he turned and walked away from her.

It gave her no comfort to know that he was as disturbed and caught off balance by what had happened

as she was herself. Fear and excitement—where did
one begin and the other end? She started to walk back
to the restaurant uncomfortably conscious of the heavy
dragging sensation in her lower body and the ache in
her breasts.

Lust! She had *never* imagined herself experiencing
such a feeling but right now she was quite definitely
lusting after Nick Crighton. Lusting after him; for him;
to be *with* him, to have *him* within her.

Sara heard herself groaning out loud at the torment
her own wanton thoughts were causing her.

JENNY GLANCED AT Queensmead's kitchen clock. Almost half past three, Max should be arriving back soon
with the children. He had rung her earlier to say that
he would pick them up from school on his way back
from the hospital.

Jenny looked from the clock to the telephone.
Should she try to ring Livvy now?

All day long she had been thinking about her niece,
worrying about her as well as about Maddy. She felt
wretchedly guilty about what had happened that morning. She *knew* how sensitive Livvy was, how much at
times she was still inclined to feel the pain of her
growing-up years. Did Jon think of that, and of Livvy
and Jack at all, now when he made such a fuss of
David, Jenny couldn't help wondering a little bitterly.

She desperately wanted to speak to Olivia and to
put things right between them. No one knew better
than she did just how much the break-up of their mar-

riage must be hurting Olivia, but she wanted to do so face to face and somewhere where she could give Livvy the time and attention Jenny knew she must be needing.

Sadly she remembered how happy and vibrant her niece had been when she and Caspar had first married. They had seemed such a well-suited couple, ideal for one another. Jenny could remember visiting them; their home had seemed full of laughter and love, especially when Livvy had first been pregnant with Amelia. When had it all started to go wrong for her and why hadn't Olivia felt able to confide in her?

Had Livvy *tried* to? Had *she*—Jenny—been too involved with other things, other people, to notice? These last few years had been increasingly busy ones for all of them—but she *couldn't* let Livvy go on thinking that she didn't matter to her.

The kitchen door was opening and Max and the children were coming in.

'How's Maddy?' Jenny asked anxiously as she went to relieve Leo and Emma of their school bags and coats and take Jason from her son's arms.

Max's terse, 'They're still battling to bring her blood pressure down,' warned Jenny that there had been no improvement as yet in Maddy's condition.

Conscious of the children and the need to maintain the security of their normal routine for them she hugged them and told them that their milk and biscuits would be ready just as soon as they had changed out of their school clothes and washed their hands.

'I'm not hungry,' Leo denied. His lower lip was trembling slightly and Jenny's heart sank as she saw the fear in his eyes. He had always been a very sensitive child, closer to his mother than his father in the earliest years of his life, although now he and Max had formed a very strong loving bond.

'When is Mummy coming home?' he demanded of Max now.

'Just as soon as she's well enough,' Max answered him.

'I want her to be here *now*,' Leo told him tearfully.

'Oh, so do I, son,' Max agreed, swinging Leo up into his arms, his voice muffled against the little boy's hair as he hugged him fiercely and kissed him.

'Mummy isn't going to die, is she?' Leo pleaded.

'Of course she isn't, Leo,' Jenny denied chokily when she saw that Max was too overcome by his own emotions to answer him properly.

It tore at her heart-strings in a way that nothing else had ever done to see this man, her tall, strong, formidable son, who was so very dear to her show his emotions so openly and vulnerably.

'I'm sorry,' he apologised to Jenny five minutes later when she had taken over from him, soothing and calming Leo with a lifetime's experience of maternalism and then sending the children upstairs to follow their normal after-school routine.

'I didn't handle that well,' he continued bleakly. 'Oh God…if anything happens to Maddy…'

Jenny could hear the anguish in his voice. Instinctively she reached out to him.

'I know how worried you must be,' she told him. 'But she's in the very best hands, Max....'

Max looked away from her. He had seen the consultant earlier in the day when he had gone to visit Maddy. *No. I'm afraid that as yet there hasn't been any real change,* the consultant had responded in answer to Max's anxious question.

Every day was taking them closer to the twenty-week deadline and closer, too, to the danger of him losing Maddy.

After he had spoken with the consultant he had sat in Maddy's room next to her bed, listening to her telling him how guilty she felt about 'being so lazy lying here.' His gaze was drawn against his will to her stomach, a small mound beneath the hospital bedcovers.

Within her body lay the new life that he was responsible for, its heart beating, its body forming, growing. A new life whose existence threatened that of its mother. If there were to be a natural spontaneous end to Maddy's pregnancy now—it did happen after all—Maddy would be grief-stricken, he knew; but in time she would accept what had happened as an act of nature in a way that she would never ever accept a man-made termination of her pregnancy.

Please, God, let her blood pressure come down, Max prayed as he reached for her hand and held it tightly, but still his gaze returned to her stomach.

'Are you thinking like me how lucky we are?'

Maddy whispered to him as she lifted their clasped hands onto her belly. 'I tell the baby every day how much we love it.' A softly sweet smile curled her mouth. 'They say that it's impossible for a baby to be aware of emotions at this stage, but I don't agree. I think that a baby can sense when it's loved and wanted.'

Every word she said increased Max's guilt and fear. Even if he hadn't already known how Maddy would react to the suggestion of a termination of her pregnancy just listening to her now would have told him.

He could feel his fingers tensing against hers. It wasn't love he felt for this baby, it was…

He could see Maddy looking at him in concern as he pulled his hand away.

'MAX?' he could hear his mother saying worriedly.

'Maddy's blood pressure isn't coming down properly. If it doesn't…' Max felt as though he were trying to speak with a throat full of splintered glass.

'If things don't improve the only way to guarantee her safety would be to terminate her pregnancy.' He heard his mother's indrawn shocked gasp.

'Does Maddy know…?' Jenny began, but Max shook his head.

'No, the consultant's thinking up to now has been that to tell her would make the situation with her blood pressure even worse than it already is. What the hell kind of sense can it be to let a woman like Maddy die,' Max cried out in anguish. 'I'm going back to the hospital,' he told Jenny when he had himself back under control. 'I'll probably be there all evening. God knows what we'd have done without you, Ma....' he told her gruffly.

Jenny *had* been intending to suggest that Max stay with the children for a couple of hours that evening so that *she* could go and see Olivia but now she could see how much he needed to be with Maddy. She would have to ring home instead and ask Jon to come over she decided when the children came back into the kitchen.

As Max went across to the table and kissed each child Jenny's heart ached for him. Maddy was the most maternal woman Jenny knew. She would rather die than destroy the life of her own child. A small icy shudder ran through Jenny's body as that thought formed. Please, God, let Maddy get well. Spare them that! She prayed mentally as Max drove away. Oh, please, please God.

FOR THE UMPTEENTH TIME Annalise Cooke removed Jack's now crumpled letter from her school bag and started to re-read it. Not that she *needed* to, she knew every word of it off by heart, but still she had to read it, to touch the paper Jack had written it on, just for the reassurance and comfort it gave her.

School was over for the day now and she was on her way to the station to meet Jack's train.

'I'm going to come home. We can talk properly then,' he had written to her in response to her own frantic tear-stained letter to him. 'I'll be arriving at half past four so try to meet me at the station if you can.'

She had never dreamed that the wonderful weekend they had spent together what felt like a lifetime ago now would result in anything like this. Jack had been so careful! She had been almost sick with excitement the day she had travelled north to be with him. They had had his room at university to themselves and she had felt so grown-up going out with him for a meal and then going back there with him. Her father hadn't known what she was doing. He had taken her brothers away on a short fishing holiday and Annalise had telephoned Jack almost incoherent with excitement to tell him that at last they were going to be able to be together. Jack had already told her that he fully intended that they should wait longer before they made love, but this opportunity to be alone together had presented itself and it had been the most wonderful experience, perfect in every way, *everything* she had imagined and more.

Jack had made love to her as though she were the most tender, the most precious, the most loved girl in the whole world and it hadn't hurt a bit. She had giggled a little with nervousness as she had watched him put on the condom he had told her so seriously they must use. Afterwards, once she had come down to earth, she had asked him a little anxiously if he was sure that it was safe. He had insisted that it was and just to prove it he had made love to her again and twice more that night and she had felt as though she had died and gone to heaven, so blissful and perfect it—he—had been.

She had, of course, felt guilty about deceiving her father, especially when Jack had told her almost sternly that he would have preferred him to know and that *he* wanted to tell him that he loved her and that one day he planned to marry her. But Annalise knew her father far better than Jack did and she knew he would never accept that she was grown-up enough at seventeen, to do what she and Jack had done.

And even once she had come home, her blissed out exultation hadn't left her. Every night when she went to bed she had imagined that Jack was there with her, reliving everything he had done, everything he had said, each kiss and touch…each whispered promise of love and commitment. But then her feelings had changed to anxiety, and from anxiety to dread and fear as the days and then the weeks crept by and still she had not had her period.

She was two weeks overdue now. Her heart started to thump frantically against her ribs. She had wanted to ring Jack but she had been terrified that someone might overhear what she had to say and so she had written to him instead, begging him not to telephone but to write back which he had done and by return post, telling her that he was coming home. And now she was on her way to the station to meet him.

She had no idea *what* they were going to do. Her whole world had become a place of terrified dread. She had felt so sick at school today—in fact she felt sick every day!

CHAPTER SIX

'THE TRAIN IS now approaching Haslewich. Please stand clear of the doors.'

Grabbing his hold-all Jack made his way to the end of the carriage. Would Annalise be there to meet him? She should have received his letter.

The ink smudges where she had cried had torn at his heart making him ache with fierce protective love for her—and with shocked fear for himself.

She couldn't be pregnant. He had been so careful about using the condoms, wanting to be responsible about what they were doing, wanting to protect her and their love.

One day he and Annalise *would* have a family together but Jack shared his uncle Jon's old-fashioned moral beliefs. When he and Annalise became parents he wanted it to be within the security of a committed established relationship. He wanted them to be married and he wanted it to be when he was in a financial position to take care of his wife and child.

Right now he was still a student in his first year at university and it was unthinkable that he and Annalise, who was still at school, should become parents. But somehow something had gone wrong and it seemed that the unthinkable had happened.

A rash of nervous sweat broke out on his forehead. He had had to lie to his tutor about his reasons for coming home and although he had no immediate lectures, he suspected that he had not been believed. But he had had to come home to see Annalise. There was no way he could leave her to worry on her own.

It had been lucky that he had still had the fifty pounds David, his father, had given him just before he had left for university.

Jack had felt slightly uncomfortable at the time for taking the money but it had seemed easier to accept the gift than to upset and embarrass his father by refusing it.

Now, from the maturity of his nineteen years, a schoolboy no longer but legally now, in the eyes of the law and himself, an adult man and a man in love as well, he was wryly aware of how immature he had been when he had left home some years ago to go in search of his missing father.

Now that David had returned to his family and Jack was able to judge him man to man, he had discovered that his father was neither the despicable villain his sister Olivia claimed nor the hero he himself had secretly hoped he might be, but simply another human being. The cautious tentative roots of a new relationship had been put down between them but they were nothing when compared with the sturdy dependability of the relationship he shared with Jon and Jenny. *They* were the two who had really parented him, who had shown him what family could and should be and it was *their* marriage and *their* family life that Jack knew instinctively he would one day base his own on.

Not that he didn't *like* his father. He did, and he also liked Honor, his stepmother, too. He was glad that his father had come back and even more happy to see the close bond that existed between his uncle Jon and his father. He had just wished that his sister Olivia had been able to be more cool about the whole thing.

But he had far more to worry about now than Olivia's determination to hold their father at a distance.

If Annalise was right... His stomach churned with sick anxiety. It wasn't just Annalise and himself he was concerned for. There were Jon and Jenny, who he knew would be saddened that their trust in him had been misplaced—and Annalise's father who was so very, very strict with his daughter.

He would have to leave university and try to find a job; something that would pay enough for him to support himself and Annalise and the baby, but what he had no idea. They would have to get married, of course. Grimly he blinked away the moisture threatening to film his eyes. Mentally he could picture his aunt Jenny's face and hear the quiet sadness in her voice as she talked about the plight of the young girls who she tried to help through the agency of Ruth Crighton's charity.

'They love their babies, but some of them are so young themselves...too young, and so very often they don't understand that love on its own just isn't enough.'

His heart started to bang in heavy painful thuds. There was no way he wanted his Annalise to be one of those girls.

Oh, God, *why* hadn't he been more careful? But it was easy for him to ask himself that now when at the time… When, at the time, his whole world had been filled with the intensity, the immensity, of what he and Annalise were sharing, the wonder of their love, the wonder of her and the special gift of herself she was giving him.

The train had stopped. He got off, immediately scanning the platform for Annalise, blinking in the bright sunshine.

And then he saw her, a small, forlorn figure, standing with her back to him several yards away. She was wearing her school uniform and a feeling of intense guilt flooded through him.

He was shamingly aware that there had been a moment, a second of time, when he had first read her letter when he had wanted to reject what she had written, when his own shock and panic had made him want to simply pretend that nothing had happened, when he had forgotten that he was now an adult and a man and that Annalise and their baby were *his* responsibilities, when he had desperately wanted to be able to lay the burden of what had happened on someone else.

She was turning her head looking for him, and squaring his shoulders Jack called her name.

As he reached her he put down his hold-all to embrace her. Tears filled Annalise's eyes as she felt the fierce reassurance of Jack's hug. Only now could she admit to herself how afraid she had been that he might not come.

'Not here,' she whispered chokily. 'Someone might see us.' But still she clung desperately to him and Jack could feel her body trembling.

'Nothing's happened?' he guessed. 'You haven't...?'

As she shook her head he tried not to acknowledge how much he had been clinging to the hope that by some miracle she was all right.

'No,' Annalise told him. 'Oh, Jack, what are we going to *do?*'

Wordlessly they clung together whilst Jack stroked the smooth thickness of her hair. She was so vulnerable, so dependent on him. Fear filled him.

'I don't know,' he admitted honestly.

Fresh tears filled Annalise's eyes.

'Oh, Lise, please don't,' Jack groaned in despair. 'Look, let's go for a walk down by the river, we can talk down there....'

'I don't want anyone to see us,' Annalise told him anxiously. 'Do your aunt and uncle know you're here?'

'Not yet. I didn't...' Jack stopped. 'I wanted to talk

to *you* first,' he told her gently. 'Have you done anything yet? Been to see a doctor…or…'

Annalise's face paled as they set off towards the river.

'No. No, I couldn't. I wanted to telephone you but I daren't,' she told him. 'I wanted to ask you to get one of those test things and bring it with you. I daren't go into a chemist and ask for one here….'

Inwardly Jack berated himself for not thinking of that for himself.

'We could go to Chester to get one,' Jack offered. Annalise shook her head.

'I can't, not until next weekend.'

They had reached the river now and Annalise turned towards him, her face sharply grave and mature as she told him unsteadily, 'I've been thinking about one of those places…you know, they advertise them in the back of magazines…where you can…'

'No!' Jack denied forcefully, the colour draining out of his face.

'But what else can we do?' Annalise asked him pitifully. 'We *can't* have a baby, Jack…and my father will *kill* me if he finds out….'

'*I'm* the one who's to blame—not you,' Jack told her fiercely. 'I should never…' He stopped. 'I'll make everything all right, Lise, I promise. We'll get married. I'll leave university. We'll find somewhere to live. I'll get a job….'

The look in her eyes of someone already world-weary with the burden of her knowledge and yet at the same time full of the anguish and fear of a child, tore at his guts.

'*Don't* look at me like that,' he begged her.

'We can't do those things,' Annalise told him sadly. 'We're too young. They won't let us…. Your family will hate me if you leave university. You'll end up hating me, too, and our baby….'

'No,' Jack denied immediately. 'Never, *ever*… *Please* don't say that, Lise….'

There was no one else on the river path and impulsively Jack pulled her into his arms, holding her tightly against his body, his voice muffled against her hair as he told her how much he loved her and how much he would always love her.

Annalise wept quietly in his arms. Already she knew that his love on its own wasn't going to be enough to protect them from what lay ahead of them. With an immense effort she managed to control her tears. She wasn't a girl any more now…a child…she was a *woman*.

'Did you tell *anyone* that you were coming home?' she asked Jack.

Jack shook his head.

'No. I wanted to see you first,' he repeated. 'We need to make plans, Lise,' he warned her as gently as he could. 'I have to speak to your father….'

'No! Promise me you won't say anything to *any*-one—not yet—promise me, Jack,' she implored. She was so distressed that Jack felt he had no option other than to agree.

Suddenly she was a child again, terrified of her parents' anger, shivering as she moved closer to the warmth and protection of Jack's body.

'They'll make us stop seeing one another,' Annalise told him despairingly, her eyes full of fear.

'They can't,' Jack reassured firmly. 'No one can make us do anything we don't want to do, Annalise.'

'This isn't the way I wanted it to be,' Annalise responded miserably, looking away from him. 'I never wanted this.' Her voice broke over the words and Jack closed his eyes.

'I've got to go home,' she burst out. 'My father will be back soon. I wish this was all just a horrible dream and I could open my eyes and everything would be back to normal.' She was crying again, the noisy racking sobs of a child this time. Jack's own throat felt raw with pain and dread and with guilt. *He* had done this to her.

'Promise me that you'll stop worrying,' he begged her. 'We're in this together.' But Annalise could only look sorrowfully at him. It wasn't the same for him. How could it be?

As he watched her walk away from him, Jack's heart turned over. She looked so thin and frail. He wished he knew more about what was going to happen to her. Olivia, his sister, had had two children but he had not really paid much attention to the progress of her pregnancies. He was dreading the thought of having to break his news to Jon and Jenny.

Aunt Jenny would surely understand, though. She

had been pregnant herself when she and Uncle Jon had married. That was no secret. The baby had died shortly after it was born, Jack knew that.

He brushed his hand across his eyes. He had hoped that ultimately when he had qualified as a solicitor he would be able to join the family practice here in Haslewich—but that couldn't happen now.

As he made his way to Jon and Jenny's he tried to think of how he might best earn a living. The future seemed frighteningly daunting but Annalise and their baby had to be his prime concern—not himself.

EVEN NOW Saul wasn't sure just why he had turned off the main road on his way home from work, taking the side road that went past Livvy's. It wasn't because he cherished any secret forbidden passion for her. Those feelings had been completely swept away by his love for Tullah, but he *did* care about Olivia. She was still Livvy and he wanted to see her, wanted to offer her a shoulder to lean on if she should need one—he knew she was far too proud and independent to ask for help.

As Livvy's house loomed up ahead of him a cautionary voice warned him that it might have been wiser to discuss his feelings with Tullah before acting on them, but it was too late to heed that voice now.

OLIVIA'S FIRST intimation that she had a visitor came when Ally, the retriever, newly returned by the kennels where she had been staying whilst they were away, started to bark. The girls were both upstairs doing their homework and Olivia had been trying to motivate herself to start sorting through Caspar's things.

Relieved at having this task postponed she hurried to open the door.

'Saul…'

The feeling that filled her as she saw the tall and sexily handsome person of her second cousin walking towards her was the closest thing she had known to happiness in a long, long time.

Her voice caught in her throat as he reached her and then, to her own chagrin and Saul's obvious concern, she promptly burst into tears. Immediately Saul wrapped her in his arms as he hugged her tightly in a brotherly embrace.

'Hey, come on,' Olivia heard him protest against her hair as he squeezed her comfortingly.

'Let's get inside….'

Still keeping one arm around her he turned to close the front door before bending to pat Ally and then guide Olivia into the kitchen where he insisted that she sit down whilst he made them both a cup of tea.

'I heard about you and Caspar,' he told her.

'You and the entire population of Haslewich,' Olivia returned with a brave attempt at a normal bantering manner that made Saul's mouth curl in a gently reproving smile.

'This is *me,* Livvy,' he reminded her quietly. 'You can take down the defences. What the hell is Caspar thinking about?' he demanded fiercely. 'He's a fool to let you go....'

'I didn't give him much alternative,' Olivia admitted. 'It just wasn't working for us any more, Saul. We were picking fights with one another all the time and for the girls' sake...' She stopped speaking and took a deep breath. Saul was right. She didn't need to put up any defences against him. They were as close as though they were brother and sister and could easily at one time have been even closer...Saul had wanted her and she...

Saul was still an impossibly handsome and sensually appealing man, the kind of man any woman could be forgiven for wanting. He had a very special male strength about him and, right now, Olivia ached to have a man like Saul to lean on, a man like Saul to protect her, cherish her...

But Saul was married to Tullah she reminded herself sharply. Saul *loved* Tullah and she loved him and *she* had no right to be thinking what she was thinking, no matter how sorry for herself she might be feeling.

'What's wrong?' Saul asked her gently. 'And don't try telling me "Nothing." If you're having second thoughts about this separation...'

'No, it isn't that,' Olivia told him. She stopped and took a deep breath. The urge to confide in him couldn't be denied.

'Saul. I've done the most dreadful thing,' she told him in a wobbly voice. For a moment she thought he was going to respond with some teasing throw-away comment but then he gave her a penetrating look and instead said quietly, 'Tell me.'

Haltingly she did.

'...and now I don't know *what* to do,' she admitted. 'I can't bear to think what Jenny must think of me. My behaviour was so appalling.' Tears burned her voice. 'I feel so ashamed, Saul.'

'Would you like *me* to have a word with Jenny for you...explain...?' Saul suggested.

Immediately Olivia shook her head.

'No. I want to speak to her myself...to explain to her myself...I have to, I can't hide behind someone else—not even you.'

'I'm sure she'll understand,' Saul comforted her. 'Jenny *knows* you, Livvy. She loves you and she'll know how you must be feeling.'

'Then if she does, why hasn't she rung me?' Olivia asked him despairingly before shaking her head. 'Oh God, Saul, there I go again, feeling sorry for myself...being selfish. She must be *frantic* with worry about Maddy. *Has* there been any news about her yet?'

'Not so far as I know. She's still in hospital. Try not to worry,' Saul counselled her. 'Ring Jenny in the morning. She should have some news about Maddy by then and you can explain everything to her.' He glanced at his watch. 'I'd better go. Tullah will be wondering where the hell I am.'

As Olivia looked at the kitchen clock she couldn't believe that they had been talking for over an hour.

'Thanks,' she told him simply as she walked with him to the door.

'For what?' he demanded.

'For being you,' Olivia told him softly. 'And for understanding me.'

She kissed him quickly on the mouth and then stepped back. She was only feeling the way she was because she was lonely and vulnerable she told herself fiercely as she watched him walk to his car...that was all!

'MR CRIGHTON...'

Max tensed as the nurse came into the small room where he had been waiting to see Maddy ever since he had returned to the hospital to be told that the consultant had given strict instructions that she was not permitted to see anyone.

'Mr Lewis would like to have a word with you. If you'll come this way...'

Fighting to control his feelings Max strode after her down the corridor and into the room he had become so familiar with and which he knew would for ever now be for him a place drenched in the darkness of his own fear and pain.

'Please, sit down, Mr Crighton,' the consultant instructed him quietly.

'Why haven't I been allowed to see my wife?' Max demanded sharply.

'Your wife's situation, as you know, is very serious and it's vitally important that she isn't distressed or upset in any way.' The doctor started to frown. 'I have to be honest with you, Mr Crighton, she isn't responding as well as we would have liked.'

'What do you mean?' Max cut across him grimly. His mouth felt dry, acid with the taste of his own fear.

The consultant had stood up. He walked over to the narrow window of the room and fiddled with the blind, keeping his back to Max as he told him obliquely, 'When we first discussed your wife's condition you raised the question of a termination of her pregnancy....'

Max felt as though a lead weight had been tied to his heart dragging it down, sending it plummeting through his body.

'You said that wasn't an option you felt we needed to consider,' he managed to say.

'It wasn't *then*...' the other man agreed heavily before turning round to face Max.

'There's no easy way to say any of this. Your wife is very seriously ill, she's also closer to the point at which I would not carry out a termination. Do you understand what I'm trying to say, Mr Crighton? Your wife is nearly twenty weeks pregnant.'

'Of course I understand.' Max's voice was equally harsh. 'What will happen if you do nothing and the pre-eclampsia can't be controlled?'

The consultant looked sympathetic and told Max again about the risk of convulsions with both mother and baby being deprived of oxygen. 'If that happens...'

'Yes. I understand,' Max interrupted him harshly.

'If, in the next few days we can get your wife's blood pressure down to an acceptable level and keep it down, then should it recur in the latter stages of her pregnancy we can always opt to deliver the baby by Caesarean section.'

'...and if you can't get it down?' Max demanded.

The consultant looked away from him.

'If there is to be a termination of her pregnancy then it has to be carried out soon.'

'So what you're saying is that if she's shown no sign of responding to the treatment within a week then...'

The consultant sighed.

'Three days, Mr Crighton...that's all we can allow her. The termination has to be carried out *before* the twentieth week,' he repeated as though he were trying to explain something to a child.

Three days.

Helplessly Max rubbed his eyes. They felt as though they were rimmed with acid, dry and sharply painful.

'Have you told Maddy any of this?' he asked hoarsely.

The consultant shook his head.

'Not yet.'

For the first time he looked Max in the eyes.

'However, if in three days' time there has not been an improvement... Look, why don't you go home and try to get some rest?' the doctor was suggesting. 'There's no point in staying here. I'm afraid we can't

let you see your wife. She might sense...something...
and it's critically important that we keep her calm.'

Max bowed his head.

THE BABY WAS already asleep and Jenny had just finished reading Leo and Emma a story when Max rang.

'I'm coming home,' he told her.

'Maddy? How is she?' Jenny began but Max cut
her short.

'Not now, Ma,' he responded tiredly. 'I'll tell you
everything once I get back. I'm leaving now so I
shouldn't be very long.'

'I'll start supper,' Jenny suggested but on the other
end of the line Max fought against the nauseous rejection filling his stomach at the thought of food. Eating, doing *anything* to sustain his *own* life seemed almost a form of blasphemy in the light of what he had
just been told.

JACK WAS JUST cooking himself something to eat
when the telephone started to ring. The house had felt
oddly cold and unfamiliar without the welcoming
presence of his aunt. He assumed that she must be at
one of her committee meetings and that his uncle Jon
was still at work.

With one eye on his stir-fry he reached for the receiver and spoke into it. On the other end of the line
Jenny frowned as she recognised her nephew's voice.
What on earth was Jack doing at home? He was supposed to be at university.

'Jack?' she questioned in concern.

'Aunt Jenny.' Guilt filled Jack's voice.

'Are you all right?' Jenny asked him anxiously.

'Er, yes…I'm fine,' Jack responded but he sounded so unconvincing that Jenny immediately felt sharply anxious. If he was fine then *what* was he doing at home?

'Is your uncle Jon there?' she asked him.

'No,' Jack replied. 'Do you want me to give him a message if he comes home before you?'

'Mmm, yes…yes, please,' Jenny confirmed. 'Just tell him please that Maddy's still in hospital but that Max is on his way home and once he gets here I'll be coming back.'

She didn't say anything to Jack about her plans to go and see Olivia, primarily because she couldn't now decide what was worrying her more, Olivia's uncharacteristic behaviour that morning or the disturbing discovery that Jack was not at university where he should be but at home.

A sudden thought struck her.

'Jack, this unauthorised "exeat" you've given yourself,' she asked, keeping her voice as light as possible, 'wouldn't have anything to do with Annalise would it?'

His sharp intake of breath gave him away even before Jenny heard his carefully casual but wholly unbelievable, 'No…no why should it? I just had some spare time in my schedules and I thought I might as well spend it at home. Look, I've got to go, my stir-fry is about to burst into flames.'

As she replaced her own receiver Jenny closed her eyes. It had been obvious to her that Jack was lying to her and that Annalise *was* the reason he had come home.

They were both far too young for the intensity of the relationship that had developed between them. Jon and Jenny had already agreed that, but they knew all too well themselves the trauma of teenage heartaches to want to see Jack suffering from them.

Although he had tried manfully to keep it from her, Jenny had heard the note of despondency, of desperation almost, in Jack's voice and she ached with love and pity for them both. The last thing she wanted to see him do was to ruin the whole of his life by giving up his studies so that he could be with Annalise. Not that she didn't like Annalise. She did. But she and Jack were so young. Too young. And Jack had to understand and accept that he simply could not come rushing home every time he and Annalise had a falling-out.

What was happening to them all, Jenny wondered unhappily as she waited for Max to arrive. Suddenly it seemed as though their lives had plunged from happiness into danger and darkness.

Since David's return... Since David's return... Jenny stiffened. She knew that what she was thinking was illogical and more than a tad influenced by her

own very ambivalent feelings towards the man who
was now her brother-in-law but who had once been
her lover. She felt no desire whatsoever for David
now. *Jon* was the man she loved but David's return
had marked a sharp change in the previously gentle
happiness of all their lives—and not for the better—
and illogical or not, for that she could not help blaming him and wishing that he had stayed away.

'YOU'RE LATER than I expected,' Tullah commented
absently as Saul uncorked the bottle of red wine they
were having with dinner.

'Mmm…' he agreed non-committally. He would tell
her about his visit to Olivia later when they were on
their own and when he could do so without compro-
mising the confidence Livvy had given him about the
situation with Jenny. As a woman Tullah would probably have a more insightful view on how Livvy might
deal with the situation than he did himself.

'Am I going to be allowed a glass of wine tonight?'
Jemima asked Tullah hopefully.

She was the eldest of his three children from his
first marriage and Saul was ruefully aware of how fast
she was growing up. During the summer she and Tullah had made a 'secret' female shopping trip which
had resulted in a certain bashful mixture of self-
consciousness and smugness as she started to wear her
first bra.

'No. Not tonight,' Tullah answered her. 'It's a school night. Perhaps at the weekend…'

Jemima pulled a face but accepted Tullah's veto.

'Jem, can you tell the others that supper's ready please,' Tullah called out to her.

As Jemima left the kitchen, Nick walked in raising his eyebrows in appreciation as he saw the bottle of wine Saul was holding.

'Good choice,' he approved, adding carelessly, 'Is Livvy okay? I saw your car parked on her drive when I drove past earlier….'

Immediately Saul could sense Tullah's tension although she hadn't moved.

'You've been to see Olivia,' she asked him sharply. 'You never said…'

'No. I just called on impulse.'

Saul could see Nick looking at them both and starting to frown.

'Have I put my foot in it?' he asked.

'No.'

'Of course not…'

Both of them spoke at the same time but Saul knew that the flush darkening Tullah's face wasn't wholly caused by the heat of the meal she was removing from the oven.

Going over to help her he told her quietly, 'Look, I'm sorry I didn't say anything. I'll explain why later….'

Tullah's smile was tight and unforgiving. Saul heaved a sigh.

'HOW ARE THINGS at the hospital?' Jenny asked Max as she handed him the mug of coffee she had just made him.

'Maddy still isn't responding to the treatment,' Max told her bleakly.

All his life Max had possessed an aura of personal strength that had seemed indomitable but now, for the first time, Jenny was aware that a pall of defeat seemed to have settled around him.

Like any mother she instinctively wanted to help and reassure him.

'There must be *some* improvement,' she insisted, 'otherwise they would not have allowed you to come home.'

Max sighed.

'The reason they sent me home is *not* because of any improvement in Maddy's condition, Ma, but because they wanted me out of the way in case *I* inadvertently made her worse.' He paused and then burst out, 'Do you think I'd be here if they *hadn't* sent me away? Oh God, Ma...if I were to lose her...'

The sheer torment in his voice brought tears to Jenny's eyes. She could see how close he was to the edge of his own self-control and she could see, too, now just why the hospital *had* sent him home.

'These things take time,' she soothed him.

'Maddy doesn't *have* time....' Max grated. '*Neither* of them do.'

Just before he buried his face in his hands, Jenny saw the tell-tale sheen of his tears.

'Try to have faith, Max,' she counselled him gently.

'Look,' she continued softly, 'I *had* intended to go home.' She didn't tell him why, there was no point in telling him about Jack's unscheduled return home or her concerns for his young cousin, 'But if you'd prefer me to stay…'

Immediately Max shook his head.

'No, you go home. Dad must be cursing me for keeping you here this long.'

Jenny hesitated, torn between staying and going.

'Go home, Ma,' Max insisted seeing her indecision. 'I'll be fine…'

'Promise me you'll ring us if you need us,' Jenny begged him.

'I promise,' Max confirmed.

'I'll be back in the morning, anyway,' Jenny told him. 'You'll want to go back to the hospital then and I can sort out the children for you.'

Much as she hated to leave him she knew that this might be her only opportunity to speak to Jack and to find out exactly what was going on.

As she gave Max a fierce hug and headed for the back door she acknowledged unhappily that it was going to be almost impossible for her to go and see Olivia.

'JENNY…you're home…'

At any other time the relief and pleasure in Jon's voice would have brought a teasingly loving comment to her lips but on this occasion she simply pursed them in irritation.

'Jack's home,' Jon told her.

'Yes, I know,' Jenny responded. 'Has he told you why?'

'He said something about having a gap in his lectures,' Jon offered.

'I think it's because of Annalise,' Jenny corrected him grimly. 'I think they must have had a quarrel.'

Jon looked perturbed.

'Surely he wouldn't come home during term time because of that?' he asked her.

'They're in love, Jon,' Jenny reminded her husband, giving him an exasperated look as she added, 'Where's Jack now?'

'Upstairs in his room. How's Maddy?'

'There's no change,' Jenny admitted.

Jon walked over to her and put his arm round her, turning her to face him.

'You look worn-out,' he told her gently. 'Come and sit down. I'll make us both a drink.'

'No. I can't. I've got to go and talk to Jack—find out what's going on,' she refused Jon firmly. 'You'll need to talk to him, as well,' she insisted. 'You'll have to make him see how important it is that he goes back to university, Jon.'

'Jenny, it's nearly ten o'clock, I haven't seen you in days…. Jack isn't going anywhere. Surely he can wait until tomorrow…' He was about to tell her how much he was missing her but Jenny was already pulling away from him saying disapprovingly, 'You're beginning to sound as irresponsible as David always was.'

As she hurried towards the kitchen door her eyes were blurring with tears. She hated this disunity that had sprung up between them but she seemed powerless to be able to do anything about it.

OUTSIDE JACK'S bedroom, Jenny paused before knocking on the door. When Jack opened it she realised that in the short time he had been away he had grown even taller and broader but the hug he gave her was still that of a boy, no matter how much of a man he might look physically.

'I'm sorry,' he apologised, his voice muffled as he released her. 'I know I shouldn't have come home but I had to.'

The anguish in his voice increased Jenny's concern.

'I know how much Annalise means to you, Jack,' she began carefully. She felt both physically and emotionally drained; these last few weeks with David's return and marriage and then Maddy's illness had taken their toll on her and she had to remind herself of just how important his own present feelings would be to Jack and to treat them as seriously as she would have done were he ten years older.

'She means *everything* to me,' Jack responded gruffly. 'I *love* her Aunt Jenny and she loves me...I know that....'

Jenny closed her eyes. She could hear the desperation in his voice but for once her intuition did not tell her the cause of it and she misinterpreted the anguish she could hear as being caused by his fear of losing Annalise and not his fear *for* her.

It was the kind of mistake anyone could make…the kind of mistake that Fate delights in as she tauntingly throws down a life-changing card.

Jack ached to be able to confide fully in his aunt, but he had given his word to Annalise. The determination and the strength he had shown Annalise herself earlier had now been replaced by a natural feeling of fear. He badly needed the comfort and reassurance that spilling his anxiety and guilt out to Jenny would have given him but he was not going to break his word to Annalise.

At the back of his mind he knew that a part of him was hoping that somehow Jenny would guess what had happened and that she would tell him so and tell him, too, that he was not to worry and that everything would be all right, but instead Jenny told him tiredly, 'No matter how much you love Annalise, Jack, you cannot simply leave your studies and come home to see her, no matter *what* has happened between you…. Have you seen her yet?'

'This afternoon,' Jack acknowledged. Aunt Jenny had every reason to be angry with him—he knew that. Manfully he tried to respond to her questions. 'I wasn't making it up when I said that there was a gap in my lecture schedule,' he insisted truthfully. 'I *do* have a window of a few days.'

Jenny looked at him and saw in his eyes that he was

telling the truth. If it wasn't for Maddy's problems she would be planning to bundle Jack into her car in the morning and drive him right back to university but she simply didn't have the time to make that length of journey.

'I promise you that I'll go back just as soon as I need to,' Jack was telling her earnestly. 'I just must have a few days with Annalise to...to sort things out....'

Jenny could feel her exasperation and her tiredness increasing.

'Jack, Annalise has to understand that *you* are a university student,' she told him severely, 'and *that* means that you have to stay *at* university.'

Jack looked away from her. He could see how angry and upset she was and his heart sank. What was she going to say...how was she going to feel when he had to tell her that he and Annalise were going to become parents?

Jenny saw the look in his eyes and her own heart softened.

'Jack, I *do* understand. I *know* how hard it must be for you.' She gave a small sigh. 'You and Annalise are so young and I know you won't believe me when I say this but...' She stopped. He *wouldn't* believe her and she wasn't sure that she believed herself that the pains of one's youth faded into insignificance with age and experience. Look how long it had taken her and Jon to come to terms with their youthful traumas.

'I know how much things can hurt,' she told him

gently. 'But, Jack, you really do have to put your studies first at this stage in your life.' She broke off and picked up one of his large hands in her own smaller ones.

'Come downstairs and have some supper. We're probably better talking about all of this tomorrow when we've all had some time to sleep on it.'

Jack blinked hard. What would she say if he were to tell her that he didn't *want* to sleep on what he had to tell her and his uncle Jon.... No, he didn't *want* to but for Annalise's sake he *must*.

SAUL EXPELLED an irritable breath as Tullah walked into their bedroom from their en suite bathroom, deliberately refusing to look at him. She had been giving him the cold shoulder treatment all evening and he was becoming increasingly fed up with it.

'Look, Tullah, you're over-reacting,' he told her.

'Am I?' she challenged him. 'You go to see a woman, a *woman* you were once desperate to take to bed—without saying a word to *me* about your visit and you've got the gall to say I'm over-reacting.'

'I went to see Olivia, my *cousin*,' Saul corrected her firmly, 'and I went to see her because I thought... because I felt...'

'Yes?' Tullah pressed him acid sweetly. 'You *felt*...'

'Oh, for God's sake, Tullah,' Saul exploded. 'You're making an unnecessary melodrama out of the whole thing.'

He had shaved and showered ready for bed and ludicrously almost, Tullah who never ever wore anything to conceal her body from him in the privacy of their bedroom, was wrapped from her neck to her ankles in a thick fluffy towel.

To his own chagrin he discovered that there was something about the sight of his beautiful wife so clad that was having a disconcertingly distracting effect on him.

'Yes, with hindsight, I *should* have rung and told you…discussed with you,' he corrected himself as he saw her expression, 'what I was planning to do. Yes, I acted on impulse, but impulse is exactly what it was, Tullah, and not some latent desire to resurrect a relationship with Olivia that never existed in the first place. I thought she might want someone to talk to, a shoulder to lean on if you like. I felt sorry for her, concerned for her. I *like* her….' He stopped.

'Then why didn't you tell me you'd been to see her when you came in?' Tullah asked him reasonably.

'Because I wanted to wait until we were on our own and the reason for that was…' Briefly he related to her what Livvy had told him about Jenny.

'Livvy did *what?*' Tullah demanded. 'No wonder she feels reluctant to get in touch with Jenny.'

When she saw Saul's expression Tullah relented. 'It's okay,' she conceded, 'I'm being unfair. Livvy *is* going through a bad time. I saw how shocked she was today, too, when I told her about Maddy.'

She started to walk across the room whilst Saul

gazed distractedly and hungrily at her towel-clad body.
He could hear in her voice that the crisis was over.

'Friends?' he asked wryly.

She smiled as she came towards him, reaching out
to trace a small circle on his bare chest with her fin-
gernail.

'Maybe…' she allowed.

'You can't really be jealous of Livvy,' Saul murmured thickly as he tugged at her towel.

'You should be flattered that I still feel so passionate
about you that I *get* jealous,' Tullah teased him.

The towel gave way to the pressure of his fingers
and dropped to the floor. Saul drew in his breath.

'Mmm…so you feel passionately about me, do
you?' He could hear his own voice thickening and feel
his body hardening.

'Sometimes,' Tullah agreed dulcetly.

'Would now be one of those times?'

He was reacting like a boy, all hungry heat and
intensity, letting her run circles round him, Saul acknowledged humorously as Tullah leaned closer to
him and murmured judiciously, 'It could be…'

'*Could…*' Saul groaned hoarsely against the lips she
had placed against his.

'How will I know…' he began, but she stopped him,
one hand on his chest as she firmly held him just far
enough off her body so that she leaned forward to
brush her lips against his skin, the hard tight points of
her nipples brushed tantalisingly against his flesh, her

other hand... Saul closed his eyes and groaned as he felt what her other hand was doing.

'Oh, you'll know,' she was breathing in a soft whispery little voice between her kisses and as he felt his body responding to the silky stroke of her fingertips Saul decided that he had had enough of being teased and swept her up into his arms carrying her over to their bed.

'Don't forget Nick's here,' Tullah warned him as she saw the look in his eyes.

'Three bedrooms away.' Saul grinned.

One of the first things they had had to learn to do as lovers had been to make love without waking his sleeping children.

'So you don't really want Livvy, then,' Tullah asked him sensually as Saul's body settled down over hers.

'Who's Livvy?' Saul responded huskily, before capturing one of the nipples that had been taunting him so provocatively earlier with his lips, lapping it with his tongue as he fought to hold off his own rioting desire, wanting to build Tullah's desire to match his own, but as she reached for his hand and guided it between her legs he recognised that she was as aroused as he was himself. As he entered her he told her thickly, 'I'll *never* love or want anyone the way I do you, Tullah... Never...'

'You'd better not,' Tullah responded as she felt her body begin to shudder with the first strong contraction of her orgasm.

MAX WAS DREAMING.

He was running, or rather trying to run, along a vast white sandy beach but his feet kept being sucked down into the sand impeding his progress. Behind him he could feel the dark malevolent shadow that was pursuing him gaining on him. He could see on the sand the shadow of his unknown assailant and the knife he was holding in his upraised hand.

Frantically Max tried to avoid the downward plunge of the knife, turning as he did so to fend off his attacker, but as he turned round he saw to his horror that Maddy was behind him and that the knife was aimed at her.

In his sleep he cried out, a tortured sound, ripped from his throat at his own inability to protect her as the knife slashed down towards the unprotected mound of her pregnant body.

Abruptly Max woke up reaching out to switch on the bedside lamp. His body was drenched in sweat and he was shuddering as viciously as though he were gripped by a life-threatening fever. The normally warm private cocoon of this bedroom Maddy had created for them was filled with the acrid scent of his own agonising fear.

He looked at his watch. Two o'clock in the morning. The death hour. His body felt icy cold now but was still drenched in sweat. He had no need to question where the horror of his nightmare had come from. The setting had been that of his own vicious attack in Jamaica when he had travelled there in search of David, but with the substitution of Maddy and their baby as its victim rather than himself. Max buried his head in his hands.

How well he could understand right now the feelings and needs that drove those who believed that they could bargain with fate. There was no way he could go back to sleep now. Getting out of bed he pulled on his robe. He might as well go downstairs and do some work. But as he headed for the bedroom door he knew the shockingly brutal images conjured up in his nightmare would haunt him for the rest of his life.

As he reached for the door handle he closed his eyes and sent a silent plea to Maddy to get well.

CHAPTER SEVEN

'HURRY UP, girls. We've got to leave for school in
five minutes,' Olivia reminded her daughters.
'Where's Ally?' she asked as she realised that the dog
wasn't in the kitchen.

Without waiting for a reply she went to the back
door and opened it calling the dog's name and then
groaning in dismay as Ally came bounding happily
towards her and she both saw and smelled just what
the retriever had been doing. Sneaking into the field
and rolling in cow manure was one of the most blissful
and forbidden pleasures in Ally's life and the moment
she saw Olivia's expression the retriever's waving tail
dropped and she changed course, going straight to
where the hose pipe was attached to an outside tap.

'Oh, Ally,' Olivia reproached her helplessly as she
followed her and started to hose her down.

Five minutes later a chastened dog was standing in
the laundry room whilst Olivia reached for one of her
towels to rub her dry. As she grabbed the towel Olivia
saw Caspar's fishing basket. The Barbour he wore
when he walked Ally and went fishing was hanging
just above it. A feeling of intense sadness and loneli-
ness overwhelmed Olivia. Absently she reached out

and touched the Barbour, a mist of emotion hazing her eyes. They had bought this jacket together, Caspar protesting that it was far too British for him and Olivia insisting that it suited him. They had almost not made it to the shop, one of the few remaining traditional stores in Haslewich which still had a half-day closing.

A rare day off together had led to them staying in bed much later than usual—Olivia had woken up to find Caspar teasing her by tickling her skin with a small feather that had escaped from the duvet. She had reached out to grab it off him so that she could retaliate in kind and then play fight which had inevitably led to them making love.

Afterwards Caspar had gone downstairs to return with tea and toast and then... The shimmer in Olivia's eyes became an aching blur as she remembered the slow sweetness of the second lovemaking which had followed the first. They had been so much in love then, their lives together so filled with that love. Where had it gone? When had it gone?

'Mummy, we're going to be late for school,' Amelia called out from the kitchen.

Angry with herself, Olivia banished her foolishly weakening memories giving Ally a brisk rub and an even brisker caution not to repeat her offence. Her 'daily' would let the dog out when she came in later in the morning and as Ally tried to give her a remorseful lick Olivia chided her sternly, 'No, it's no use trying to get round me now.' But nevertheless she gave the retriever a forgiving pat before heading back to the kitchen where the girls were waiting for her.

There was no way now that she was going to have time to go and see Jenny, she acknowledged as they all hurried out to her car; and deep down inside Olivia knew that a part of her was relieved to be able to put her ordeal off.

Saul would never know just how tempted she had been to give in and weakly allow him to act as her go-between.

As she drove towards the girls' school, she wondered how Maddy was and offered up a small mental prayer for her cousin-in-law's swift recovery.

JACK FROWNED as he watched his aunt rushing round the kitchen. His uncle Jon had already left for work and Jenny had explained to Jack that she was going to Queensmead and that she didn't know when she would be back.

As he watched her Jack asked her uncertainly, 'Aunt Jenny, is everything all right with you and Uncle Jon?'

Jenny, who had been searching for her car keys, turned round to look at him.

'Of course it is,' she said. 'What on earth makes you ask such a question?' she demanded, but in her heart of hearts Jenny already knew.

What did surprise and disturb her, though, was that Jack had somehow picked up on the tension between her and Jon.

'Nothing,' Jack shrugged, looking both awkward and slightly embarrassed. His aunt was normally so concerned for her husband's welfare, so happily at one with him and he with her and Jack had immediately been aware of the small prickle of discord between them.

'Nothing's wrong,' Jenny reiterated more firmly. 'We're just both a bit on edge because we're worrying about Maddy...and not just about Maddy,' she added pointedly.

Her own increasing sense of anger and resentment towards Jon was something she herself couldn't explain. Trying to do so just made her feel even more guilty and angry and right now she didn't have time for the self-indulgence of such emotions. Part of the cause was Jon's growing relationship with his brother, of course. The new closeness growing between them made Jenny feel vulnerable and afraid; but these were feelings she didn't want to explore too closely, feelings she didn't have *time* to explore, she defended herself as she finally located her keys and picked them up.

By rights one of them ought to be sitting down with Jack and finding out more about this quarrel he had had with Annalise. By rights *she* ought to be on her way to see Olivia right now... By rights *Jon* ought to be playing a far more supportive role in their family traumas instead of escaping from them to spend his time with David.

AFTER HIS AUNT had left, Jack picked up the local paper and anxiously turned the pages until he found the Jobs Vacant columns. He had hoped to be able to borrow his aunt's car so that he could drive Annalise somewhere where they could talk more privately together. She was plainly terrified of telling her father what had happened, but sooner or later they were going to have to tell him and his own family as well. Wildly Jack wondered if it would be possible for them somehow to live on his grant if he could supplement it with a part-time job. Both of them and a baby as well? He clenched his hands in despair.

'YOU CAN SEE your wife now, Mr Crighton.'

White-faced with tension, Max hurried towards the door of Maddy's room. He had hardly been able to believe it when he had arrived at the hospital to be greeted by the news that Maddy's condition was showing a small improvement.

'A *very small* improvement,' the consultant had warned Max, his face relaxing into an unexpected smile as he added, 'Your wife is an extraordinary woman. She told me that if it will help her baby she's prepared to lie without moving a muscle for the remainder of her pregnancy, but hopefully that should not be necessary. If her blood pressure continues to improve we could be talking about allowing her to return home just so long as she continues to rest.'

Max had said nothing. The grim trauma of his nightmare still hung over him like a black pall.

MADDY WAS LYING in the middle of her narrow hospital bed, her pale face framed by her hair, her eyes luminous with love and understanding as she looked at Max.

He forced himself to smile as he reached for the hand she was holding out to him. In the few short days she had been in hospital it seemed to him that her already delicate bone structure had become even more fragile. He could circle her wrist so easily, her veins darkly blue beneath the whiteness of her skin. Almost clumsily he kissed the inside of her wrist, a give-away gesture if he had but known it, for Max was never clumsy and that he should be so now told Maddy just how concerned and upset he had to be.

Her heart and the baby lying underneath it gave a nervous little flutter. If *Max* was concerned... But the doctor had assured her that her blood pressure was coming down.

'How are things at home?' she asked him.

'Fine,' Max told her and she could see that he meant it. 'The kids are missing you, of course....'

'Mr Lewis said that if my blood pressure continues to come down I can see them later,' Maddy told him with a beaming smile. 'Try not to worry,' she begged him softly, 'It makes me feel so guilty....'

Max couldn't bear to look at her. *He* was the one with the burden of guilt.

'Poor baby,' Maddy crooned now patting her stomach, 'He or she isn't having a very good time.'

Max's guilt increased. He couldn't bring himself to

look at Maddy's stomach. For her sake he would have been prepared to sanction the termination of the new life she was carrying had he been permitted to do so, but *he* knew that Maddy herself would never have willingly countenanced such a course of action.

'I'd better go before the nurse comes in and throws me out,' Max told her gruffly. 'The doctor warned me that I could only have a few minutes with you.'

Maddy frowned uncertainly as he lifted her hand to his mouth and pressed a kiss into her palm. She felt as though he were keeping something from her, as though he were keeping him*self* from her, she recognised. But the anguish and the love she could see in his eyes as he turned to leave her were real enough.

As he walked towards the door, Max had to fight not to turn back and tell her how afraid he was of losing her and how haunted he now felt by his feelings towards their coming child. He felt as though his guilt would never leave him.

'I'M SORRY,' Sara apologised automatically as she pushed open the bookshop door, realising too late that someone was about to walk in, her expression changing as she recognised that that 'someone' was Nick.

'Oh,' she began stiffly, immediately starting to turn away, her body registering both her shock and her determination to distance herself from him.

She hadn't seen him since their meeting on the river path. Not that she had wanted to see him. She hadn't wanted to think about him, either, or to continually almost obsessively dwell on the way he was making her feel, she reminded herself ironically, but that hadn't stopped her from doing so.

'Sara.'

An outside observer, hearing that charged, almost passionate, note in Nick's voice could quite easily have got totally the wrong idea, Sara decided grimly as she fought not to allow herself to react to it. Behind her someone tut-tutted as they had to circle round them to get into the shop but neither Sara nor Nick were aware of their disgruntlement.

She had the most beautiful skin Nick had ever seen. He ached to reach out and touch it, to touch *her*. Her hair, thick and vibrant, hung sleekly to her shoulders. She was wearing a long camel-coloured coat; cashmere he suspected, over plain black trousers and a fitted black top. She smelled of fresh air and a subtle delicate perfume that made him want to move closer to her.

'Come and have a coffee with me.'

His abrupt invitation startled him as much as it did Sara. He could see the shock registering in her eyes along with the rejection. What the hell had possessed him? He knew there was no place in *his* life for what she represented.

'I…' Sara paused, the refusal she was about to utter somehow impossible to say. A chilly little breeze had sprung up making her shiver.

'Come on,' Nick announced firmly, slipping his hand beneath her arm. 'It's too cold to stand here and argue. My car's parked round the corner right outside the coffee shop.'

Somehow Sara found she was walking alongside him. What on earth was she *doing?* She *loathed* him, *detested* him and the last thing she wanted to do was to have coffee with him. But somehow that was exactly what she *was* doing, breathing in a rich heavenly scent of the freshly ground beans as they walked into the coffee shop, virtually empty apart from a very obvious pair of lovers seated in one corner and holding hands across their table.

'I don't know why I'm doing this,' Sara protested faintly as they were led to a table by one of the waitresses.

'Perhaps we're more alike than you think,' Nick suggested wryly as they sat down, enlarging when she looked sharply at him, 'Maybe we *both* like living dangerously.'

Living dangerously! Sara's stomach clenched betrayingly. What she was doing *was* dangerous, she acknowledged. Dangerous and downright reckless.

Scanning the menu Sara ordered hot chocolate, braving the look the stick-thin waitress gave her curves as she asked disapprovingly, 'With marshmallows or without?'

'With please,' Sara told her defiantly.

She could see Nick grinning at her as he gave his own order of espresso.

'Hot chocolate *and* marshmallows…somehow I thought you were going to be a café latte girl.'

'Really? Well I'm sorry to disappoint you,' Sara began challengingly, stopping when Nick asked her softly, 'Who said I was disappointed?'

Sara moved restlessly in her chair. Just in her line of vision the lovers were leaning closer to one another.

Curiously Nick turned his head towards the lovers and then looked back at her.

'Poor souls, they're obviously aching for something more intimate and we both know how *that* feels, don't we?'

'You're absolutely crazy,' Sara hissed at him furiously as the waitress brought their order.

'No,' Nick corrected her when the girl left, 'I'm, *honest.* You want me as much as I do you, Sara. No, don't bother to perjure yourself, there's no point.'

'Perjure myself. This isn't a court case. I'm not on trial. Oh, this is ridiculous. I...'

'You know the best thing you and I could do don't you?' Nick interrupted her.

'Yes, move to opposite ends of the country, or better still the universe....' Sara answered him flippantly.

'Actually I was thinking of something more radical than that,' Nick told her grimly.

Sara stared at him. She wished she hadn't ordered the chocolate. It tasted too sweet and sickly, clogging her already tight throat.

'The best way for us to get this whole thing out of our systems might not be for us to fight it but to go along with it—a quick, short, sharp fling a no-holds-barred sex thing, intense enough to burn itself out...'

Sara focused on him, her drink forgotten. 'You've got to be joking,' she interrupted him sharply. 'That's the oldest line in the book and if you think for one minute *I'm* going to fall for it...'

'Calm down. It wasn't a serious proposition,' Nick reassured her wryly. 'You've got to understand this situation is as unfamiliar to me as it obviously is to you....'

'You mean women actually still exist who *have* fallen for it,' Sara derided him.

'No,' Nick checked her instantly. 'I mean that I have *never* experienced what I am experiencing right now... *I* don't like what's happening any more than you do, Sara.'

'*Nothing* is happening,' Sara denied immediately.

'Prove it,' Nick challenged her. 'We can go back to your place now and I can take you in my arms and kiss you and you can show me just how much "nothing" is happening between us....'

'No,' Sara told him forcefully.

A short, sharp fling...a swift sexual liaison based on lust. It was alien to everything she believed in, everything she had felt she could ever want and yet, the images Nick's words had conjured up were tormenting; alluring and enticing; a hot body-drenching fantasy of sex and desire that teased her with dangerously illicit images of the two of them together and which had a devastating physical effect on her. Torn between shame and longing she tried to control her unruly thoughts. If Nick should even begin to guess what they were!

'I have to go,' she told him, feverishly getting up and almost bolting for the door knowing that Nick wouldn't be able to follow her until he had paid the bill.

Ruefully Nick watched as Sara made her escape. That comment he had made to her about them having a sexual fling had been said more as a challenge to his own feelings than as an option he had intended to promote *seriously,* but the expression on Sara's face, the brief betrayal he had seen in her eyes had been like adding petrol to the fire he himself had already started.

The resulting conflagration was still making itself felt within his body. Feelings so intense had *surely* to burn themselves out. Oblivious to the waitress's pouting disappointment at his total lack of interest in her, Nick made his way back to his car. If it wasn't for this wretched ridiculous ban that his doctor had placed on him returning to work he could have found some relief from what he was experiencing first by putting a safe distance between Sara and himself by returning home, and second by immersing himself in the most complex and demanding case he could find. But with big brother Saul watching his every move, he knew he wasn't going to be allowed to leave until the medics had given him the all clear.

OLIVIA STARED frowningly at the half-eaten sandwich on her desk. She couldn't remember buying it, never

mind starting to eat it. What *was* she going to do about
Jenny? She ached to have someone to confide in, but
who was there now?

Her mobile rang. Frantically she dived in her bag
to answer it, the colour leaving her face as she heard
the headmistress of the girls' school telling her crisply,
'Mrs Johnson, it's Briony Howard here. You were due
to pick your daughters up at six. That's when our after-
school crèche closes. It's now six-fifteen....'

Stammering an apology Olivia assured her that she
would pick the girls up within fifteen minutes.

How *could* she have let that happen? What kind of
mother *was* she, she asked herself guiltily as she
stuffed the mobile back into her bag and grabbed the
papers she had been working on.

It was just gone six-thirty when she pulled up outside the school. Amelia's and Alex's pale anxious
faces told their own story. Olivia apologised to the
grim-faced headmistress.

'Places at the crèche are limited,' she told Olivia
warningly, 'and I'm afraid that when we have parents
who abuse our time limits we have to ask them to
make alternative arrangements. On *this* occasion I'm
prepared to make allowances, but in future...'

Scarlet-cheeked, Olivia bowed her head as she accepted the other woman's justified rebuke.

As she hurried them towards the car she could see
that both girls were close to tears as indeed she was
herself. A memory of her own childhood came back

to her. She had been meant to be going to Brownies but her mother had been out shopping all day returning too late to take her and her father had flatly refused when Tania had complained that she was too tired, saying that he had an appointment.

They had started to argue and Olivia could remember how upset and close to tears she had felt, but when her father slammed out of the house Tania herself had started to cry and somehow Olivia had found that *she* was the one comforting her mother instead of the other way around. Later her father had come back grimly bowling her into the car without a word and then driving to the church hall far too fast but miraculously on time for the Brownie meeting.

He had even given her one of his terse hugs before driving off again. If she closed her eyes she could still capture the warm, secure feeling that had given her— the sense of belonging and of being loved; but such instances had been very rare and she was convinced her father had never really loved her.

There was no way she ever wanted one of her own daughters to think that!

'I'm sorry,' she apologised to them both as she unlocked the car door.

'It's all right, Mummy,' Amelia told her quietly. 'We told Mrs Howard that you would be busy working....'

Busy working! *Too* busy to remember that her daughters were waiting for her. What kind of person was she? What kind of mother was she?

Who knew, once she and Caspar were actually divorced perhaps he would remarry and provide them with a far better mother, one that the girls deserved.

Angrily she shook herself and her thoughts returned to her father. Why had he come back into their lives? She hated him for being here…hated him, hated him, hated him….

'I'm hungry,' Alex complained as they drew up outside the house.

Olivia glanced at the car clock. It was just gone seven. Normally Caspar gave the girls their tea at around five.

Caspar…

Olivia closed her eyes. She didn't want to think about her husband right now—so why was she doing so? Why was she sitting here in the car, reluctant to open the door and go into a house which she knew was going to feel cold and empty?

Cold…with the kind of central heating bills she was paying? And as for being empty… As she hustled her daughters towards the house, Olivia reminded herself that she had been the one to make the decision to separate from Caspar and it was a decision she was very glad she *had* made.

Once she had sorted out her child-care arrangements she would feel better. Right now she felt so guilty about the anxious expressions she had seen on her daughters' faces when she had arrived to pick them up.

'I'm sorry I was late coming for you,' she apologised huskily to them again.

'It's all right, Mummy,' was Amelia's same immediate response.

Olivia closed her eyes as guilt smote her. Amelia was a child still, a little girl, yet the tone of her voice, the look in her eyes, were those almost of an adult.

Fiercely Olivia refused to let herself cry in front of them.

'I wish Daddy was here,' Alex piped up, 'then he could have picked us up from school....'

She gave a small indignant gasp as Amelia nudged her and sent her a warning look.

'You hurt me,' she protested indignantly and then stopped, her face going bright-red, tears filling her eyes.

Olivia could feel her head starting to pulse with sickening tension.

'Girls, please don't fight,' she begged them. 'I'll make us something special for supper, shall I? What would you like?'

'A hamburger,' Alex clamoured with relish, her tears forgotten as she danced up and down.

A hamburger? Olivia's tension increased. That meant driving back into town and Caspar, who had virtually grown up on fast food courtesy of the complicated and haphazard child-care arrangements of his spectacularly involved mish-mash of stepparents, had always been very firm about making sure the girls ate what he termed 'proper food,' allowing them only one fast-food chain meal per month.

However, before she could say anything Amelia was telling her younger sister sharply, 'You know Daddy never let us have hamburgers during the week.'

'No...that's right,' Olivia agreed quickly, bustling both girls inside whilst she tried to ignore both Amelia's victorious told-you-so smirk at her younger sibling and Alex's sullenly angry complaints.

In most households Olivia knew it was the mother who dealt with these particular areas of negotiation and discipline, but because Caspar's work as a lecturer had enabled him to spend more time at home than she could herself, he had taken on that role in their family.

But *she* was the girls' mother she reminded herself stubbornly.

'BYE, GRAMPS.' Sara smiled fondly into her mobile telephone. Her grandfather had rung her, having learned from her parents where she was.

'Haslewich,' he had commented, asking doubtfully, 'Are you sure that's a good idea. Oh, I know your father thinks I'm a silly overprotective old fool,' he had continued whilst Sara had remained silent.

Although on the surface her father and grandfather got on well, Sara knew from what her mother had told her that Gramps had been something of an overprotective parent to her and that there had been arguments and discord when she had first met Richard Lanyon.

'That's why someone like Tania is the ideal person

for him,' Sara's mother had confided. 'Dad needs someone he can cosset and cherish, someone who won't feel overwhelmed and constrained by that kind of love as I'm afraid I did. I once accused him of always wanting to keep me as his little girl, which was both unfair and untrue, but my mother, your grandmother, was very similar to Tania.'

After that conversation Sara had been even more grateful to her own father for his robust parenting which had involved encouraging her to both act and, even more importantly, think independently.

Even so she still had a soft spot for her grandfather who had been the donor of many very enjoyable childhood treats and a shoulder to cry on when she had felt the need.

Perhaps she had inherited from him a watered-down version of his own desire to protect because she, too, felt very sympathetic to and protective of her stepgrandmamma.

'Have you told Tania where I've ended up?' she had asked her grandfather.

'No, and I don't intend to,' had been his prompt response. 'It would only upset her, arouse unhappy memories for her.'

'Tania has a son and daughter living in Haslewich,' her father had reminded Sara during their own telephone conversation. 'If you were to meet them you could find yourself in a potentially difficult position. No child enjoys being deserted by its parent.'

'Tania *didn't* desert them,' Sara had defended

fiercely. 'You know that, Dad. She *wanted* to see them but her ex's family made it too difficult for her and she felt, especially with her son, that he was at an age when it wasn't fair to him to disrupt him and cause him any conflict of loyalties...'

'Mmm...' had been her father's brief but telling response.

The Crightons. She had sworn before she met them that it would be impossible for her to like them—and now...

And now what...? She *liked* Nick Crighton. Sara made a taunting face at her reflection as she walked past a mirror. *Like* was hardly the word to describe the maelstrom of emotions *Nick* aroused within her.

No, maybe not, but a lot of them began with *L* didn't they? *Longing...lusting...loving...*

Loving! No. No way did she feel that. Admitting to the lusting bit was bad enough!

A short, sharp, sexual fling. A hot, sweet, mad, self-indulgence. A wild, wanton abandonment of her old teenage fantasies and beliefs that loving someone and wanting them could only go hand in hand. No it was unthinkable, impossible and yet, she only had to close her eyes to see Nick in her mind's eye: strongly muscled arms, broad shoulders, a very male torso—and he would look even better undressed than he did dressed, she suspected.

A soft little groan that was almost akin to an aroused-female growl escaped her lips. Guiltily she looked over her shoulder and then derided herself. She was alone in the flat, wasn't she, and Nick Crighton, whatever other skills of legerdemains he might possess did *not* have the power to simply materialise in front of her.

Not in person, perhaps, but he was quite definitely exerting a very strong pull on her senses and he certainly had the ability to 'materialise' to devastating physical effect in her imagination.

A short sexual fling! She must be mad to even contemplate such a thing. But she *wasn't* contemplating it. No. Not for one minute, even though she strongly believed that women were as entitled to acknowledge the sexual side of their natures as any man, even if she herself had never previously indulged in such a freedom.

She knew girls who had, though. Girls who quite openly and unashamedly stated that they had slept with a man simply because they had desired him physically, and so far as Sara had been able to judge, they had emerged from the experience not just totally emotionally unscathed but shockingly and almost enviably glowing with pleasure and self-satisfaction.

No, it was often the girls who swore that for them sex could only go hand in hand with love who were the ones who seemed to suffer the most traumas, investing so many hopes and dreams in their relationships that the discovery that their partner did not share them was a humiliating and devastating experience.

At least a sex-only fling could be ended cleanly and

tidily with a 'Thank you, I've had enough now and goodbye.'

And she *would* be glad to say goodbye to Nick Crighton, glad to say that she had totally burned out any desire for him. But, of course, it wasn't going to happen. She wasn't going to get any more involved with Nick Crighton than she already was—was she?

CHAPTER EIGHT

'YOU'RE VERY preoccupied,' David commented lovingly to Honor as he brought her the cup of herbal tea he had just made for them both. 'Is something wrong?'

'Not *wrong* exactly,' Honor said slowly.

Frowning David put down his own tea untouched. Honor had not been her normal self for several days and now his concern showed in his voice and face as he insisted, 'But something *is* bothering you? What is it, Hon? Are you having second thoughts about Father Ignatius being with us?'

'No, no...' Honor smiled immediately. 'I love having him here. He was telling me a fascinating story the other day about some of the remedies people use in Jamaica—and as for him being *here*... He's spending more time up at Fitzburgh Place than here. He and Freddy have really hit it off together.' She gave an amused smile. 'It's obvious they've got an awful lot in common.'

'An agnostic and a Jesuit. Yes. I suppose they must have,' David agreed wryly before adding, 'Stop trying to change the subject. What's wrong?'

Honor gave him a rueful look before warning him, 'You're not going to like this.'

'There isn't anything you could do I couldn't like,' David told her truthfully. 'You've given me so much, Honor. First and most importantly your sweet, delicious, wonderful self, but as well as that you've given me back my self-respect by accepting me, loving me as I am.... You've helped me grow, too, into a new better self. Because of you I've begun to build bridges between myself and my family. You've given me two wonderful stepdaughters...'

'Ah...' Honor intervened, her voice trembling slightly, 'Not just two stepdaughters, David.' She paused whilst he waited, puzzled.

'I think I'm pregnant,' she told him shakily. 'Well, not so much *think*,' she amended, talking quickly and slightly nervously. 'The symptoms are exactly the same as those I had when I was carrying both girls and I've done a test. I know how shocked you must be. I was myself and...'

'Not shocked,' David denied, walking over to her and taking her in his arms. His voice was muffled as he held her against his body. Honor wasn't sure which of them was trembling most—David or herself.

'Are you annoyed with me?' he asked her gruffly. 'You have every right to be, I know. I should have taken more care.'

'Me—cross with *you*?' Honor checked him. 'You mean you don't mind?'

'Mind...? I can only think of one thing that could make me happier than I feel right now,' David told her emotionally.

As she looked at him Honor knew that he was thinking of Olivia, but before she could say anything David was wrapping his arms gently around her and holding her tenderly as he told her softly, 'For you to have my child is surely far, far more than I could possibly deserve. He or she may not have been planned,' he continued as he raised one hand and gently stroked her face, 'But I can assure you that he or she will be very much loved. Oh, Honor…' His control broke and tears filled his eyes. 'For you to give me a child when you have already given me *so* much…'

'I still can't properly take it in myself,' Honor admitted, happy tears of her own filling her eyes. 'I thought I'd be too old and I know that the girls will certainly think so! We're going to have to make some sort of an official announcement, I suppose. Perhaps the best thing to do would be to invite everyone round…. I just wish…' She stopped, not wanting to upset David by saying that she was concerned that Olivia's refusal to have anything to do with them was going to make it difficult for them to give her any advance warning of what was going to happen. By rights, as David's daughter, she should be one of the first people to know, Honor believed.

She stopped speaking as David started to kiss her with passionate tenderness.

'I love you so much,' he whispered huskily to her, but as his eyes started to cloud a little Honor guessed what he was thinking.

'This is going to be very difficult for Olivia, isn't it?'

'I hate knowing how much she's hurting and not being able to do anything to help her,' David admitted as he released her. 'I can't blame her for feeling the way she does and I don't, but I just wish she'd let me talk to her.

'Just thinking about how much I want this baby, *our* baby, makes me feel like hell knowing how little either Tiggy or I wanted Olivia. Her conception was an accident and then somehow or other I convinced myself that she was going to be a boy. Dad wanted her to be a boy, of course, and...

'I can remember taking her to Dad's once. She wasn't feeling very well. She was screaming and feverish. I suppose she'd have been about ten months old. Tiggy and I had had a fight about who would go to her and whilst we were arguing Jon went and picked her up and took her over to Jenny. The moment Jenny held her she stopped crying.... I've never forgotten the look Jon gave me—a look I thoroughly deserved. Poor Livvy.'

'Yes,' Honor agreed. She hadn't expected to conceive and the timing couldn't have been worse but she could see in David's eyes that already, like her, he loved the child they had both created, even though their shared joy was shadowed by their knowledge of Olivia's pain.

'No, DON'T you dare move,' Max warned Maddy as he brought the car to a halt outside the front door to

Queensmead. He had picked her up from the hospital half an hour earlier and of the two of them, the doctor had remarked sardonically that Max looked more traumatised by the experience they had just been through than Maddy.

'You know what the doctor said,' Max reminded her as he opened the passenger door of his car for her. 'Totally, absolutely, no way are you to do anything other than rest....'

'That doesn't mean that I can't walk,' Maddy protested laughing as Max insisted on lifting her out of the car and carrying her into the house.

She had never seen him so emotionally affected by anything, not even when they had both thought their marriage had to end and it made her ache with love for him to know how much he cared.

The children and Jenny were waiting to welcome her home and tears filled Maddy's eyes as she saw the way her sitting room had been rearranged to provide room for a pretty day bed.

'From now until the baby arrives I'm going to be working quite a lot from home,' Max informed her firmly after Jenny had swept the children back to the kitchen for something to eat. 'Ma will be on hand as well if we should need her. Between us we'll sort out the school runs and everything else. All you have to do is to make sure that you follow the doctor's instructions and rest!'

Maddy waited until he had finished before saying

softly, 'Max, I'm not so fragile that you can't kiss me, you know.'

Emotionally she could see how much he loved her but physically he had been oddly and unfamiliarly distant with her and she had noticed, too, how much he was avoiding even looking at, never mind touching the bump that was their child.

She had wanted to ask him if anything was wrong but the journey home had tired her more than she wanted to admit. For their baby's sake she had to do as the consultant had instructed.

As he watched her and listened to her Max knew that their lives together could never be the same. The burden of the guilt he felt lay too heavily against him for that. Maddy would hate him if she were ever to know what he had thought, wished for, when he had feared that he might lose her.

Anxiously Maddy studied him. She had never known him so remote and withdrawn. Even in the early years of their marriage when she had felt he hated her, his reactions had still been blazingly passionate. Was he perhaps angry about the disruption her condition was causing? Things had not been entirely easy for him since David had returned. Did he perhaps secretly wish that this fourth child had not been conceived?

'Max,' she began huskily.

But he shook his head telling her firmly, 'You stay here and rest. I've got to go and help Ma get the kids ready for bed.'

JACK TRIED to focus on what his uncle Jon was saying to him. They were eating supper together, just the two of them because Aunt Jenny was still at Queensmead and Jack was heavy-heartedly aware of just how little progress he had made with his plans during the day.

Annalise had insisted on going to school. He had met her afterwards, not from school but on the river path because she didn't want anyone to see them together.

'Annalise, we *can't* keep what's happening a secret for much longer,' he had warned her gently, hating himself when she had burst into tears. It seemed unbelievable that they were going to be parents.

Sympathetically Jon watched Jack. It was obvious that the lad had his mind on other things. Teenage love could be traumatically painful, especially when it went wrong.

THE PAIN WAS so strong that it brought Annalise out of her deep sleep of emotional exhaustion. At first her mind blurred; she simply lay in her bed suffering the waves of sharp cramping discomfort then, as the fogginess of her sleep cleared she realised what they were and what was happening.

Hardly daring to believe what her body was telling her, she hurried to the bathroom. The proof that she was right and that her period had started made her feel giddy with joyous relief. She *wasn't* pregnant...she *wasn't* going to have a baby.

Automatically she did the things that were necessary

whilst all the time the relief inside her expanded like a bubble. Once she was back in bed she didn't want to sleep. Hugging her arms around her body she savoured the pain washing through her, welcoming it.

She had prayed so desperately for this to happen and now that it had… Now that it had, she was never, ever going to have sex again she told herself fervently. At least not unless she was one hundred percent sure that she was properly protected from *any* risk of pregnancy. A cold shudder ran through her as she allowed herself to acknowledge properly for the first time just what it would have meant if she *had* been pregnant. Jack might have said that they would get married and that everything would be all right, but she knew it wouldn't have been so easy.

Jack… She would telephone him first thing in the morning to give him their good news, she decided tiredly as the painful cramps slowly started to ease and she drifted back to sleep.

JACK HAD JUST woken up when his mobile rang. Reaching for it he answered the call, his heart pounding heavily as he heard Annalise's voice.

'What is it? What's wrong?' he demanded anxiously.

'Nothing,' Annalise responded, the happiness bubbling through her voice as she told him, 'nothing's wrong at all. In fact, everything is wonderfully, fabulously all right. I'm not going to have a baby, Jack…I'm not pregnant…we're safe….'

It took several seconds for her excited words to reach his brain.

'What?' he demanded. 'When...? How...?'

Quickly Annalise explained.

'Look, I've got to go,' she told him.

'I'll meet you after school,' Jack began. 'We can talk properly then....'

'I've got to go,' Annalise repeated. 'Jack...you won't tell *anyone* about any of this will you?' she begged him. 'I couldn't bear anyone else to know.'

Jack frowned. His first thought when he realised what Annalise was telling him had been one of relief that he could now honestly explain to his aunt and uncle just why he had come home, why he had no option *other* than to come home.

'Promise me, Jack,' Annalise was insisting. Jack could hear the tension in her voice and the anxiety. Reluctantly he gave in.

'I promise,' he told her.

Annalise's hand shook as she put down her own mobile. All she wanted to do now was to forget how frightened she had been and why and for her life to go back to normal.

THE MOMENT Jenny saw Jack's face when he walked into the kitchen she could see how much happier he was. She knew that he had seen Annalise the previous day and she guessed that they had made up their quarrel. Even so...

'You look a lot happier this morning,' she commented.

'I am,' Jack agreed, going over to her and giving her a fierce hug as he told her in a muffled voice, 'I'm sorry, Aunt Jen, but I *had* to come home and see Annalise.... Please don't worry, though, everything's fine now and I'll be going back to uni tomorrow.'

'Everything's fine now,' Jenny repeated wryly. 'But what happens the next time you have a falling-out, Jack? This *mustn't* happen again,' she insisted firmly.

Jack released her, his eyes unhappy. He ached to be able to explain to her that it was no mere quarrel that had brought him home but something far more serious, but he had given his word to Annalise and he could not break it.

'It won't,' he assured her.

Jenny wished she could be as sure.

'How's Maddy?' Jack asked her.

'Improving,' Jenny replied.

Max had told her that he could manage without her help today, which meant that she could have a much needed day in her own home and the first thing she intended to do just as soon as she had stripped the beds and filled the washing machine was to go for a supermarket shop for both herself and Queensmead.

'DAVID,' Jon exclaimed in pleasure as his brother walked into his office. 'I wasn't expecting to see you today.'

'No,' David agreed. 'I was up at Fitzburgh Place

earlier and Frederick asked me if I would drop some papers off with you.'

'Got time for a coffee?' Jon asked as he took the papers from him.

'Mmm...I wouldn't mind.'

'You look rather distracted. Is anything wrong?' Jon asked.

'Not *wrong* exactly,' David told him, taking a deep breath before saying hesitantly, 'The fact is—' a rueful almost boyish smile of pride and pleasure curled his mouth '—Honor's pregnant.'

Outside Jon's half-open office door Tullah, who had just been on her way into Jon's office to ask him something, came to an abrupt halt.

'Pregnant... You mean with a *baby?*' Jon demanded in bemusement.

'Pregnant...with a baby,' David confirmed straight-faced. 'It wasn't something we'd planned,' he confessed, 'but I have to say that as accidents go, *this* one *is* pretty wonderful. We're going to organise a family get-together to make an official announcement.'

A new love, a second family, a whole new role and purpose in life. Jon couldn't help but be pleased for his twin, whose happiness he now felt was set fair to match his own.

Embracing him warmly he told him, 'Congratulations.'

But then he frowned. 'I take it that neither Livvy nor Jack know as yet?'

'No,' David confirmed soberly. 'God, Jon, I hope I

make a better father this time around than I did for
them. I've tried to talk to Jack about it, to explain to
him. He listened to me like an adult listening to a
child, politely but unconvinced. But then, why should
either he or Livvy care about my guilt? From their
point of view, I haven't done much caring about
them.'

Outside Jon's office door Tullah suddenly realised
that she was eavesdropping. Quickly she hurried away.
She felt as shocked as Jon had sounded by David's
news.

'How *is* Livvy?' David asked Jon anxiously. 'I wish
there was something I could do to help her.'

'Well, she's obviously very unhappy,' Jon acknowledged. 'Although what with Maddy being so ill and
Jack coming home unexpectedly from university, there
hasn't been the opportunity to talk in any depth to
Livvy about anything.'

'Jack's home?' David questioned sharply.

'Yes, but he's going back tomorrow,' Jon reassured
him. 'He and Annalise had a falling-out apparently but
everything's okay now.'

As David listened to him, his feeling of guilt increased. His daughter was battling on her own with
the trauma of her broken marriage. His son had had a
row, serious enough, with his girlfriend, to bring him
home from university and yet neither of them had
made any attempt to turn to him for help or comfort.
But then, when had *he* ever indicated to them that they
could do, when had he *ever* made time for them or

their problems? When had he *ever* let them see that he cared...that he loved them?

Heavy-hearted, David acknowledged the extent of his own failings. He ached to make amends, to build a closer relationship with Jack and Olivia, to be a proper grandfather to Olivia's girls and to Jack's children when he should have them, but he couldn't blame Jack and Olivia for holding him at a distance.

He had changed so much since his cowardly flight from Haslewich, grown so much, but proving that to himself was not enough where his children were concerned. They needed, especially Olivia, to have it proved to *them*. But how could he do that, he wondered in wry frustration, when Olivia wouldn't allow him anywhere near her?

'What about Maddy? How is she?' he asked Jon, momentarily putting his anxiety for Olivia to one side.

'Getting better—slowly,' Jon told him. The news that Honor and David were expecting a child had brought a problem to the forefront of his mind that needed to be addressed.

'Dad is giving Max and Maddy a hard time at the moment,' he confided. 'We're all anxious about Maddy with this pre-eclampsia problem. She's home now but only on the strict understanding that she doesn't overdo things, but the fact that Dad keeps threatening to leave Queensmead to someone else isn't exactly helping.'

'To me, you mean,' David responded. 'Look, Jon, I've already told you, so far as I'm concerned I have no right whatsoever to Queensmead…I don't even want the place.'

'Mmm…*I* know that, but Dad…'

'Do you want me to have a word with him?' David offered.

'Well, you could try but once he knows that you and Honor are having a child it will probably make him worse than ever. Jenny is furious with him. No one could have looked after him better than Maddy.'

'No, Honor was saying that he's lucky to be in the position he is in,' David agreed.

OLIVIA LOOKED at the baguette she had just bought. She wasn't really hungry even though she hadn't had a proper breakfast and the small quiet garden overlooking Haslewich's churchyard was hardly the place to sit and eat at this time of year. Huddling deeper into her coat she started to re-wrap her unwanted lunch. She could have taken it back to her office to eat, of course, but she had felt in need of some fresh air—and an escape from the distracting and unwanted images of Caspar that had been coming between her and her work all morning.

It had been spotting his fishing basket that had done it, made her remember and see them as a loving couple again through the surely far-too-rosy-tinted lenses of the early days of their relationship.

Jenny was crossing the church's small garden on her way back from visiting the grave of her first child. The sharp sadness of his long-ago death was gone now and she found it comforting to sit and talk to him, updating him with their family news as she tidied his grave. Then she saw Olivia, seated on one of the benches, apparently staring sightlessly into space.

Immediately she started to hurry towards her.

'Jenny!' Olivia couldn't keep the shock or the guilt out of her voice when she felt her aunt's hand on her shoulder. 'I didn't see you coming.'

'No. You were miles away,' Jenny agreed.

Olivia bit her lip as Jenny sat down next to her.

'I feel dreadful about the way I behaved…and what I said,' Olivia confessed. 'I had no idea about Maddy, but that doesn't…' She stopped and shook her head, her voice suddenly thickening with tears.

'Livvy, it's all right,' Jenny reassured her. 'I can imagine how you must have been feeling. I felt dreadful myself that I didn't explain properly.'

'I've been meaning—'

'I wanted—'

Both of them started to speak at once and then stopped.

'I was going to get in touch,' Olivia began, 'But I was afraid…I wouldn't have blamed you if you'd refused to accept my apology. My behaviour was unfor—'

'Livvy, Livvy, I would *never* do that,' Jenny protested, so plainly distressed by what Olivia had said that the younger woman felt some of her weary tension start to ease away.

'I think we can all appreciate what a difficult time

you've been having,' Jenny continued gently. 'The break-up of any relationship is traumatic.'

As she heard the loving compassion in Jenny's voice Olivia's eyes began to smart.

'Oh, Aunt Jenny…'

As she saw the way Olivia's body was shaking Jenny reacted instinctively, putting her arms around her and holding her close.

'It's all right, Livvy, it's all right….' She soothed her, much as she would have done had Olivia still been a little girl who had so often come to her with her problems. Wisely Jenny let her cry, sensing that Olivia needed the release.

'Are you having second thoughts about separating from Caspar?' she asked her forthrightly when Olivia had eventually pulled back from her and accepted the tissue Jenny had proffered.

'It's too late for that,' Olivia responded. Not even to Jenny could she bring herself to admit to the chaotic turmoil of her feelings or the grief that was threatening to overwhelm her. But grief from what? Not for the sterile hostile territory their marriage had become. No, her grief was for what their relationship had once been and for the love they had once shared but had now lost.

'Livvy,' Jenny said as Olivia got herself back under control. 'I wish I could do something to help you with the girls but at the moment…'

'It's all right. I *do* understand,' Olivia assured her immediately—and meant it.

'I've got them into an after-school crèche for now but that can only be a temporary measure. Do you think it's worth asking Chrissie Cooke if she knows of anyone? Her husband is related to more than half the town one way or another.'

'I'll ask her for you, if you like,' Jenny offered immediately. She hesitated. She held no brief for David but her conscience forced her to point out quietly, 'Have you thought of asking David and Honor, Livvy? I'm not trying to lecture you, but David *is* the girls' grandfather and I know from what Jon's said that he desperately wants to be able to get to know them properly.'

'My *father*...' Livvy's face had gone white with angry rejection. 'Do you *really* think I'd do that, no matter how desperate I was?' She gave her aunt a small tight bitter smile.

Jenny knew just how Olivia would react but she had felt duty bound to make the suggestion.

'Oh, Jenny,' Olivia began, abruptly burying her head in her hands.

'*Why* did he have to come back? *Why* couldn't he have stayed where he was? Just knowing he's here in Haslewich makes me feel...makes me want...' Olivia turned her face away. How could she explain the feelings of alienation and anger that had possessed her since her father's return when she couldn't fully understand them herself?

'I'm so sorry, I've got to go,' Jenny told her with regret. 'I've got my own supermarket shop to do and

Queensmead's, and I want to get Jack's things ironed before he goes back to university tomorrow.'

Jack's home?' Olivia demanded in surprise.

'An unofficial visit,' Jenny told her wryly, briefly explaining what had happened.

'Well it's no use expecting Dad to talk to Jack about moral values and obligations,' Olivia told her aunt bitterly. 'I'm sorry,' she apologised to Jenny, 'But I just can't help it.'

'I'll be in touch,' Jenny told her as they both stood up. 'And I'll have a word with Chrissie and ask her if she knows of anyone suitable to help out with the girls.'

'You're the best,' Olivia told her gruffly. 'You don't know how much I've been hating myself for—'

'It's over…forgotten,' Jenny told her quietly, 'And Livvy…don't ever think that *you* don't matter or that your uncle Jon and I don't care. You're *very* special to us and you always will be.'

As they turned to go their separate ways, Olivia's heart felt infinitely lighter than it had done.

BEFORE HEADING for the supermarket Jenny dialled Chrissie's number on her mobile and quickly explained the problems Olivia was having finding someone to help her with her daughters.

'Well, I don't *know* anyone, but I'll certainly ask around,' Guy's wife confirmed immediately.

They chatted for a few more minutes and Chrissie, like everyone else, was anxious to know about Maddy, asking Jenny to pass on to her her good wishes for her continued recovery.

SARA AND Frances were sharing a working lunch when Chrissie arrived, kissing her sister-in-law warmly and shaking her head over her offer of something to eat.

'I'm trying to watch my weight,' she groaned. 'Guy is taking us to Tuscany next summer and I'm determined to fit into my pre-baby bikinis!

'Look, I know it's a long shot,' she continued, 'But Jenny Crighton rang me earlier. Olivia is desperate to find someone to help her with the girls now that she and Caspar have separated and she was wondering if *we* knew of anyone.'

Frowning a little Frances shook her head. 'I know of plenty of potential baby*sitters,* but there isn't anyone old enough or experienced enough to act as a proper help.'

'No, that's what Jenny thought. She feels very guilty that she can't offer.'

'Poor Livvy, I feel so sorry for her,' Frances sighed. 'Catch me not being there to help any of *my* children if they needed me. I know that Jenny has been like a mother to Livvy but you'd think that Livvy's *own* mother would be only too delighted to offer her help.'

'Well, you'd certainly think so,' Chrissie agreed, 'but from what *I've* heard, Tania was never much of a mother to either Livvy or Jack and by all accounts she's shown no interest in her grandchildren at all.'

Sara had started to stiffen when they began to discuss Grandmamma Tania. She was dying to defend her, to put *her* side of the story, but how could she? How would it look if she suddenly admitted to a relationship which she had never previously mentioned? Frances had been more than kind to her and Sara acknowledged that the older woman would have every right to feel that Sara had behaved deceitfully in not mentioning the relationship earlier. Not that she *had* intended deliberately to conceal it, *but*... But she now found herself in a position which was making her feel both guilty and uncomfortable.

'Perhaps Olivia's mother doesn't know she needs her help,' was all she dared allow herself to say.

'Well, she certainly knows that she's a grandmother,' Chrissie answered pithily, 'and despite Olivia's offers to take the children to see her she's always managed to come up with some excuse not to see them.'

Sara was stunned. This wasn't the way her grandmamma told the story. Though she remembered her father had sometimes been acerbic in his reaction to Tania's never getting to see either her children or her grandchildren. Perhaps there was some truth in his comments after all.

'I do feel so sorry for Livvy,' Chrissie was saying now. 'She had such a raw deal when she was growing up and now to have her marriage break down as well...'

'Yes, she hasn't had an easy life,' Frances agreed.

ANNALISE DAWDLED across the supermarket car park
with her shopping. She was going to be late meeting
Jack. She ought to be looking forward to seeing him
she knew, to sharing with him her sense of joy and
relief that she was not, after all, pregnant, but for some
reason she felt almost as though she didn't *want* to see
him.

Jenny had just loaded her shopping into her car and
was on her way to park her trolley when she saw the
girl.

'Annalise,' she called out, frowning a little as she
noticed the almost despondent hunch of her heart-
achingly vulnerable narrow teenage shoulders.

With her own daughters and Olivia grown-up Jenny
had almost forgotten how endearingly coltlike teenage
girls could be.

Annalise stopped as she heard Jenny call her name,
turning round to look at her.

Jack's aunt! A paralysing sense of guilt and apprehension filled her, an atavistic female sense of wrong-
doing and responsibility, too deeply ingrained for Annalise herself to be able to understand or analyse it.

She just knew somehow that of the two of them,
she would have been the one who both Jack's family
and her own would have blamed if she had been pregnant.

Jack might have tried to convince her that his aunt
would understand and want to help them but Annalise
had not been able to believe him.

Annalise looked far from happy, Jenny recognised

as she caught up with her and her heart went out to her.

'Have you got time for a chat?' she asked her.

Annalise wanted to refuse but Jenny was already leading the way to her car. Reluctantly Annalise went with her. Her tummy still ached and she felt vaguely sick.

Annalise was looking at her as though she were expecting her to be angry with her, Jenny thought ruefully. She *had* been angry, it was true, with Jack as well as with Annalise, but now suddenly she was remembering how it felt to be Annalise's age and in love.

Jenny could see from Annalise's strained expression just how much the quarrel between her and Jack must have upset her. The older woman had no wish to add to that upset but since fate *had* given her an opportunity to talk frankly to Annalise, Jenny felt that she had to take it—and not just for Jack's sake.

'Jack told me what happened,' Jenny began gently, frowning when she saw Annalise's white-faced shocked reaction.

'What's wrong?' she prompted her quietly.

'He promised me he wouldn't *tell* anyone,' Annalise burst out. She couldn't believe that Jack would lie to her, especially not about something so important. Her hands curled into two small frustrated fists of pain.

'It was *private*…. He had no right….' She stopped, fighting back her tears of shock and anger. She had been on an emotional see-saw all day, one minute euphoric and giddy with relief, the next half-afraid that she might have imagined it and that she *was* pregnant after all.

'Annalise, I'm his *aunt*,' Jenny reminded her firmly. 'His uncle Jon and I are his legal guardians. He might be over eighteen now but we still feel responsible for him. I'm sure that both of you consider yourselves to be grown-up but I think you know that it wasn't a very grown-up thing for Jack to do to come home from university in term time.'

'*I* didn't ask him to....' Annalise protested, sensing that Jenny was blaming her.

No doubt Jack's family would have preferred it if she hadn't said anything to him at all, if she had simply kept her shame and his unwanted baby out of his and their lives she decided bitterly.

'As it happens, everything has worked out for the best,' Jenny was continuing, 'but this must not happen again Annalise and we have told Jack so.'

'*Again...*' Annalise turned huge anguished eyes in Jenny's direction. Her gaze, full of bitterness and pain, caught at Jenny's heart, but she knew she had to stand firm.

'I *know* that both you and Jack consider yourselves to be in love,' Jenny continued carefully, 'but you're very young...and we'd hate to see either of you ruining your lives. It's vitally important that Jack gets his degree, Annalise. He'll have told you, I know, how much he wants to become a solicitor.'

Annalise knew what Jenny Crighton was telling her.

She was telling her that Jack's family did not want his life ruined by an unwanted pregnancy. She might be pretending to be equally concerned about *her,* but Annalise knew that she wasn't. How *could* she be? *She* meant nothing to the Crightons. She probably didn't mean all that much to Jack, either. How could she, when he had broken his promise to her and told his aunt?

Inwardly she writhed in hot shame at what his aunt must be thinking. Annalise's father was old-fashioned and he held old-fashioned views about girls who became pregnant outside marriage—views which he had made very plain to his daughter.

Annalise couldn't bear any more. She turned and hurried away, ignoring Jenny's anxious, 'Annalise… please wait,' as the girl tore across the car park clutching her shopping.

'Well, you made a fine mess of that,' Jenny berated herself as she watched her go. She hadn't meant to upset her, only to try to make her understand how vitally important it was that Jack did not repeat his behaviour of this week and come rushing home every time they had a falling-out.

Sighing, Jenny switched on the engine of her car.

CHAPTER NINE

'WHAT DO YOU mean—it's over?' Jack asked Annalise in bewilderment. He had been waiting for her for over half an hour and five minutes ago when she had eventually arrived she had sidestepped his embrace telling him flatly, 'I mean it's over,' Annalise reiterated sharply 'Over...finished...us...'

'Annalise,' Jack protested. 'Look, I know this pregnancy business upset you, but...' He tried to reach for her hand but Annalise shook her head and stepped back from him, the expression in her eyes cold and rejecting. She ached to challenge him about his broken promise to her but she was afraid that if she did she would break down in tears.

'I don't understand what's happening,' Jack told her quietly. 'I love you.'

How could she believe *that?* How could she believe *any*thing he said to her now?

'I thought *you* loved *me,*' Jack coaxed. There was a hard lump in his throat, a sharp, savage pain in his heart. He couldn't understand what was happening or why.

Annalise looked away from him refusing to say anything. She was angry with him—Jack could see that.

But why? Because he had not been careful enough?
She couldn't reproach him any more for that than he
did himself.

'Annalise, please…' He begged her.

'I don't want to talk about it any more,' Annalise
told him. 'There isn't any point. I don't want to see
you again, Jack…I just want you to leave me alone.'

She couldn't look at him. She knew if she did her
control would break and she would burst into tears.
She hadn't known that life could hold this much pain.
She felt angry, abandoned, frightened, torn between
hating Jack and wanting him to take her in his arms
and tell her that everything was going to be all right.
But how could it be all right? He had lied to her,
broken his promise to her—and even if he had not,
Annalise knew that she could not go through the
trauma she had just experienced again. Jack might
have promised her that everything would be all right
but right now, everything was far from all right.

Jack ached with remorse and love. His emotions
burned the backs of his eyes, but he was a man now
and men didn't cry.

Annalise was already moving away from him.

'Annalise…don't go….' he begged her, but she was
ignoring him, hurrying back down the tow path.

He wanted to go after her and plead with her to give
him a second chance but a couple were coming the
other way walking towards him. The river path was
too public a place to say what he wanted to say to her.
The frustration of not having the privacy he needed,

of being looked on by others as being too young tore
at his heart.

He loved Annalise and he would always love her.
He wasn't too young to know that.

But she didn't want him any more. She had told
him so. She blamed him for the fear the thought of
being pregnant had caused her and she blamed him,
too, for not being able to protect her from it, Jack
knew. And he knew it because he, too, felt the same
way. He, too, blamed *himself*. In making love with her
and not making sure she was properly protected he
had been selfish and now he was paying for that selfishness. Annalise had stopped loving him.

Fiercely he knuckled the dampness from his eyes.
The last thing he wanted to do now was go back to
university but he knew he had no choice. He had let
Annalise down but he wasn't going to compound his
sin by letting his aunt and uncle down, as well.

HALF-BLINDED by her own tears, Annalise ran down
the river path. It was over, finished, and she was
glad…glad…she told herself fiercely. How *could* Jack
have told his aunt what should have remained their
own painful secret—and how could *she* even think
about still loving him after what he had done?

'YOU'RE LOOKING very pensive,' Saul commented to
Tullah. He had just arrived home from work to find
her on her own in the sitting room standing staring
into space. 'Something wrong?'

'Well, not wrong exactly, but…' Her forehead pleated in an anxious frown, Tullah proceeded to tell him what she had overheard. 'There was a message on the machine when I came home from Honor inviting us over there at the weekend.' She took a deep breath, 'I was thinking about Olivia.…'

'Yes,' Saul agreed grimly.

'I got the impression that David *wanted* to tell her before the party but that he was afraid she would refuse to see him.'

'I'm sure she would,' Saul acknowledged.

'What do *you* think we should do?' Tullah asked him.

'What do *you* think we should do?' Saul retorted.

Tullah took a deep breath.

'Well, in her situation *I'd* want to know and…and before the news became public knowledge. I couldn't tell her. We get on well enough together but we aren't close. Not like…'

'Are you trying to say that you think *I* should tell her?' Saul asked her.

'Yes,' Tullah confirmed, 'And soon, Saul…like tonight.…'

OLIVIA HAD SEEN the message light on her telephone bleeping when she walked into the house. For one idiotic moment she had actually thought that Caspar might have rung her and when, instead she had heard her father's voice, anger had overwhelmed her unwanted and very betraying disappointment.

'Olivia. I need to talk to you,' he had said. 'There's something—'

Olivia had cancelled the message without listening to any more.

Had Jon perhaps spoken to him suggesting that this might be a good time for him to get in touch with her…a time when she felt weak and vulnerable? Well, she had meant what she had said to Jenny. Her father was someone she would *never,* ever ask for help.

She had just given the girls their final good-night kisses and switched off their lights when Saul rang the front doorbell. Her pleasure at seeing him brought a happy sparkle to her eyes, lifting her mood. She wasn't foolish enough to really think that Saul wanted to resurrect their long-ago relationship, but she *was* woman enough and all too vulnerable enough to need to boost her ego with the attention of a handsome sexy man.

'Come in,' she invited him. 'I was just about to make some coffee.'

Saul wasn't looking forward to what he had to do and Olivia's uninhibited pleasure at seeing him made him feel even worse.

He waited until she had made them both a drink before starting to speak.

'Livvy, there isn't any easy way to do this,' he began quietly whilst Olivia's heart turned over at the ominous tone of his voice.

'What is it? What's happened? Caspar…' she demanded and then stopped, her face flushing as she realised from Saul's surprised expression just how wrong and revealing her reaction was.

'No. This doesn't have anything to do with Caspar,' Saul denied.

He took a deep breath.

'It's David—your father…'

For a moment it felt as though everything stood still. The shock and pain that then rushed over her were confusing and unexpected.

'He's had another heart attack,' she guessed.

'No. No, it's nothing like that.' Saul cursed inwardly. He was making a complete mess of this.

Putting down his coffee he reached across the table and took both of Olivia's hands in his. His grasp felt warm and reassuring. Comforting… The touch of a friend, Olivia recognised ruefully but quite definitely not that of a would-be lover.

'He and Honor are expecting a child.'

There, it was out. He had said it.

'What?'

The shocked look of white-faced disbelief Olivia was giving him was every bit as bad as the reaction Saul had dreaded.

'Honor is pregnant…. I can't believe it….' Olivia protested, wrenching her hands out of Saul's grip and standing up to pace the kitchen angrily. 'I *can't* believe she would be *stupid* enough to have a child with him knowing the way he treated me and Jack.'

'People change, Livvy,' Saul told her as gently as

he could even though his heart was going out to her for the pain he could see in her eyes.

'People change.' The blank look on Olivia's face worried him. 'You mean my father's *pleased* about *this* baby…. Is *that* what you're trying to tell me?'

Saul wished he was anywhere but where he was.

'From what Tullah overheard him telling Jon—yes, he is,' he was forced to admit.

'He couldn't have cared less about me and Jack. He couldn't be bothered with us. We meant *nothing* to him—nothing at all,' Olivia raged.

So *that* was why her father had wanted to speak to her…. Not to try to persuade her to allow him into her life and the lives of her daughters, but no doubt to tell her that he didn't need them now…now that he was going to have *another* child of his own…a child he *wanted*…a child he would love.

'Honor's planning to announce her pregnancy to the family at the weekend. She's inviting everyone round. Tullah happened to overhear David telling Jon about it at work and she felt…we *both* felt…'

The look in her eyes made him ache with sadness for her. What she was feeling had to be compounded by the breakdown of her marriage but Saul knew there was no real comfort he could give her.

'If we've done the wrong thing…' he told her gently.

Olivia shook her head.

'No. No you haven't…I'm grateful to Tullah for sending you to tell me, Saul. It's just…I never thought… When I was a little girl, I wanted so much for him to love me,' she told him, her voice empty of expression. 'I wanted that *so much*, almost as much as I wanted him and Ma to be happy together, to be *normal* parents like Jon and Jenny… I wanted that *so badly*…and I used to feel that I was to blame in some way because they weren't…that it was *my* fault…'

'Livvy…' Saul protested, his own voice thickening with emotion.

'I'm sorry,' Olivia apologised. 'You can't want to hear any of this.'

'You can talk to me any time, but I can't stay any longer just at the moment,' Saul told her regretfully. 'Will you be okay?'

The brittle smile she gave him tore at his heart.

'Yes. Yes, of course I will,' Olivia told him.

As he went to hug her she stepped back. For a moment Saul hesitated and then turned and headed for the door.

Olivia waited until she was sure he had gone before allowing the emotion racking her to have its head, her whole body convulsed by uncontrollable shudders of anguish.

Honor was expecting her father's child. *Her* father was going to be a father to someone else. Well she just hoped for the baby's sake that she wasn't a girl, Olivia reflected bitterly.

Once the baby arrived Honor would soon see David in his true colours and so would everyone else. Her father had no right to subject yet another child to the misery and lack of love she and Jack had experienced. But what if this time things *were* to be different...? What if her father *were* to follow in the path of so many second time around fathers and absolutely adore the progeny of his middle age?

A cold shudder shook Olivia's body. What was the matter with her? Why should *she* care *how* her father behaved? He was *nothing* to her any more. *Nothing!*

Panic. Pain. Fear, abhorrence of her own emotions as well as a furious anger against her father consumed her, refusing to allow her to concentrate on anything else. If Caspar had been here... Caspar... Why on earth was she thinking about *him?*

CASPAR GRIMACED as he answered the sharp summons of his mobile phone. Just for a second he had hoped...thought...that perhaps it might be Olivia. He had lost count of the number of times he had been tempted to call her. He ached for the sound of the girls' voices...and for Olivia's.... Grimly he reminded himself of all the reasons their marriage had started to fall apart, the most destructive of which was the fact that Olivia was totally and completely hooked up in her memories of her childhood and that she refused to either let them go or acknowledge how destructive they were.

Sure, he understood that she had had a bad time. He hadn't had the best of childhoods himself, but they were adults now and hell, he had hated and resented the way Olivia had picked on everything she considered he was doing wrong and made a link between it and her father's behaviour as though somehow they were one and the same.

''Scuse me, are you going to be staying in this parking space long? It *is* reserved for medical staff at the centre and I *do* happen to have clients waiting to see me....' The sharp crispening of the soft female voice as its owner reached the end of her sentence alerted Caspar to his transgression.

'I'm sorry,' he apologised adding truthfully, 'I didn't realise I was in a reserved space. In fact, I only stopped because my mobile was ringing.'

As he turned to look properly at the woman whose battered station wagon was now blocking his own exit his eyes widened appreciatively. She was every red-blooded male's dream of perfect American womanhood and then some. Tall, slim but with all the right kind of curves in the right kind of places. Honey-blonde hair, widely spaced dark-blue eyes, a voluptuously full soft pink mouth.

Dressed casually in jeans and a check shirt she looked about eighteen at first glance but Caspar guessed from her demeanour that she had to be quite a lot older.

'I'll be out of your way just as soon as you can reverse to let me pass,' he told her.

'Okay... I can tell from your accent that you're a stranger in town and I guess that the reserved markings aren't too clear, but that doesn't let you off the hook

GET 2

HOW TO GET YOUR 2 FREE BOOKS AND FREE GIFT!

1. Peel off the MIRA sticker on the front cover. Place it in the space provided at right. This automatically entitles you to receive two free books and an exciting mystery gift.

2. Send back this card and you'll get 2 "The Best of the Best™" novels. These books have a combined cover price of $11.00 or more in the U.S. and $13.00 or more in Canada, but they are yours to keep absolutely FREE!

3. There's no catch. You're under no obligation to buy anything. We charge nothing – ZERO – for your first shipment. And you don't have to make any minimum number of purchases – not even one!

4. We call this line "The Best of the Best" because each month you'll receive the best books by some of today's hottest authors. These authors show up time and time again on all the major bestseller lists and their books sell out as soon as they hit the stores. You'll like the convenience of getting them delivered to your home at our special discount prices . . . and you'll love your *Heart to Heart* subscriber newsletter featuring author news, horoscopes, recipes, book reviews and much more!

5. We hope that after receiving your free books you'll want to remain a subscriber. But the choice is yours – to continue or cancel, anytime at all! So why not take us up on our invitation, with no risk of any kind. You'll be glad you did!

6. And remember...we'll send you a mystery gift ABSOLUTELY FREE just for giving "The Best of the Best" a try.

SPECIAL FREE GIFT!

We'll send you a fabulous surprise gift, absolutely FREE, simply for accepting our no-risk offer!

Visit us online at
www.mirabooks.com

BOOKS FREE!

Hurry!

Return this card promptly to GET 2 FREE BOOKS & A FREE GIFT!

The Best of the Best™

▶ DETACH AND MAIL CARD TODAY! ▼

Affix peel-off MIRA sticker here

YES! Please send me the 2 FREE "The Best of the Best" novels and FREE gift for which I qualify. I understand that I am under no obligation to purchase anything further, as explained on the opposite page.

(P-BB3-01)
385 MDL C6PQ   185 MDL C6PP

NAME   (PLEASE PRINT CLEARLY)

ADDRESS

APT.#   CITY

STATE/PROV.   ZIP/POSTAL CODE

The Best of the Best™ — Here's How it Works:

Accepting your 2 free books and gift places you under no obligation to buy anything. You may keep the books and gift and return the shipping statement marked "cancel." If you do not cancel, about a month later we will send you 4 additional novels and bill you just $4.24 each in the U.S., or $4.74 each in Canada, plus 25¢ shipping & handling per book and applicable taxes if any.* That's the complete price and — compared to cover prices of $5.50 or more each in the U.S. and $6.50 or more each in Canada — it's quite a bargain! You may cancel at any time, but if you choose to continue, every month we'll send you 4 more books, which you may either purchase at the discount price or return to us and cancel your subscription.

*Terms and prices subject to change without notice. Sales tax applicable in N.Y. Canadian residents will be charged applicable provincial taxes and GST.

If offer card is missing write to: The Best of the Best, 3010 Walden Ave., P.O. Box 1867, Buffalo, NY 14240-1867

BUSINESS REPLY MAIL

FIRST-CLASS MAIL   PERMIT NO. 717   BUFFALO, NY

POSTAGE WILL BE PAID BY ADDRESSEE

THE BEST OF THE BEST
3010 WALDEN AVE
PO BOX 1867
BUFFALO NY 14240-9952

NO POSTAGE
NECESSARY
IF MAILED
IN THE
UNITED STATES

altogether,' she told him severely. 'It says as plain as day over there that this is a medical centre....'

Ruefully Caspar saw that she was right.

'I really am sorry,' he apologised again. She wasn't wearing any kind of uniform and he wondered just what she did.

'You work here, right?' he asked encouragingly.

'Right,' she told him, giving him a cool look. 'I *do* work here but I *don't* pick up strange men, even if they do ride Harley-Davidson motorbikes....'

Caspar couldn't resist it, a wide grin illuminated his face as he teased her, 'No, but surely that's your job if you work here...picking up strangers, nursing them, doctoring them....'

'I'm a counsellor...a psychiatrist...not a medic,' she responded crisply. 'And since it looks as though you could do with a bit of free advice, let me tell you that that kind of line just doesn't cut it with today's woman.'

'No? Then what does?' Caspar asked her softly. He couldn't remember when he had last enjoyed himself so much, when he had last felt so alive, so much a man...so challenged and yes, downright excited in a very basic and totally male way by a woman who wasn't Olivia. Appreciatively he watched the delicious sway of her hips as she walked determinedly away from him and towards her car without dignifying his comment with a response.

Well, what had he expected? She was right not to respond to him. The world was full of potentially very dangerous men and it made good sense for her to be cautious.

She was in her car now and trying to start it. *Trying* to start it… Caspar frowned as he recognised from the dull whine he could hear that there was no way the station wagon was going to start without the aid of a mechanic and a new starter motor.

He watched as the station wagon door opened and she got back out. It was hard for him to repress his totally male smile as she clasped her hands together and told him with obvious irritation and embarrassment, 'It won't start. I'm going to have to call the garage and arrange for a tow.'

'How long is that going to take?' Caspar demanded, trying to look severe. 'I'm only just passing through here and I need to find myself a room for the night and get something to eat.'

'It isn't my fault,' the woman told him recovering her equilibrium a little. 'Like I said, *you* shouldn't have parked here in the first place.

'Where are you passing through to?' she asked him curiously and then looked self-conscious as though her own interest in him was a betrayal she regretted.

'Wherever the road takes me,' Caspar told her, promptly adding, 'I'm trying to fulfil a teenage ambition I had to ride from coast to coast.'

'On a Harley-Davidson?'

'Yup,' he agreed, giving her a mischievous smile as he added, 'It's a pity you aren't a medic, I'd forgotten that a certain area of my body was a good deal more resilient at sixteen than it is now at close on forty!'

'Doesn't your wife mind you taking off without her? I can see that you're wearing a wedding ring,' she told him, nodding in the direction of his hand.

'It's over… We… She's gone back to the UK with our daughters. She's a lawyer…a solicitor they call it over there and her parting words to me were that she wanted everything to be "legal." That's how we met…through the law. I lecture in it now and…' Caspar stopped, shaking his head. 'I'm sorry…I guess this is what happens when you've been riding the road solo for too long, you start boring every stranger you meet with your life story.'

'I'm a psychiatrist. We don't *get* bored,' she told him. 'I'll have to wait here for the garage but if you like, once they've been I could show you a really great place in town to eat—Italian…they have rooms as well.'

Caspar took a deep breath. His instincts warned him that he could be stepping into very deep water indeed but then why shouldn't he? He was a free man now, wasn't he? Olivia didn't want him….

'Sounds good to me,' he responded. 'I'm Caspar Johnson, by the way,' he introduced himself.

'Molly Reilly.'

Reilly, so that explained those wonderful Celtic eyes, the flawless skin, though the perfect teeth were pure American, Caspar acknowledged as he went to shake the hand she had extended towards him.

One of the worst rows he and Olivia had had, had ridiculously been over the girls' teeth. He had wanted them to have orthodontic work done on them and Olivia, he remembered, had been horrified.

'Why?' he had objected when she had refused. 'Look, *all* American kids get their teeth fixed.'

'Amelia and Alex are *not* American,' she had responded, 'And *I* do not want them growing up with a set of teeth that appear so perfect that they look...like they belong to...to a film star.'

Caspar hadn't understood either her passionate reaction or her argument then and he didn't now.

'It's taking away their natural character,' Olivia had protested. 'Remaking them, Caspar, and that will make them feel that they aren't good enough, that they have to be perfect to be worthy of being loved and I don't want that for them.'

'For God's sake, Livvy, we're talking about fixing their teeth, that's all,' he had exploded in exasperation.

'I THOUGHT you said it was over....'

Molly's comment caught Caspar off guard, making him change colour defensively.

'How did you know—?' he began and then stopped.

'I'm thirty-four,' Molly responded dryly, 'and I guess that's more than old enough to be able to recognise when a married man is thinking about his wife.'

'Actually, I was thinking about my daughters,' Caspar corrected her. 'Now, about this Italian...'

'COME ON, Jen, we're going to be late,' Jon exhorted. 'David said to be there for three and it's gone that now.'

Jenny shook her head. She hadn't wanted to go to David and Honor's party in the first place and she had told Jon so.

'Not go! We've *got* to go. David is my brother.'

'Yes, and he's also Livvy and Jack's father,' Jenny had reminded him simply. 'How do you think they're going to feel, especially Livvy when she hears about this baby?'

'Jen, Livvy is an adult,' Jon had expostulated. 'David's invited her and the girls.'

'She won't go,' Jenny told him positively.

'DO YOU THINK she will come?' David asked Honor anxiously. There was no need for Honor to question who the 'she' was he was referring to.

'Don't get your hopes up too high,' she advised him gently.

'Oh, God, Honor, I just wish… I wanted to tell her myself…before…before anyone else…to make it something special we could share—just as you did with Abigail and Ellen.'

Honor smiled sadly as she listened to him. The relationship she had with her daughters was a world away from the one David had with his, but even they had expressed shock and in Ellen's case, almost outright hostility to the news that she, their mother, was to have a child.

'But have you thought of the danger, the risks to both yourself and the baby?' Ellen had demanded practically, 'As an older mother...'

Abigail had reminded her sister, 'Don't forget, Mum knows a lot more about having babies than we do. After all, she's had both of us.'

'Yes, but that was over twenty years ago,' Ellen had pointed out acerbically.

Now that she was over her initial shock, though, she had apologised for her original hostility.

If her daughters, who knew how much she loved them, could both feel slightly threatened and upset about the news that she and David were to have a child, then how on earth was Olivia going to feel?

It grieved Honor, not just that their child should be born into such a situation but that the birth of a child which should be such a joyful and hopeful event should be the cause of unhappiness and pain.

She had discussed the matter with Father Ignatius whilst they had been working together in the still room. She loved using the old-fashioned word to describe the room where she stored her herbs and made up her remedies with its connotations of mediaeval times and the skills of its herbalists.

'I just wish there was a herbal I could make for Olivia that would help her,' she had exclaimed ruefully.

'The answer to Olivia's ailment surely lies within herself,' the priest had responded. When Honor had looked questioningly at him, he explained, 'Her father's love is there for her and his sorrow and regret for the pain of her past, but David cannot force them on her, he can only offer them to her.'

'…and if Olivia continues to refuse to accept them?' Honor had asked him.

Father Ignatius had sighed and shaken his head. 'If she does, and I am very much afraid she might, then both she and David will continue to suffer.'

And now, here she was, compounding that suffering for Olivia with the child she was carrying.

Honor's hand went to her stomach—still flat as yet—her pregnancy might have been unexpected and unplanned but her baby was already a source of great joy to her.

OLIVIA WASN'T going to come. David knew.

'We can't stay too long,' Jon was saying. 'Jenny's on grandparent duties tonight at Queensmead.'

Grandparent. He, *too*, was a grandparent, a grandfather, just like Jon but he doubted that his granddaughters even knew he existed.

As he took a sip of his drink he studied the room. The priest, predictably perhaps, was chatting with Ben and Freddy. Honor was laughing at something Jon was saying to her. They had deliberately kept the numbers down, just immediate family.

'JENNY!' David exclaimed warmly as he walked into the kitchen and saw his sister-in-law there.

'I'm glad you could come. It means a lot to Honor.

I know how busy you are at the moment with everything. I just wish that Livvy could have brought herself to come.'

'Livvy can't go anywhere,' Jenny told him quietly. 'She's got two children to look after, she's working full-time and she doesn't have a husband to help and support her.'

'Do you really mean Livvy can't go anywhere?' David asked Jenny quickly.

'Surely you must be aware of the problems she's having,' Jenny insisted. 'Jon *must* have told you. Normally *I'd* help but… Jon's told Livvy to take as much time off work as she needs but, of course, she won't…. She's been trying to find the right kind of help…a nanny…although it's proving hard. But why am I telling you this, David? *You're* her father. You should *know,* but you don't care, do you? All you care about is your *new* life.'

'Jenny!' The horror in Jon's voice shocked Jenny into silence. She hadn't heard him come into the kitchen but there was no mistaking the anger and chagrin in his expression as he turned to David and started to apologise.

'It's all right, Jon,' David soothed him. 'And Jenny *does* have a point, even if she is wrong about one thing. I *do* care about both Jack and Livvy, Jenny, and I care very much.'

David was still frowning. Jenny's outburst had shocked him but nowhere near as much as the information she had given him about Olivia. He had known things weren't very good for her, of course, but Jenny's words had painted a picture of someone so totally alone and isolated that he had immediately felt the strongest urge to do something to help and protect her. Flesh of his flesh…his daughter…his child. David closed his eyes. He had to do something…he must….

'JENNY, how could you speak to David like that?' Jon asked in bewilderment as they drove home having taken Ben back to Queensmead first, both of them sitting in a mutually hostile silence as they waited to be alone to vent their true feelings.

'Like what? I simply told him the truth,' Jenny defended herself. 'There he is celebrating the conception of another child when poor Livvy…'

Jon frowned. If he hadn't known better he might almost have suspected that Jenny was jealous of Honor and David and the baby they were expecting.

'HONOR, I've been thinking, about this problem that Livvy is having finding someone to help with the children. Well, I've got plenty of spare time and they are my grandchildren. Since Jenny can't help her…' David's voice trailed away as he saw the way Honor was looking at him.

'You don't think it's a good idea,' he guessed disheartened.

'I think it's an *excellent* idea,' Honor assured him. 'But I doubt that Olivia will.'

'It's worth going to see her and offering to help,'

David told her eagerly. 'This could be the break-through I've been looking for, Honor, a way of show-ing Livvy, *proving* to her how much I regret... And I want to see her, anyway,' he added gruffly. 'I owe it to her and to...him or her, whichever it turns out to be,' he smiled as he touched her stomach gently, 'To tell her about our baby myself.

'You don't want me to do it, do you?' he asked her quietly when he saw her expression.

'I don't want you to be disappointed or...or hurt,' Honor countered. 'I know how much it would mean to you to mend the rift between you, David, and I know, too, how much Olivia needs to have that rift mended even if she herself won't admit how much she needs the healing that forgiving you and herself will give her.' She paused and sighed. 'But I just don't feel that she's ready yet.'

'You're a wonderful woman—have I ever told you that?' David whispered as he kissed her. 'I understand what you're saying, Honor,' he acknowledged when she smiled. 'But I'm still going to try. From a practical point of view, if nothing else, Livvy needs help and, after all, I am her father. I'll go and see her tomorrow. It's Sunday and she won't be at work. You must curse me sometimes for bringing you so many family prob-lems.'

'Your family is nowhere near as problem-driven and -riddled as mine,' Honor told him with a grin.

Leaning over, she kissed his forehead and then his

nose, sighing in soft pleasure as he drew her down against him.

'Is this all right?' he asked her in a whisper, brushing his fingertips against her stomach. 'I mean…'

'It's fine,' Honor assured him. Making love with David wasn't going to damage or harm their baby, but at some stage she would have to take the decision whether or not to have the kind of tests that could potentially do so. As an older mother it was sensible to check that everything was progressing well for the baby. But right now she didn't want to think about that. Right now she simply wanted to enjoy what there was…what she had in the here and now…right now.…

'Mmm…that feels good,' she told David huskily as he stroked her breast, snuggling closer to him as she whispered, 'Do it again.…'

CHAPTER TEN

SARA SMILED happily to herself. It was her day off and she was on her way to the exclusive health and golf complex near Chester where Frances and her family were members to spend the day at their expense enjoying the spa's facilities.

'It's the least we can do after the terrific job you've done for us with the paperwork,' Frances had assured her.

And so here she was armed with Frances's careful directions, making her way through the pretty Cheshire countryside.

Along with her derogatory and unflattering comments about the Crighton family, Tania had been equally unenthusiastic about their home town, condemning it as a dull country backwater, but Sara had found it to be anything but and Tania had neglected to mention the town's historic past.

Just as soon as she could, Sara had promised herself that she would explore the town's environs, walking the route of its ancient walls, visiting the salt mine museum and the castle; but today she was content to be in her car on her way to her destination.

Frances had raved about the club's beauty treatment

facilities whilst her husband had been equally enthu-
siastic about its golf courses.

'You'll love the swimming pool, and the restaurant
is pretty good as well.'

'But not as good as yours, of course,' Sara had responded with a grin.

'Of course not,' Frances had laughed back.

And now here she was turning in at Camden Park's
gates and driving down the curving drive that mean-
dered through the greens.

Smiling a little ruefully to herself she pulled up her
small car in a car park which seemed to be full of top-
of-the-range BMWs, four-wheel drives, Jaguars and
Mercedes—had no one in Cheshire heard of compact
cars?

The spa's receptionist, though, couldn't have been
more pleasant or helpful, inviting Sara to choose from
a range of options available from the beauty treatment
rooms.

Having made her choice, a long luxurious massage
and a facial, Sara decided to use the time beforehand
with a healthy, invigorating swim.

The pool area was as luxurious as Frances had said,
its walls painted with Italian frescoes. A long col-
umned arcade led to the Jacuzzi and steam room and
the human beings adorning the area were equally as
decorative as the backdrop, Sara acknowledged as she
studied the women in their obvious designer leisure
wear, their menfolk... Suddenly she froze. There,
standing at the opposite end of the pool, thankfully so

deep in conversation with his female companion that he was unaware of her presence, was Nick Crighton.

She had been right about one thing, she decided shakily. His body *was* every bit as sexily male and muscular as she had imagined, his skin sleekly brown and still damp from his swim. Sara could hear the woman laughing at something he had said to her as he shook the water from his hair, a soft deliciously feminine sound that matched her appearance.

Enviously Sara discreetly studied her. She was tall, possibly even six foot, Sara recognised, with a tiny waist and firm curves which her swimsuit revealed subtly rather than clinging to it in any obvious kind of way. Her hair was clipped up but Sara guessed that it might be long—and whoever she was, it was obvious to Sara that she and Nick Crighton knew each other very well. When she lifted her hand and placed it on Nick's arm, he moved closer to her. A white-hot sheet of envy enveloped Sara, shocking her with the explicitness of the message it carried. *She* wanted to be the one who was touching Nick. She wanted—

Nick was walking away from the woman now and diving cleanly into the pool. Compulsively Sara watched him as he swam. A strong powerful crawl took him easily down the length of the Olympic-size pool, each movement clean and strong, droplets of water glinting on his bare arm as he raised it. A scar, old and silvery, made a jagged line on his upper arm. Sara winced as she saw it—how had it happened? A sensation of sweet hot weakness poured through Sara's

body like a dark forbidden narcotic. She wanted to go
to him, hold him, touch him, be held and touched by
him. She wanted to lick the droplets of water from his
skin, cling to him, wrapping herself around him. She
wanted…

Helplessly she closed her eyes, mocking her own
weakness by telling herself with mental derision, 'He's
just a man swimming…that's all….'

Against her will her gaze was drawn back to him.
He was swimming on his back now, again with long
powerful strokes. The images that the sight of such
thoroughly sensual male strength and control were cre-
ating inside her were causing havoc in her senses. She
could imagine him…*feel* him almost…. Aghast, she
licked her suddenly dry lips. Her heart was pounding,
her pulse racing, her insides…

Jealousy twisted through her. Who was the woman
he was with and what right did he have to be with her
after what he had said to her—Sara? Her own thoughts
shocked and appalled her. What was happening to her?
She scarcely recognised her normal sane self in this
tortured creature of sensual need and jealousy that she
had suddenly become.

Nick was climbing out of the pool now and as he
did so, for the first time Sara saw the long jagged scar
on his torso.

Helplessly she expelled her breath on a sharp surge
of vocal shock.

Even though he was surely too far away to have
heard her, suddenly for some reason, he went still and

stared in her direction frowning. Immediately Sara stepped back and turned on her heel. She could hear Nick calling her name but there was no way she was going to give him the satisfaction of knowing she had been watching him…wanting him.…

It was only a few yards to the ladies' showers and changing rooms but by the time she made it to their sanctuary Sara's heart was pumping fiercely as she tensed her body against her fear of Nick catching up with her before she reached it.

ON THE OTHER SIDE of the pool, Nick exhaled fiercely. Seeing and recognising the transfixed male look in his eyes, Bobbie Crighton was amused. She and Luke had bumped into him by accident earlier. They were club members and Luke was playing golf with some friends whilst Bobbie had been intending to enjoy a swim followed by the luxury of a manicure. Her children were spending the day with their grandparents and she had just been on her way to the second-floor beauty treatment rooms above the swimming pool when she had bumped into Nick, who had explained that his brother Saul had insisted that he use their membership facilities to help build up his damaged muscles.

'Someone you know?' she remarked *sotto voce* now, following the direction of Nick's hard-edged glare.

'Sara Lanyon. She works for Frances Sorter,' he told Bobbie grimly. 'She's related through marriage, in a roundabout sort of way, to David's ex-wife, from whom it seems she's picked up some idiotic antipathy to the Crightons in general and male Crightons in particular—and this Crighton male—in extreme particular!'

'Oh, dear,' Bobbie sympathised, but there was a rueful look in her eyes. After all, hadn't *she,* in what now seemed like another lifetime, arrived in Haslewich with very much the same attitude?

Intriguing that another woman should come to Haslewich sharing a similar antagonism. Would she undergo the kind of change that she, Bobbie, had experienced? Bobbie's smile deepened as she remembered how Luke Crighton had been instrumental in her own change of heart.

'How's Olivia managing?' she asked, switching the subject. 'If we hadn't arranged to take the children to the States for Christmas I'd have offered to help.'

Bobbie had originally helped to look after Olivia's children when they were younger and she and Olivia had remained very close until Olivia had gone back to work full-time, after which Bobbie had seen less and less of her.

'According to Saul there was never any way Livvy was going to feel good about David coming back, but neither he nor Tullah talk about her too much. After all, there was a time when Saul and Livvy were pretty close....'

'Yes, but that was before Saul had met Tullah,' Bobbie pointed out.

'Ah, but you women can be pretty possessive where your men are concerned,' Nick teased her deliberately.

'Us *women,*' Bobbie began and then laughed, recognising when she was deliberately being baited.

'Female jealousy is nothing when compared to that of the male of the species,' she warned him. 'Just you wait! I'd better go,' she added, 'otherwise I'll be late for my treatment.'

'See you at one for lunch then,' Nick reminded her.

He had promised himself a session in the gym to work on his damaged muscles but suddenly all he could think about was Sara.

He had received a letter this morning, forwarded to him by Ffion Davies, the wife of a local landowner in Pembrokeshire where he lived. Ffion acted as his assistant-cum-secretary and had a spare key to his cottage. She had typed a note to accompany the letter which had read, 'this looked urgent—and interesting!'

The letter was from a man who had refused to identify himself other than by saying that he was a senior diplomat. He had given a box number for Nick to reply to and he was asking for Nick's help in securing the release of his daughter who was being held hostage by a break-away religious group in the Far East.

His request was a little outside Nick's normal field of operations in that he was being asked to use his negotiation skills and familiarity with the politics of the area in question rather than his legal expertise. The government of the country concerned had already made it clear that they were not prepared to negotiate with the rebels and the writer feared for the safety of his daughter. Nick didn't blame him; there had been too many incidents of hostages being killed in such situations for him not to do so.

Strictly speaking, there were other agencies better equipped to deal with this situation than he was himself but... But it was just the kind of challenge he needed right now...and it would take him away from Haslewich and Sara...if he could get himself fit enough to take the task on.

SARA SMILED voluptuously to herself as her body relaxed under the skilled hands of the masseuse. She was daydreaming that she was lying on a tropical beach watching as Nick swam towards her through the clear aquamarine water.

On the other side of the thin partition separating her treatment room from its neighbour she heard a familiar warm female laugh—the woman she had seen with Nick. Suddenly her daydream changed. Another woman came walking down the beach coming between her and Nick. She was tall and magnificently curved and Nick was turning away from her to swim to the interloper.

'There,' the masseuse smiled, bringing Sara back to reality, 'all finished.'

Thanking her, Sara slid off the bed. By rights she ought to have been feeling totally relaxed but instead, thanks to Nick Crighton and his sexy female friend, she was feeling anything but.

Who was she? Were she and Nick already lovers? She was extraordinarily striking looking. The intensity of her own jealousy bewildered Sara, but no matter how hard she tried she could neither drive it away nor analyse it.

In the end, in desperation, whilst she redressed and brushed her hair she reminded herself sharply that it was ridiculous for her to feel like this. Just because she had spent going on for close on a week fighting as hard as she could against the sharp pangs of longing Nick aroused in her, that was no reason for her to start over-reacting like a possessive lover. No, she had no reason to feel such jealousy, Sara acknowledged. Just as she had no reason to feel such need and desire...such...hunger...she told herself angrily. Give what you feel its proper name, she challenged herself mentally, because that's exactly what you are feeling—lust!

She had never thought of herself as a sensual woman; but then, she had never thought of herself as a jealous one, either.

She looked at her watch. It was time for her to go and have her lunch.

Lust. The word even tasted scalding hot and dangerous on her tongue, sending shock waves of wanton imagery through her thoughts.

Sara wanted to wrench it out of her mind, to subjugate and destroy it. But how could she? The best way to fight fire was supposed to be to turn and face it, not run from it...to fight it with its own self. Was

Nick right? Was the best way to rid herself of her unwanted hunger for him to give in to it and let it burn itself out?

The café bar where she had booked her table was busy, families enjoying a shared lunch, couples energised and glowing with health from their morning's exercise. She was just about to follow the waitress to her table when she saw them walking towards her—Nick and his lady friend, arm in arm, smiling intimately at one another. This time the jealousy that hit her was like the kick of a mule. Instant, hard and horridly painful—so painful in fact that she actually had to gasp for breath.

'Isn't that the girl we saw this morning?' Bobbie asked Nick as she spotted Sara.

Nick, who had already seen her and had decided for his own sanity to ignore her presence, agreed grimly, 'Yes.'

'It looks as though she's on her own. Let's go over and join her,' Bobbie suggested, hiding her amusement with an innocent smile when Nick started to frown.

'I don't think—' he began, but Bobbie didn't let him finish. She was intrigued to meet Sara after what Nick had told her about her, and even more intrigued by Nick's reaction to her.

'It would look awfully rude if we didn't,' she told Nick. 'After all, she is practically family.'

Nick's eyebrows rose but he could sense that Bobbie wasn't going to be dissuaded.

When she saw that Nick and his companion were heading for her table Sara could barely contain her outrage. How could she possibly want a man who could be so brazen, so blatant?

His companion, she noticed, was wearing a beautiful engagement ring *and* a wedding ring.

'Sara,' Nick began as they reached her table. 'May I introduce you to Bobbie—'

'Do you mind if we share your table?' Bobbie took over, promptly sitting down before Sara could object.

Sara stared at her with a glazed look. Close up she was even more stunningly beautiful than Sara had imagined. What was she doing with Nick? She was *married*. How *could* he? How *dare* he? Did he love her…? Was he…? Was she…?

Lost in her own angry thoughts, Sara didn't see Nick reaching towards her until it was too late and he was actually touching the bare flesh of her arm. She jumped as though she had been burned, trembling from head to foot, her face going from red to white as her body reacted helplessly to his touch. She could see from the look in Nick's eyes that he was as shocked by her reaction as she was herself and then, to her own disbelief, she heard her own voice coming from what seemed to be a long way away as she said huskily, 'That proposition you put to me the other day. I've changed my mind.'

Nick stared at her. He knew exactly what 'proposition' Sara meant. She was referring to that idiotic throw-away comment he had made about them having a short, sharp sexual fling.

It took him several seconds to believe what he had heard. Sara was agreeing that they should have sex.... Just like that...without any...without them...

'I have to go now.' Awkwardly she edged away.

Sara couldn't believe what she had done...what she had said. She felt as though a totally alien life form had somehow taken her over, made her behave in a way that was totally out of character.

Amused Bobbie watched the by-play between them in silence. She could feel the heat and sexual tension they were both generating.

'Sara,' Nick protested, but it was too late, she was already hurrying away.

'Mmm... Now you *have* whetted my curiosity,' Bobbie teased Nick. 'Are you going to enlighten me?'

'There isn't anything to enlighten you about,' Nick told her forbiddingly. Bobbie laughed.

'Oh, no? And what about a certain proposition?'

'It was just a small business matter,' Nick fibbed dismissively.

'If you say so,' Bobbie accepted dulcetly, but Nick could see that she was still smiling.

Sara had agreed to have sex with him—so why wasn't he feeling more triumphant? Why this cold feeling of shock and dismay in the pit of his stomach? Because she had totally misunderstood his comment— that was why. Yes—he wanted to take her to bed, but he was an old-fashioned kind of man who preferred to do his own hunting rather than have his quarry offer herself to him. Rubbish! So why then this feeling of disappointment, of disillusionment almost?

So he had been wrong to assume that Sara was the kind of woman for whom sexual desire and emotional love went hand in hand. Why should that arouse so many negative feelings for him?

SARA WAS TREMBLING uncontrollably by the time she reached her car. There was no way she could stay at the spa now. She couldn't understand what had driven her to act in such a way but she knew her pride would never allow her to recall her reckless words.

What was going to happen now, she wondered. At the very least Nick was going to have some explaining and appeasing to do to his companion and yet she had looked more amused than shocked or hurt by Sara's challenge. And she had certainly not displayed any of the agonising jealousy that she herself had felt. Jealousy that had motivated her, driven her, invaded her personality and taken it over.

DAVID COULD HEAR the noise as he opened his car door on Olivia's drive. A child was crying, screaming. Instinctively he hurried towards the source of the noise, checking when he saw his two granddaughters, the elder leaning protectively towards the younger who was holding her knee, her hand covered in blood.

As he crouched down beside them, Amelia told him shakily, 'Alex has hurt herself.'

'Yes, I know,' David agreed steadily. 'Look, why don't I stay here with her whilst you go and get your mummy?'

Obediently Amelia left her younger sibling's side and started to run towards the house.

Carefully David smiled at Alex. 'Why don't you let me have a look?' he suggested gently.

'It hurts,' Alex sobbed.

'I know,' David sympathised. He could see a piece of glass on the path smeared with blood and he went cold. She had obviously cut herself, but how badly, how deeply?

Very gently David reached for her, soothing and calming her as he persuaded her to let him look at her injured leg. When he saw that the cut was relatively minor, he expelled his pent-up breath in relief.

'You! What are *you* doing here?'

David tensed as he heard the antagonism in Olivia's voice but Livvy wasn't looking at him. Her face had gone white as she hurried anxiously towards her younger daughter.

'Alex… Oh, Alex…'

'It's all right,' David assured her. 'It looks much worse than it is. It's just a flesh cut….'

'…and you're an expert, of course,' Olivia stormed bitingly at him.

'Not an expert, no,' David responded with quiet dignity, 'But I do know enough to recognise a relatively minor wound when I see one. However, it will still have to be cleaned. Shall I carry her to the house for you?'

'No!' Olivia denied immediately, but to her chagrin as she reached for Alex the girl shook her head and told her, 'No, I want him to carry me.'

Angrily Olivia gave way, preceding David up the path towards the house as he carried Alex in his arms.

As SHE WATCHED her father dealing deftly with Alex's cut leg whilst Amelia looked on in almost doting hero-worship, Olivia felt as though somehow she had been transported back in time and that she was the one in her father's arms.

She would have been about Alex's age—perhaps a little older. She had, she remembered, been playing in the garden at Queensmead with Max out of sight of the adults. They had been arguing about something and Max had pushed her over. She could still remember how hard she had fought not to cry whilst Max taunted her saying that she was a soppy cry-baby girl. It had been Jenny who had found them, exclaiming in concern as she saw Olivia's scraped and bleeding knees, picking her up and carrying her back towards the party of grown-ups on the other side of the garden.

'Tania, Livvy's fallen and hurt her knees,' Jenny had told Olivia's mother.

But as Jenny had held the girl out towards her sister-in-law, Olivia could still see the look of irritation and distaste in her mother's eyes as she had recoiled from her exclaiming, 'Oh, no. Don't give her to me, Jenny, my clothes will be covered in blood and this dress is new. Give her to David. He can deal with her. David...' she had called, and Olivia could remember how her father who had been talking with Ben and Jon had turned impatiently to look at them.

'Olivia's cut her knees. You'll have to take her inside and clean her up,' Tania had announced.

And as her father's frown had deepened her grandfather had complained, 'Wretched child. Let one of the women deal with her, David.'

Olivia had shrunk away from her father as he had taken her from Jenny, carrying her indoors without saying a word to her and upstairs to the bathroom where he had sat her down whilst he cleaned her knees of the grit embedded in them, frowning whilst he did so.

'How did this *happen?*' he had asked her whilst tears welled in her eyes from the sting of the antiseptic he was using.

When she made no response, unwilling to tell him that Max had pushed her in case he refused to believe her, he had shaken his head and told her with a sigh, 'Well, try not to be so clumsy in future.' He had picked her up then, giving another sigh whilst Olivia had fought back her tears.

It had been Jenny who had comforted her later, giving her a cuddle and asking if she was feeling all right, but Olivia had still ached for it to be her father who was holding her.

And now, here he was carrying *her* daughter with

every evidence of that tenderness and concern she had once so much longed to get from him and had felt was withheld from her. He looked every inch the loving caring grandfather, but it was an image Olivia flatly refused to believe in.

How could she? He had never been a loving caring father to her—not in her eyes and yet now, here he was preparing to become a father again, but this time... But this time the child he had helped to create would be loved by him in a way that she never had been.

The intensity of her emotions frightened her. She was an adult now, a parent herself, surely way beyond caring about the traumas of her childhood.

Protectively she reached out to take Alex from him but to her consternation her daughter insisted, 'No,' clinging to David and turning her face away from her mother.

'Let me take her upstairs for you,' David offered gently.

Olivia looked so shocked, so stricken that his heart went out to her. He ached to be able to gather *her* into his arms along with her daughters. He could see so clearly in her expression that she was hurting and angry and, he recognised with the maturity he had lacked when she had been a child, the pride and hurt were warring inside her.

Other than physically wresting Alex from his arms, Olivia recognised she had no alternative but to agree.

Giving David a curt nod she led the way upstairs leaving him to follow her.

It was a good half an hour before the girls allowed David to leave. He had to be shown their computer and their homework before Olivia could settle them in their room and take David back downstairs with her. She was on her way to the front door when he asked her quietly, 'Olivia, why didn't you return my phone call?'

Olivia tensed. She had her back to him and she refused to turn round as she responded sharply, 'Why should I? After all, what could you possibly have to say to me that I would want to hear—*Father?*'

David winced as he heard the bitterness in her voice. She already knew what he had to tell her; he could see, not just from her challenging response to his question, but from the angry rejection of her body language as well.

'Maybe *you* didn't want to hear what I had to say Olivia but *I* wanted...' He stopped.

'Look, I know that I wasn't the best of fathers to either you or Jack and I can understand how you must feel....'

Olivia swung round, her face pale with angry disbelief.

'No you can't,' she denied. 'How *could* you. Your father *loved* you.... He practically worshipped you and he still does. At best you treated me as though I were...an...an inconvenience...at worst...'

'Olivia.' David couldn't help himself, instinctively he went towards her but immediately she retreated.

Olivia couldn't believe what was happening—that he had actually dared to come here to her home.

'Livvy,' David groaned. 'You have no idea how guilty I feel…how much I wish—'

'Guilty! Why, because you're afraid that I might tell Honor what an uncaring father you are? Yes, I know about the baby.' She practically spat the words at him.

'Honor already knows about all the sins and failings of my past,' David interrupted her quietly, but with such gentle strength that Olivia felt the tide of anger sweeping over her momentarily still. As a child she had known and seen her father in every kind of mood, euphoric when things were going well for him, sulky and uncommunicative when they weren't, demanding, insensitive, callous almost when dealing with anyone's emotions other than his own, a man who, as an adult, she had judged as vain, selfish and weak. But the man facing her now was none of those things. She could feel the quiet resolution of his own inner strength reaching out to hold her. She took a deep confused breath whilst David held his.

He wanted so desperately to reach out to her, to begin to build a bridge between them which eventually would give them both an easy passage over the chasm of the pain of her childhood.

'Honor and I *are* expecting a baby,' he continued, 'Your half-brother or -sister, Olivia.'

The unexpectedness of the pain his words brought

her cut through and broke the spell she had been under.

'I don't want to know,' she began furiously, 'and if you only came to tell me something I already knew anyway…'

'Telling you about the baby wasn't the sole purpose of my visit,' David denied.

He took a deep breath.

'When I mentioned to Jenny that Honor and I were disappointed that you couldn't make it at the weekend, Jenny told me about the problems you've been having finding someone to help out with the girls. Honor and *I* could help, Olivia. *I* could pick the girls up for you from school. I thought…'

Olivia clung to the worktop as shock and fury poured through her.

'You thought what? Do you *really* believe I would *ever, ever* allow *my* daughters anywhere near *you?*'

Olivia realised that she was practically screaming the words at him, her self-control slipping away so fast that she felt sick, but somehow she couldn't stop herself.

'You *need* help Olivia,' David pressed on as calmly as he could.

'Yes, but not from you, never from you. What is it you really want? To practise your parenting skills on *my* children so that you can perfect them in time for the birth of *your* new child?'

She gave a bitter laugh.

'My God. How dare you, of all men, bring another

life into the world? Haven't you done enough damage to Jack and me?'

'Livvy.' There was pain and guilt as well as protest in David's voice as he listened to her. He had known...expected...that she would object to his suggestion, but the raw agonising hostility and anger she was expressing made his throat ache with pain for her.

He had done this to her...caused her to feel like this.

'Livvy, I know how you must feel.'

'What?' Olivia stared at him. 'No, you don't.... How *could* you? How could *you* know what it feels like to be rejected by your parents...to be unwanted by your father, to be despised and disparaged because of your sex? The unwanted female child. Grandfather always used to say that Max should have been your child and I could see in your eyes that you thought so, too.'

'No, Livvy, that isn't true,' David denied. 'I...I was weak and...and immature enough to agree with my father when he said that Max should have been my son—yes—he always did seem closer in nature to me than to his real father, Jon. I'm not using that as an excuse but as an explanation. But I certainly never hated you. Never!'

'Yes, you did,' Olivia contradicted him flatly. 'Not that I care. Who would want the love of a father who's a thief and a liar?' She gave a small dismissive shrug.

'No matter how much you might have wished Max

was your son it can't have been as much as I wished that Jon and Jenny were my parents.'

If she had meant to hurt him then she had succeeded, David acknowledged. Not because of what she had said, but because of the mental picture she had unwittingly drawn for him of a defenceless hurting child who had given her love to her aunt and uncle because she felt her own parents had rejected it. What he was hurting for was her.

'Livvy, listen,' he begged her tenderly. 'We all know what a wonderful mother you are, but we know, too, that without Caspar... You have a full-time job.'

'You've been talking about me...behind my back.' She gave David a bitter hostile look. 'Oh, yes, I can just imagine what must have been said. Poor Olivia...her parents didn't want her and now it looks like her husband doesn't, either. Well, for your information, *I* was the one who decided to end our marriage.' She held her head up proudly. 'They say, don't they, that a child is programmed by the relationships it experiences as a child...driven to replicate them in adulthood, no matter how damaging or destructive they may have been. If that's true, I suppose it's no wonder that my marriage didn't work out.'

'Livvy,' David protested in shocked concern.

'Don't call me Livvy,' Olivia told him sharply, her voice starting to rise with the tension and pain she was experiencing. 'You don't have the right.... You don't have any rights where I'm concerned. How dare you come here, patronising me, pretending to be concerned for me? Trying to whitewash over the past. Don't think I can't guess why. The new perfect David Crighton you've somehow managed to convince the rest of the world you've become—but can't possibly be—just has to do the right thing, doesn't he? The perfect son. The perfect brother. The perfect husband and now, the perfect father. Well, maybe that's what you'll be to Honor's baby, but you certainly never were to me or Jack.'

Just the thought of her father being a parent again, starting a brand-new life…a brand-new family… caused her such an intensity of savage, dark, self-destructive emotion that Olivia felt as though she were drowning in her own pain and grief.

Quietly David listened, wanting to give her time to express her anger and pain before he tried to comfort and reassure her, but before he could do so she took a deep breath and told him sharply and fiercely, 'I want you to leave. Now. This is my home. Just as the children are my children.'

'And my grandchildren,' David reminded her quietly.

He could see from her expression that he had said the wrong thing.

'You need help, Livvy,' he insisted. 'Please let me do something.'

'The only thing I want you to do is to keep out of my life,' Olivia cried. 'I hate you…I hate you….'

WEARILY DAVID massaged his temple as he drove back to Honor. He had failed at many things in his life but no other failure had made him ache with guilt and remorse like this one did.

More than ever now he knew just how much Olivia was hurting, how alone she was, how abandoned she felt. And he had sensed, too, for all her pride and defiance, that she still had some very strong feelings for Caspar.

And it wasn't just Livvy's pain that was making him long to gather her up in his arms and comfort her with all the tender fatherly love he had never shown her as a child. There were her daughters, as well…his grand-children, especially Amelia the elder one with her wary eyes and anxiety for her mother. He didn't blame Olivia for not being aware that her elder daughter was taking on the role she herself had found so onerous, the role of a child having to protect an adult. But he would certainly blame himself if he didn't protect Amelia…if he turned his back on her as he had done on Livvy.

CHAPTER ELEVEN

DESPAIRINGLY, Olivia watched as both her daughters played with their food. They had been subdued ever since David had left and she knew that they were as aware of the atmosphere of heavy tension filling the kitchen as she was herself.

'Will Daddy be home for Christmas?' Alex suddenly asked her in a loud voice, ignoring the look Amelia was giving her.

Olivia took a deep breath. She had by now carefully explained to both girls that she and Caspar were going to be living separately from now on and assured them that once Caspar had found somewhere permanent to live they would be going to see him. Whatever her private feelings, there was no way she was going to stop them from seeing their father.

'Darling, we've already discussed Daddy is going to be living separately from us.'

'I don't *want* him to live anywhere else, I want him to come home and live with us.'

Alex's manner was almost aggressive, her mouth pouting as she glared angrily at her mother.

Olivia closed her eyes and mentally counted slowly to ten.

AT LEAST she seemed to have reassured the girls that
they would be seeing Caspar again as well as explaining why it was not possible for them to have Christmas
together, Olivia decided thankfully as she finished
reading the chapter of their shared bedtime story and
started to get up.

'Mummy…'

Olivia tensed.

'Yes, Alex…' God, but she was so tired and there
was still so much she had to do before she, too, could
go to bed. Far too much fortunately for her to have
any spare energy left to think about that unexpected
and unwanted visit from her father. How dare he simply think he could walk into her life…their lives…?
And as for that pseudo loving offer of his help…

'That man who came today who looks like Uncle
Jon, is it true that he's our grandfather?'

Olivia froze. How on earth…? Anger seared her in
a white-hot sheet of hate. Had her father actually
dared…?

In the other bed Amelia was making a strangled
anxious noise. Frowning, Olivia looked at her.

'Alex, I told you not to say anything about that,'
Amelia snapped, glaring at her younger sister.

Olivia sat down heavily on Amelia's bed. She was
trembling violently but she tried to suppress it, worried
that the girls might see.

'What makes you ask that, darling?' she asked Alex
carefully.

'Leo said that he was,' Alex replied openly. 'He

called him ''Uncle David'' and when I said that we didn't have an uncle David he said that he was *his* uncle David but *our* grandfather.'

'I see.'

Frantically she wondered what to do. She had never discussed her father or her childhood with her daughters. They were far too young to understand the complications of her relationship with her own parents for one thing and for another she never saw her mother and had not expected that her father would ever dare to come back to Haslewich.

'Is it true?' Alex was persisting.

Olivia paused; her throat had become dry, she ached to deny her father, but how could she without blatantly lying?

'I…yes, he is,' she agreed huskily.

She could see the troubled look on Amelia's face and had a sudden unwanted recollection of herself at Amelia's age watching over her mother as she slept off what Olivia recognised now must have been one of her bulimic attacks.

She closed her eyes momentarily. If only Caspar were here, *he* would know what to do—what to say.

Tears clogged her throat. He had been so furious with her when he had discovered that she hadn't told him that her father had come home. Confusing muddled thoughts were filling her head. Why was she feeling regretful about their quarrel? *Caspar* was the one who had been at fault—not her.

'But how can he be our grandfather?' Alex was saying plaintively.

'He's our grandfather because he's Uncle Jon's brother, stupid,' Amelia cut in sharply, avoiding looking directly at Olivia as she spoke.

Alex glared back at her sister.

'But if he's our grandfather then why don't we see him? Leo sees Uncle Jon and Aunt Jenny all the time.'

'That's enough. Go to sleep, both of you,' Olivia instructed them shakily.

Just hearing them talking about her father, comparing their lack of any kind of relationship with him with the warm intimate love that existed between Jon and Jenny and their grandchildren made Olivia feel sick and angry and guilty. She had tried to compensate, to provide her children with the grandparenting she wanted them to have and she had thought she had succeeded, that they were finding surrogate grandparents in Jon and Jenny just as she had found surrogate parents in them; but just recently she had found herself watching her aunt and uncle, afraid that she might see that they preferred their 'real' grandchildren above Amelia and Alex.

'But I want to know how he can be our grandfather when we've never seen him?' Alex was continuing stubbornly.

'That's enough,' Olivia shouted, immediately ashamed of her anger when she saw the shocked look in Alex's eyes and the way she clung to her bedclothes.

'I don't want to hear another word about...about any of this,' she continued in a more gentle voice.

Kissing them both good-night she walked over to the door. Just as she was closing it she thought she heard Alex whispering fiercely to Amelia, 'Well, I don't care what you say, I liked him.'

'NICK—are you feeling all right?'

Nick frowned as he looked across the room at his brother.

'Yes. I'm fine. Why?'

'You've been in a world of your own for the last ten minutes. If you overdid it at the gym earlier and—'

Nick grimaced.

'Will you please stop fussing. There is nothing wrong with me and if you weren't such a worrier—'

'So,' Saul said softly. ''What *is* absorbing your attention to the exclusion of everything else just now?'

Nick refused to be drawn. The truth was that he had been thinking about Sara and her unbelievable acceptance of his preposterous proposition. Because she genuinely wanted to have a 'no strings—no-holds-barred' sex fling with him or because she was playing a very subtle game of brinkmanship?

Irritably Nick wondered just why he was finding it so hard to take on board the idea that Sara might simply want to have sex with him as opposed to a relationship. Most men would have been overjoyed to take her up on her offer; after all, wasn't sex without emotion or commitment every determined-to-remain-single man's fantasy—and he *had* to remain unattached. There was no way he could continue to do the job he loved if he wasn't. Oh, at first he imagined a woman would accept that there would be times when he would simply have to pack his bags and disappear for an unspecified length of time, but gradually things would change. Inevitably in a committed relationship the subject of children would arise, and once the relationship included children there would be pressure on him to put their needs first, to give up a job that didn't just take him away from them in terms of time but which also was dangerous enough to contain a risk that he may never return.

One day maybe he would feel ready to exchange his current work for a stay-at-home desk job, but that day was still a long, long way off and Sara had struck him as the kind of woman who would be very specific about what she expected from her man—her mate....

There he went again, bringing emotion into the equation.

Perhaps he should try to out-manoeuvre Sara and double bluff her, agree that they should opt for a sex-only relationship and see just how long it took her to change her mind and backtrack.

Grimly he wondered how many other men in his position would be feeling so ominously heavy-hearted about the thought of going to bed with a woman who made them ache so much just to think about her that their longing for her was a tight, taut physical pain.

'BUT OVER the years things changed, Livvy changed....'

'It's something most people do,' Molly told Caspar dryly. 'It's called maturing.'

'I'm sorry, I'm boring you,' Caspar acknowledged shortly.

His original one night stop-over in Williamsville had become four and counting. The original meal at the Italian restaurant Molly had recommended had proved so energising and exciting and the ancient sedan so recalcitrant and stubborn about refusing to be fixed, that Caspar had found himself offering to pick Molly up from her home and drive her to work as a thank you for recommending the restaurant to him and because she had laughingly admitted that he had not been the only one to harbour a teenage fantasy of riding a Harley-Davidson.

Now, after just a matter of days, Caspar felt as though he had known her all his life and in a way he had. She was very much the type of girl he had dated through college, feisty, self-confident, proud of herself and her opinions although as a woman she presented those assets of her personality in an appealingly softer way than he remembered his collegiate dates doing.

'No, you're not boring me,' she corrected him firmly, her smile saying that she was refusing to play games and take offence at his remark as he had done at hers.

'I was simply pointing out that it's a healthy part of the human condition for us to change. To resent such a natural process in those close to us suggests to me—'

'Now, you're starting to psychoanalyse me,' Caspar groaned.

'It's my job,' Molly reminded him.

'And that's how you see me, is it?' Caspar asked her ruefully. 'As a potential patient?'

It was several seconds before she replied, an uncharacteristic hesitation that exposed a potential hint of vulnerability that aroused all Caspar's male hunting instincts.

Whilst she played with the froth on the top of her cappuccino Caspar waited. He would be lying to himself if he tried to pretend that he didn't find her attractive; that his body and his mind were both excited and aroused by her. But he would be lying to himself, too, if he tried to ignore the fact that admitting those feelings caused him to feel guilty—even though he had no reason to be. He and Livvy had separated—Livvy's idea not his, and so he was now perfectly free to…to what? To enjoy the company of another woman, to flirt with her, desire her…go to bed with her…form a relationship with her?

It was Molly who brought a halt to his stampeding thoughts by telling him quietly, 'The way I see you is as a man who is still very much working through the problems in his relationship with another woman—in your case your wife, but marriage doesn't come into this. Olivia is on your mind…in your thoughts virtually ninety-nine percent of the time.'

'Because I can't understand what the hell was wrong with her,' Caspar exploded.

'Did you try *asking* her?' Molly asked him calmly, adding before he could answer, 'or did you simply assume that you knew and then proceed to put her right, tell her how she should behave?

'You would be amazed at how many of my clients complain to me that they aren't listened to, that their complaints, their attempts to make themselves heard are simply swept aside.'

'Of course I listened to her,' Caspar defended himself, adding jokingly, 'I'm a lawyer. I'm used to listening.'

'*Is* that what lawyers do?' Molly asked him ruefully.

Caspar had the grace to laugh.

'Well, occasionally they do other things,' he teased, 'like riding Harley-Davidsons and enjoying good Italian food and being with stunningly beautiful clever women...'

'Beautiful and clever. How else do you see me I wonder, Caspar? Perhaps as someone who can fill the empty space in your bed that's beginning to make you ache just a little bit too much for comfort?'

Caspar hesitated. For this woman nothing other than the truth would suffice. She wouldn't accept it and he knew he would be insulting her if he tried to offer her anything less than her due. And he already knew that she just wasn't someone he wanted to insult or hurt in any way.

'I see you as someone unique and special,' he told

her gravely and honestly. 'Yes, I want to take you to bed. What man wouldn't? But I enjoy being with you for its own sake, Molly. I like listening to your voice, seeing your smile, watching you. I like that fearsomely clever mind of yours and I like the delicious way your sweater fits over the curves of your breasts. I like the championing look in your eyes when you talk about people you want to help and I like the authority in your voice when you want to make a businesslike point. I like the way you drive that wretched beat-up old car instead of something that's a status symbol. I like the way you've made a life for yourself here in this small country town instead of taking those remarkable and highly marketable career skills of yours to somewhere like Washington. What does keep you here, by the way?'

She looked down at the table, long, long eyelashes lying vulnerably against the purity of her skin.

When at last she looked at him he could see an emotion in her eyes that tore at his heart.

'I grew up here,' she told him quietly. 'Whilst I was away at college there was an accident at a local chemical factory. They made stuff for farmers—pesticides, that sort of thing. The explosion caused a gas cloud that passed right over the town.

'My younger sister was in school that day. She was four years old—a menopause baby for my mother— we all adored her. She and a lot of the other kids in school that day breathed in that poisonous stuff.... She started having fits and suffered severe brain damage and so did some of the other kids.

'They all got compensation of course, but how can you compensate someone, anyone, for the loss of their ability to enjoy life to the full?' There was a wry twist to her mouth as she added, 'Up until then I had been intending to study law—I'd got it all planned. A fast-track career that would take me up to and into the White House, no less, but then I saw the way the lawyers working for the chemical company were handling the case and—'

She spread her hands '—I guess I just didn't have the stomach to be that kind of lawyer and so—' she took a deep breath '—I couldn't heal my baby sister. She lives full-time in a special home now. I go visit every week but she can't recognise me now.' Her eyes were bleak.

'My folks died some while back—of a broken heart some might say.... In my line of work you get to see all kinds of human misery and despair, but for me there's nothing out there that comes anywhere near to what a parent feels when they see their child destroyed and they just can't protect them.'

Caspar shook his head. What could he say? Any words would seem inadequate—and worse, an insult. Instead, uncharacteristically he reached out and took hold of her hand clasping it warmly between both of his own.

'Thanks.' The look she gave him as she removed her hand from his grip spoke volumes.

'I guess over the years I've become a little cynical. Telling that story...' She gave a small shrug. 'I tend to rate how much time I aim to give the person listening to it, how much access to my life by the way they react to what I've said.'

'So how did I score?' Caspar asked her levelly.

'You're off the board,' Molly told him, but she hadn't, Caspar noticed, said in which direction he was outside her scorecard.

'To tell you right now how much I miss my daughters seems kind of thoughtless and selfish,' he said quietly after several seconds of silence. 'But I do miss them...more and more every day.'

'Are you in contact with them?' Molly asked him.

'No. Not at this stage. We, or rather Olivia, decided that until things were legally settled it was best that we didn't make contact. They know that I'm driving around the States, but with Christmas coming up.... One of my half-siblings has a place out at Aspen. I'd have loved to have the girls out for at least a part of the holiday but I'm not sure the disruption would be good for them right now.'

Molly listened in silence noticing the very British 'the girls' instead of a more American and familiar 'the kids.'

He intrigued her, delighted her and drew her to him in a way that was already making warning bells ring for her.

She was in her thirties, no fool where men were concerned. There had been a youthful and very brief marriage after which she had decided that the only commitment she wanted to make was to herself, which was really just as well because Caspar, despite all his protests to the contrary, was very much still committed to his Olivia and their daughters.

'We'd better go,' she told Caspar, glancing at her watch. 'The garage promised me that they've got the right part for the car this time.'

The mishaps surrounding the repair of her ancient car had become almost a private special-couple-thing kind of a joke between them, only they were not a special couple and the loss of her ancient car was anything but a joke. She could always replace it, of course, but it had belonged to her parents and was the last remaining tangible bridge between the woman she was now and her childhood and for that reason she tended to treat it and value it much as one might a much loved elderly pet.

'If I were you I'd definitely ditch it and get a Harley,' Caspar teased her as they both stepped out into the cold, late-afternoon air.

'No way! Harleys are for teens and sad middle-aged lawyers,' Molly mock-taunted him back. The speed with which they had established an intimate verbal connection worried her a little when she allowed herself to question it.

But why worry about a problem that was soon going to disappear? Caspar had no long-term plans to stay in town and she was certainly not going to encourage him to do so. And just to reinforce that fact, as they walked towards the motorbike she asked him casually, 'What time do you plan to leave in the morning?'

'Straight after breakfast,' Caspar responded. He had been wondering about extending his journey and possibly even spending Christmas in Mexico. He'd decline the various family offers to stay because doing so would arouse far too many painful thoughts about home and Amelia and Alex.

At this time of the day—late afternoon—he would normally have collected them from school and taken them home. Just as soon as he had decided what he was going to do with the rest of his life and he had a settled place to live he was going to have them over to stay with him.

He could still visualise the way they had looked the last time he had seen them.

They had virtually reached the parked bike now but Molly had stopped to answer her ringing mobile.

'What...? Yes. Yes, I'll be right there,' Caspar heard her saying, her face was white with shock. Her voice broke up over the words as she told him shakily, 'That was the home. My sister... She...isn't well.... I need to be there.... I'm sorry, I can't delay.... It's been good meeting you, but I have to go.... Goodbye, Caspar...'

ANXIOUSLY Olivia unlocked the door of her car. Provided there were no traffic hold-ups she would just about be able to make it to the school in time to avoid another telling off.

Her nerves felt as raw as the screeching of the car tyres she could hear as another driver exhibited the frantic impatience she could feel boiling up inside herself. She had barely arrived at the office this morning when Jon had collared her. Unsuspectingly she had followed him into his office, assuming he wanted to talk to her about work only to discover that he actually wanted to try to persuade her to allow her father to 'help' her.

'Your father desperately wants to be there for you, Livvy—to make amends.... Why don't you give him another chance?'

'I already did...many many times whilst I was growing up,' Olivia had informed him bitterly.

Her mobile started to ring just as she was approaching the school. For a moment she was tempted to ignore it but what if the call was important? What if *Caspar* was ringing her?

Pulling into the side of the road she reached for the phone frowning when she recognised Jon and Jenny's number.

'Livvy,' she heard Jenny demanding anxiously.

'Yes. Yes, I'm here,' she confirmed. 'I'm just on my way to school, though, to pick up the girls and I mustn't be late....'

'Livvy...the girls are here.'

'What? But that's impossible. I booked them into the after-school crèche. How can they be with you?'

There was a small pause and then she heard Jenny

saying quietly, 'They *are* here and… Look, I think it's best if I explain once you get here.'

'Once I get there— Jenny, is something wrong? The girls, are they—'

'They're both fine,' Jenny assured her quickly. 'But there's something… I'll go now and let you get here, Livvy.'

The girls were at Jon and Jenny's…. As she reversed her car and set off in the direction of her aunt and uncle's house, Livvy's thoughts were a seething mass of maternal shock and anxiety.

How could the girls have got there? Jon and Jenny lived nearly three miles away from the school and…

A traffic jam delayed her by several precious minutes so that it was over twenty minutes later that she pulled up on Jenny's drive, abandoning her car to open the door and run towards the house.

Jenny had obviously been waiting for her because she opened the front door immediately.

'I wanted to talk to you before you see the girls,' Jenny was telling her as she ushered her into her sitting room.

'What's happened? What's wrong? Why—?'

'Nothing's wrong. They're both fine,' Jenny reassured her again firmly.

'But what are they doing here? How did they get here?'

'They walked,' Jenny told her, her eyes and her voice betraying what she was thinking and Livvy could sense the heavy cold sick feeling ricocheting through her own body as she contemplated the long country lane that led twisting and turning across the fields from the school to Jon and Jenny's home.

It was a narrow lane bordered by fields and woodlands, busy with speeding commuter traffic at certain times of the day and emptily quiet at others and it was the kind of lane that represented *every* type of danger to children that all parents feared—speeding traffic, no pavements, thick screening hedgerows which meant...

Olivia felt as though she wanted to be sick.

'They walked—on their own....' She was horrified by her negligence as a parent, a mother. How could she not have known the danger they were in?

'Apparently they left school once classes had finished somehow managing to evade their teacher,' Jenny was continuing. 'I have to admit they planned it all very well.'

'But Amelia knows she must *never ever* leave the school without being with an adult—she knows—' Olivia protested.

'As I understand it, it wasn't Amelia who was the driving force behind the enterprise,' Jenny told her ruefully.

Olivia stared at her.

'You mean Alex...' she began in disbelief. 'But she's...' She stopped. Of the two of them Alex *was* the more adventurous, the more stubborn.

'But why...why...?'

Jenny took a deep breath. This was the bit she had been dreading explaining to Olivia ever since the girls had arrived exhausted and bedraggled half an hour earlier.

How on earth they had managed such a long walk without being seen by someone and reported to the authorities, Jenny had no idea. What she did know, however, was that their guardian angel must have been watching over them to protect them.

'I know how much they've been missing you and Uncle Jon,' Olivia was saying shakily, 'But I've tried to explain to them that you've been busy....'

Jenny couldn't meet her eyes.

'It wasn't really me they came to see Olivia.... At least not in the sense that you mean. They wanted to ask me about their grandfather.'

'Their grandfather...?' Olivia couldn't conceal her feelings.

'What did you tell them?' she demanded harshly.

'I said that they should talk to you about him,' Jenny said gently.

'He came to see me yesterday,' Olivia told Jenny huskily and reluctantly. 'My father...he offered to help me with the children. I told him no. I told him that I didn't want them to have *anything* to do with him and I don't. Leo had told them that he was their grandfather.'

Olivia continued in an uneven voice.

'The girls saw him...my father.... Alex had fallen over in the garden and he picked her up.... They guessed who he was...they asked me all sorts of questions....' She closed her eyes. 'What did they say to you?'

'They asked if it was true that the man they'd met was their grandfather and that he was Uncle Jon's brother. They wanted to know why they had never seen him before.'

'And what did you tell them?' Olivia asked her faintly.

Jenny touched her arm comfortingly.

'It wasn't my place to explain the situation to them, Livvy...and they're so young. I just said that he'd been living in another country but that now he was back.'

Olivia sighed. She could well understand how impossible it would have been for Jenny to even begin to attempt to explain the truth to girls so young.

'I'd better take them home,' she told Jenny wearily. 'Thank you for looking after them.'

She sounded so forlorn that Jenny took hold of her in silent commiseration.

'MUMMY...'

Amelia saw her first.

Without any preamble Olivia told them that she was taking them home, bidding them thank Jenny for looking after them.

The car wasn't the place to ask them the question she wanted to ask. At the end of the short drive Alex was yawning tiredly and had to be carried from the car to the house, shaking her head and announcing that she didn't want any tea when Livvy asked what she would like to eat.

'Aunt Jenny gave us something to eat whilst we were waiting for you,' Amelia told her quietly.

Olivia had promised herself that she wasn't going to frighten them by getting angry but the fear haunting her of what could so easily have happened to them was driving her. Why, when they were both safe and she was giving thanks for that fact, did she still feel like screaming at them that she was furiously angry with them for leaving school in the way they had when they knew that it was expressly forbidden for them to do so?

But to her despair and shame she could see in Amelia's eyes that her elder daughter was afraid of her doing just that so instead, she dropped down on her heels next to her and gently gathering them both to her in her arms she asked as calmly as she could, 'Haven't both Daddy and I always told you that you must never leave school unless one of us is with you— or we've told you that someone else will collect you?'

Alex, still a baby really, trembled, her eyes filling with huge tears.

'When is my daddy coming home?' she whispered heartbreakingly. 'I want him to come home.'

'Oh, Alex.' Fresh guilt and a grief she didn't want to acknowledge filled Olivia.

'Daddy doesn't love us any more, does he?' Alex was continuing tearfully.

'Of course he loves you,' Olivia responded immediately and she knew truthfully.

'Then why isn't he here?' Alex demanded quickly.

'Sweetheart, you already know why,' Olivia reminded her gently.

'Daddy and Mummy aren't going to live together any more. You know that,' Amelia informed her younger sister sharply, but when she looked at her Olivia could see that if anything her elder daughter was even more upset than her younger.

She ought to have expected this and been prepared for it, Olivia knew, but somehow she had hoped... convinced herself that the girls had accepted the separation.

'Well, if we can't have a daddy then I want to have a grandpa,' Alex announced, adding challengingly, 'Other children at school have grandpas and grandmas and they—'

'Oh, Alex,' Olivia protested realising painfully that Alex's small body was resisting all Olivia's attempts to offer her love and comfort.

'Amelia...' Olivia turned to her elder daughter. She loved both her children so much that it had never occurred to her that they might start to reject her...blame her...because they felt they had lost Caspar.

'You're older than Alex.... *You* know you aren't allowed to leave school and that road...'

'I had to do it, Mummy,' Amelia told her unwillingly. 'Alex said that she would go without me if I didn't....'

The look she gave first her younger sister and then Olivia herself tore at Olivia's emotions. How well she herself could remember that feeling of being responsible for the welfare and safety of a younger sibling, the anxiety, the fear, the anger and resentment against the world that forced on her a responsibility that was too heavy for her combined with a stoical determination to carry that burden somehow.

Oh, Amelia…. What was she *doing* to her children she asked herself sorrowfully. What was she inflicting on them?

'I wanted to know about my grandpa,' Alex was telling her firmly. 'You wouldn't tell us so I wanted to ask Uncle Jon about him.'

Every word she uttered was adding to Olivia's despair and guilt. How could she possibly continue with her work now? How could she bear to allow them out of her sight for a single second?

Serpent-like the thought slipped into her mind that none of this would have happened if Caspar had been here.

Caspar…

She had dreamed about him last night—again—waking up, her face wet with tears to find her arms outstretched yearningly to the empty side of their bed.

But it had been the Caspar she had fallen in love with she had dreamed of, she reminded herself fiercely, not the Caspar her husband had become.

'Amelia and Alex, you must both promise me that

you will never, ever, do anything like this again,' Olivia told them. 'That road is very dangerous…and you…

'You're both so precious, so vulnerable,' she wanted to tell them, but of course they were far too young to understand.

She was, Olivia knew, facing the dilemma that faced so many single working mothers. She needed to work to support her children financially, to give them the lifestyle enjoyed by their peers within their family group and at school. The house was mortgaged and Caspar would do his bit she knew, but she had always been the main breadwinner. Yes, they could downscale. She could sell the house and buy something smaller in Haslewich itself, perhaps, and she was fully prepared to do so; but no matter what economies they made she would still have to earn a living…and she could not do that unless she had the kind of back-up and help that meant she need never have a single second's anxiety about the safety and welfare of her daughters.

There had been another message left from the nanny agency to say that they were unable to find anyone to meet her needs. Jenny, who she had hoped would help her, could not do so. All the other women in the family had very full busy lives of their own with their own responsibilities; and besides, there was no way she wanted her precious children to feel they were always on the fringes of other people's lives, always second best, always having to stand aside and watch others receive the love and hugs of loving parents and grand-parents whilst they...

Olivia closed her eyes. There was no other course open to her now. For her children's sake she had to put aside her own pride and bitterness.

She had seen the look in her father's eyes as he tended Alex's cut leg. Tears filled her own. For the sake of her daughters there was nothing else she could do.

SARA GLANCED at her watch. It was well gone eight o'clock in the evening and her desk was virtually clear. She could have left hours ago and been curled up comfortably in her flat watching her favourite TV programme. So what was she doing sitting here... waiting...?

She was working, that was what she told herself, ignoring the fact that she had been achieving little for the last fifteen minutes. Anyway, what had she expected? That just because she had indicated to Nick that she had changed her mind and that she wanted to go ahead with...with the ultimate cure for the affliction she was suffering from, that he would drop everything and come speeding over to sweep her off to his bed!

No, of course she hadn't.

Liar, she scorned herself with silent derision. That was *exactly* what she had expected him to do. Was he deliberately trying to torment her, to humiliate her or was he more mundanely perhaps the kind of man who lost interest in his prey once it had stopped running?

Unable to dwell logically or unemotionally on such unpalatable and unwanted thoughts, Sara got off her chair and paced her office agitatedly.

If he didn't want her, well that was fine by her. He, after all, was the one who had come on to her and not the other way around. She had noticed how sexually compelling he was of course, but... She tensed as the telephone on her desk rang. There was no telephone in the flat which was why she had remained down here in the office, finding herself work to do just in case...

She made an angry grab for the telephone receiver grimacing when she discovered that the caller was someone who had dialled the office number in error and who really wanted to make a booking in the restaurant.

Politely she asked him to hold on whilst she went into the restaurant for the reservation book.

Having taken the booking, she was on her way back to the restaurant with it when she saw him. He was just about to push open the outside door. It was a wet night and as she watched him in avid absorbed intensity she saw him shake the raindrops off himself.

He hadn't seen her as yet and so she was able to watch him, virtually rooted to the spot by the urgency and strength of what she was feeling.

NICK HADN'T intended to go to the restaurant—or indeed to make any attempt to contact Sara. He wanted, no, *needed*, time to come to terms with what she had said to him. But then he had discovered that he needed some cash and the nearest cash dispenser was only a few seconds' walk away from the restaurant and...

As he pushed open the door he saw her. She was standing looking at him. A huge swell of feeling so strong that it shocked him surged through him. He wanted to swoop down and pick her up there and then, take her away somewhere where he could be totally and completely on his own with her...then they would see just how easy she would actually find it to separate sex from emotion.

As he reached her side some dangerous impulse within her drove Sara to say in soft challenge, 'Goodness me, I'd begun to wonder if you'd changed your mind and to think that perhaps you were one of those men who was all talk but no action!'

Aghast she wondered what on earth had prompted her to say something so foolhardy. But it was too late to take back her challenging words now. She could see from the angry glint in Nick's eyes just what *he* thought of them.

'Changed my mind? No way. And as for the rest of your statement...' His voice had become as smooth as cream but Sara was very sharply aware of the acid sting that lurked beneath his soft words.

'It will be my pleasure to prove otherwise.'

His pleasure! A tiny dart of fear and insecurity stabbed through Sara's body. Unwittingly her glance lifted to his to search his eyes, her own widening and darkening with an unexpected vulnerability that made Nick catch his breath. Just what kind of a game was she playing with him? One moment the sophisticated sexually experienced woman of the world, the next a vulnerable-looking novice who trembled at the mere thought of having sex.

But, after a remark like the one she had just made to him, there was no way she could be that!

Helplessly Sara wondered how on earth she could have been so idiotic. No man liked having his sexuality challenged—she knew that.

Nick took a deep breath. What was he waiting for? She had made it plain to him just what she wanted.

'I have to return home for a few days....'

'Home?' Sara questioned numbly. What was he trying to tell her? That he had, after all, changed his mind? That he needed more time to decide? Either way...

'Yes. I live in Pembrokeshire,' he told her tersely. 'I want you to come with me.'

Go with him?

Sara wasn't sure if the weakness that filled her was caused by shock or relief.

'We could be alone there,' Nick told her quietly, forcing her to meet and hold his gaze. 'I don't think either of us want to have our private lives played out under the interested eyes of either Frances and her family or my brother and his...'

'No,' Sara agreed. 'But Pembrokeshire...'

She hadn't got as far as thinking where they would

expiate their mutually unwanted desire but had hazily assumed they would go to some hotel. Certainly, she agreed with him that she didn't want anyone else to know what was happening. After all, it wasn't as though they were going to have a proper relationship or become a 'couple,' but to go away alone with him to his home…

'If you can't trust me enough to come to my home then you certainly can't trust me and if you can't trust me enough to enter my home then you certainly can't trust me enough to enter your body,' he told her trenchantly and with such open sexual meaning that Sara flushed.

'I… When… There's Frances and my work… I'd have to take time off,' she began disjointedly.

'The weekend after next,' Nick told her immediately. 'Oh, and you'll need warm clothes. The cottage is fairly remote.'

Warm clothes! Sara gave him a startled look but wished she hadn't as he returned it with amusement, bending his head to whisper wickedly in her ear, 'What's wrong? Granted I want you like hell and I can promise you it's going to give us both very great pleasure when I prove it to you, but we shan't be spending the *entire* weekend in bed. Pembroke has one of the most famous and beautiful coastline walks in the country. If the weather's good enough we could even sail. The sea off the coast can be a little bit rough, though.'

Sara was almost beginning to get the impression

that he was subtly trying to put her off—either that or intimidate her.

Dryly she told him, 'My father's a keen sailor and I used to crew for him.'

Giving him an old-fashioned look she added in an even dryer tone, 'The year I was fourteen we both did the Round Britain race crewing for a client of my father's.'

'Did you win?' Nick asked her mock innocently.

Sara gave him a sharply incisive look but he held her gaze.

'No. We were placed tenth,' she replied calmly and then couldn't resist adding, 'But we came out with the best time for a purely amateur crewed boat.'

'I spent a couple of summers sailing off Cape Cod when I was at university,' Nick told her casually, but Sara wasn't deceived. Well, if he wanted to play 'anything you can do I can do better' games that was fine by her. *She* certainly wasn't going to back down.

FOURTEEN AND crewing in something as dangerous as the Round Britain race—Nick frowned as he left her. Her father must have been mad to allow it. She was such a slender scrap of a thing. She could quite easily have been swept overboard. Just thinking of the danger she would have been in made his whole body tense.

WHAT ON EARTH had she committed herself to, Sara wondered anxiously as she watched Nick walk away.

She tried to comfort herself by thinking that she could always change her mind and refuse to go but she knew already that her pride just wouldn't allow her to take that escape route.

Of course, there was always the chance that Frances would not want her to take the weekend off; but, predictably, when Sara mentioned it to her later Frances agreed immediately to her request.

Sara thanked her hollowly. Now there was nothing to stop her from going to Pembrokeshire with Nick.

'Thank you very much!' she silently mentally cursed fate.

'YOU'RE GOING HOME?' Saul frowned. 'Now look, Nick...'

'It's only for the weekend,' Nick assured him. 'I need to check the state of the house—that sort of thing.'

'Mmm... Well, if you've made up your mind I don't suppose *I* can stop you,' Saul acknowledged.

'No, you can't,' Nick agreed dryly.

'I can't stop you, Nick,' Saul continued quietly but with firm elder brother authority, 'but I can and must remind you of how foolhardy it would be of you to prejudice your own recovery by doing anything stupid or dangerous.'

Foolhardy and dangerous—well, that just about accurately summed up his plans for his time in Pembrokeshire, Nick acknowledged, albeit not the way that Saul meant. On this occasion it would be his emotions that would be in danger and the risks he was taking with *them* that was foolhardy rather than with his physical safety.

Still, there was always the chance that Sara would back out. A woman who as a girl had taken part in one of the most gruelling sailing races there was—back away from *any* challenge—who was he kidding?

HONOR LOOKED AT the silent telephone. She had just had the strangest feeling. Living as she did so close to and in harmony with nature, Honor had long ago ceased to question or doubt these occasional darts of 'intuition' she experienced. She and Father Ignatius had discussed this phenomenon in great detail without either of them being able to come up with a rational explanation for it other than to acknowledge, as the priest had said, that there were both historical and biblical anecdotes and written confirmation to prove its existence.

Thoughtfully she walked over to the telephone. David, touchingly, had already added Olivia's number to their personal directory.

Her hand was reaching out for the receiver when the telephone started to ring. After a look at the caller's number she cried urgently, 'David, come quickly, it's for you.'

AS SHE HEARD the familiar male voice responding to her telephone call, Olivia took a deep breath. This was the hardest and the most humiliating thing she had ever had to do.

'Hello...it's me—Olivia,' she announced herself abruptly.

On the other end of the line David closed his eyes and willed his own voice not to falter or betray what he was feeling as he prayed that somehow she would sense and accept the love he was sending to her.

LESS THAN FIVE minutes later it was all arranged. Olivia would drop the children off every morning with David and Honor on her way to work. David would take them to school and collect them again in the afternoon and she would pick them up from David and Honor's on her way home from work.

THAT NIGHT, curled up alone in her bed in a small protective foetal ball, she allowed herself to give in to her feelings. Was there something about her that meant she was destined to forever be alone, to forever be denied the experience of being truly and completely loved?

'MOLLY, wait...'

Her eyes dark with anxiety, Molly turned to look impatiently at Caspar.

'I have to go,' she repeated.

'I know that,' Caspar acknowledged. 'But how will you get there if your car still isn't ready? Why don't you let me take you?' he suggested before she could say anything.

'Let *you* take me?'

Molly's forehead pleated in a quick defensive frown.

The light-hearted flirtation they had been indulging in had been one thing, but what he was suggesting now was something else.

Gravely she looked at him.

This wasn't any time for her to be indulging in her own emotional needs, especially with a man like Caspar; but he was already walking towards her, already taking control of the situation and her and she, fool that she was, was letting him do it, luxuriating almost in the sensation as he removed from her shoulders the burden of dealing with the practicalities of the situation.

As he took charge, Caspar couldn't help contrasting Molly's behaviour to Olivia's. He couldn't remember the last time Olivia had unquestioningly allowed him to play his male role. These last few years she had seemed to challenge every decision he had made, pouring scorn on them and on him, undermining him to such an extent that it had begun to eat away at the very essence of his maleness. Molly's acceptance of his help made him feel ten feet tall and capable of doing anything and everything she might ask of him.

As he looked at her, her eyes shiny and dark with the tears she was so obviously determined not to shed, he had to fight not to take her in his arms right there and then and comfort her.

IT SEEMED TO Olivia to be hours before she finally fell asleep to dream despairingly and longingly of being wrapped securely in Caspar's arms whilst he held her and whispered to her that he understood and sympathised with everything that she was feeling. In her dream she told him truthfully that he was the only person she felt secure and safe with, the only person she could be herself with and admit her fears and failings to.

Caspar!

As she felt the tender familiar brush of his mouth on hers, tears seeped from beneath her closed eyelids.

CHAPTER TWELVE

STUBBORNLY Sara had refused to allow Nick to pick her up for the drive into Pembrokeshire, insisting instead that they made the journey to his cottage separately in their own individual cars; but now as she followed his skilled handling of his large four-wheel-drive vehicle in her own much smaller and less comfortable compact car, all the doubts and fears Sara had fought to keep at bay behind the battlements of her pride began stalking her with a vengeance.

They were in Wales now and through Aberystwyth, following the coast road. It was a wet day with a grey mist rolling in over an even greyer sea, the hypnotic sound of her windscreen wipers failing to do anything to soothe down Sara's oversensitive nerve endings.

She had, as instructed, packed warm practical clothes. When they had met up at their arranged meeting place earlier in the day, Nick had got out of his car and come striding across to her. Dressed in jeans and a casual shirt he had still had the power to make her go weak at the knees—and to suddenly and unwontedly realise just why she was behaving in such an uncharacteristic and self-destructive way.

'I thought we'd stop for lunch on the other side of

Aberystwyth,' he had told her. There's a small town that I think you'll like with a particularly good seafood restaurant.'

And now they had reached that town and Nick was pulling off the road and into the small market square.

Almost numbly Sara followed him, parking her car next to his at the harbour front in the space he had left for her.

Even in the harbour the sea was choppy, the small moored fishing boats bouncing like corks on the heavy swell of the grey foaming water.

Sara was glad of the warmth in the fleece she had pulled on over her jeans and top as she stepped out into the cold damp air, deliberately ignoring the hand Nick put out towards her. She had never felt more on edge and anxious…not even on that supposedly so important first time. Losing her virginity had been nothing when compared with what she was contemplating doing now, a mere basic rite of passage with a boy she remembered with a vague amused fondness and who had been as nervous and uncertain about the actual mechanics of what they were doing as she had been herself. She had been eighteen then, though—a girl—and now she was a woman. Woman enough for a man like Nick Crighton?

She shivered causing Nick to say irritably, 'I don't bite, you know, Sara…' before adding in a lower and far more sensual undertone, 'at least not in public.'

The restaurant he took her to was down a narrow side street between the harbour and the town square.

To reach it they had to walk past the town's charming pastel-washed Georgian houses.

The restaurant was surprisingly busy. Nick explained to her that the town was a favourite retirement area for the middle classes which explained the preponderance of hearty tweed and twin-setted couples at the other tables Sara recognised.

The waiter was waiting to show them to their table and Sara started to remove her fleece.

'Let me,' Nick offered, immediately turning to help her. Sara already had one arm out of her jacket and as she felt Nick's fingers curl round it as he helped her, her body reacted to him immediately, goose bumps lifting on her skin as a hot wave of explicit sensation shot through her. For a moment neither of them moved, their gazes meeting and meshing. The naked hunger she could see in Nick's eyes both shocked and excited her.

'For God's sake, don't look at me like that,' she heard Nick muttering thickly under his breath.

'Like what? I'm not—' Sara immediately denied defensively.

But Nick cut her short telling her rawly, 'Oh, yes, you are. For goodness sake, Sara, I know how much you're enjoying this but I'm not as fireproof as you obviously are. And if you don't stop right now it's going to be as obvious to everyone else here as it must be to you that the only thing I'm hungry for right now, the only thing *I* want to eat,' he emphasised with sexual explicitness, 'is you.'

Discreetly the maître d' had stepped back from them whilst he showed some other diners to a table. Sara could feel her whole body burning with a heat that had nothing whatsoever to do with embarrassment. Shockingly she knew, too, that if Nick were to take hold of her right now and lead her through the restaurant's reception area to where the stairs led to the rooms she had noticed they advertised she wouldn't want to stop him. But instead he was ushering her grimly into the dining room, one hand cupping her elbow as she tried to keep as much physical distance between them as she could—not easy when the spaces between the tables were so narrow, but every time she felt the heat of his body against her own her flesh reacted so explosively that she could feel herself physically trembling.

They both ordered lobster and whilst they waited for their meal to be served Sara studied the other diners. Middle class and middle-aged in the main, they exuded the air of placid calmness that only seemed to underscore the highwire tension of her sexual arousal.

'Do you eat here often?' she asked Nick, trying to bring a measure of calm ordinariness to the situation.

'It's a good stopping off point when I'm travelling back from Cheshire,' Nick responded. 'It's a journey I make fairly frequently.'

'To see your married…friend…?' Sara questioned him immediately.

'My what?' Nick frowned and then realised who she

meant. 'Oh, you mean Bobbie.' He smiled whilst Sara seethed with impotent jealousy.

Their food had arrived and Nick waited until the waiter had gone before leaning across the table and telling Sara dulcetly, 'Bobbie is married to Luke Crighton—and very happily married to him I might add.'

'But you were with her at Camden Place,' Sara argued.

'We bumped into one another by accident, she was there with Luke but he was playing golf.'

Sara put down her cutlery, the blood draining from her face. 'You mean you aren't... She isn't...'

'No, I'm not,' Nick confirmed cooly. 'And she most certainly isn't. I can assure you that if I was already in that kind of relationship I wouldn't...'

'You wouldn't what?' Sara challenged him sharply. She was still trying to come to terms with the shock at discovering that her jealousy, the jealousy which had led her to where she was right now, was apparently totally unfounded. 'You wouldn't want *me*.'

'You didn't really think I was involved with Bobbie, did you?' Nick marvelled, ignoring her comment. Leaning across the table he told her quietly, 'Well, for your information...' He paused and frowned. He had almost been on the point of admitting to her that she was the first woman he had ever invited back to his home, the first woman he had ever wanted so strongly that he wanted to take her there and be completely and totally alone with her.

'For my information what?' Sara demanded.

Nick's frown deepened. Perhaps he should be honest with her. 'This is the first time I've ever invited a woman to stay at the cottage. How's your lobster?' he asked her, determinedly changing the subject.

WHEN THEY LEFT the restaurant an hour later it was almost trying to snow, the air much colder and the rain turning to sleet.

Sara shivered inside her fleece, giving a small gasp of dismay as she started to lose her balance as they crossed the now deserted square.

Immediately Nick reached out to steady her. His touch making her skin prickle with heady excitement. She was beginning to feel very afraid, Sara recognised, not of Nick himself but of the way she felt and her inability to control the strength of her reaction to him.

The discovery that he was not having an affair with Bobbie—or anyone else—seemed to have projected her into an untrammelled surge of sensual longing and responsiveness making her ache for him with an intensity and an immediacy that thoroughly unnerved her.

Now, suddenly, panic hit her.

'I've changed my mind,' she burst out in a tremulous voice. 'I…'

'You've what?' Nick demanded, almost jerking her off her feet as he swung her round and anchored her against his body using his own to protect her from the wind-driven sleet as he looked inimically down into her eyes.

'Don't play games with me, Sara,' he warned her. 'Because right now…'

She was trembling from head to foot, unable to tear her gaze from him. Helplessly it slid from his eyes down to his mouth, her heart giving a body-rocking lurch against her ribs.

'Sara…'

She saw his chest rise and fall with the deepness of the breath he took and watched helplessly as he lowered his head, not able, not *wanting,* to escape the inevitability of his mouth covering her own.

Somewhere in the distance she could hear the forlorn cry of the seagulls, the sound as sharply piercing as the ferocity of the pain-cum-pleasure that exploded through her.

She could feel herself trembling, leaning helplessly into Nick, needing his support against the weakness that he himself was causing as their mouths clung and meshed. Her lips were as hungrily greedy for the taste and feel of his as his were for her.

Recklessly she opened her mouth beneath his, inviting, pleading, for an intimacy that shocked her even whilst his answer to it turned her bones to water and made her give a pitiful mew of strangled longing deep in her throat.

They were kissing like teenagers, so hungry for one another that they were oblivious to everything else, she recognised dizzily. And how and when had she wound her arms around his neck like that so that her body was pressed as close to his as it could possibly get? So close that she was perfectly well aware of the effect she was having on him.

'It's damn near another thirty miles to the cottage,' she heard him groaning against her mouth between kisses. 'And right now I don't think I can take another thirty seconds of this without...'

He moved, shifting both their bodies, his taking the weight of hers and for one delirious moment Sara actually thought he might touch her intimately. Her breasts ached for him to do so, ached for the touch of his hands, his mouth. She wanted...

The noisy sound of some people emerging from a pub on the other side of the square into the fresh air brought her to her senses and to the mortified realisation of what she was doing—and feeling.

'Are you all right?' she heard Nick asking her as they made their way to their parked cars.

'Of course I'm all right. Why shouldn't I be?' she rejected his concern challengingly.

'Do you really need me to answer that?' Nick returned as he waited for her to unlock her car.

No, of course she didn't, Sara admitted as she waited for him to pull out onto the main road. If she wanted to do so now there was nothing to stop her turning in the opposite direction and changing her mind. Nick couldn't *make* her go with him. Nick *wouldn't* make her go with him she acknowledged.

But...

But if she didn't, for the rest of her life she would wish...wonder... And for the rest of her life, too, she knew a part of her would always ache for him and for what might have been.

It's just sex, she reminded herself grimly. That's all.

Bitterly she wondered how on earth she could dare to even try to put the words *just* and *sex* together in thinking about what she wanted.

Her handbag lay on the passenger seat and her face pinkened betrayingly as she glanced at it. Inside it were the condoms it had taken all her self-confidence and several abortive attempts to purchase. What were the social niceties of such matters? She really had no idea, but she knew that there was no way she could possibly leave either her health or the conception of an unplanned child to chance.

That comment Nick had made about her being the first woman he had taken back to his cottage had caught her off guard and punched a huge hole in her emotional defences. Was it the truth or was it just a cynical ploy he had used knowing how such an admission was likely to affect her.

The weather was worsening, thick clouds drifting in ominously off the sea and reducing driving visibility, and Sara was shiveringly aware of what a mystical land this was. A land of legend and ancient wisdom where anything could happen.

Why was she telling herself that? What was it she secretly *wanted* to happen?

Back there in the town square of Aberaeron, locked

to Nick's body, returning his passionate kisses with hungry fervour, she had known she was aching for him physically right down to her toes. And she had known as well that the ache wasn't merely physical. A sheep loomed out of the mist causing her to grasp her steering wheel hard and remind herself that she needed all her concentration for the road.

IN FRONT OF HER as he saw the way the weather was closing in, Nick cursed himself for not insisting that they travel together. He was far more familiar with this drive than she was and, unfashionably macho though it might make him seem, he couldn't deny his very male urge to take charge and protect her.

Standing body to body with her in the town square of Aberaeron looking down into her face, knowing helplessly that he was completely unable to resist the temptation to kiss her, Nick had finally allowed himself to acknowledge that no mere desire on its own, no matter how strong or potent, could be responsible for the intensity of what he was feeling.

In that telling moment in the restaurant when Sara had unwittingly revealed her female jealousy of Bobbie's supposed relationship with him along with his instinctive urge to reassure her, had been a much less civilised and outrageously male triumph that she should feel that way about him.

They were approaching Fishguard, the small town wreathed in a blanket of sea mist. On the other side of the town lay the road to St. David's and the hinterland behind it—and his cottage. He frowned as he caught sight of his jacket on the passenger seat of the four-wheel drive. Inside it was his wallet and inside his wallet... He had felt almost as awkward and self-conscious as a teenager when he had made the journey to a large anonymous supermarket out of town to buy the condoms now concealed in his wallet. It made good sense, of course, for Sara's sake and his own to take such precautions; but he had to admit that he felt there was something a little bit too clinical and contrived about the act of having to do so. Ruefully he mentally derided that passionately romantic streak in his nature that baulked at such practicalities. And even more so at the fact that Sara was exercising her modern woman's right to have sex with him simply because she wanted sex? What was it he *really* wanted from her—a passionate declaration of love? He frowned as the mist thickened, demanding that he gave his attention to his driving and not to his own personal thoughts.

HONOR FROWNED as she listened to Ben complaining to her about Max and Maddy.

'I think you're being rather unfair,' she told him quietly, resisting the temptation to say even more as she reminded herself of her growing concern that his health was deteriorating.

As she listened to Ben she couldn't help comparing him to her cousin Freddy. Granted Freddy was a little bit younger than Ben but more importantly, Freddy

had a warmth, a love, for his fellow human beings that
Ben totally lacked.

Thinking of Freddy made Honor's frown deepen
slightly.

Two days ago he had asked her and David to have
dinner with him, explaining that there was something
he wanted to discuss with them both. That something
had been his desire to leave Fitzburgh Place to them.
Honor wasn't sure which of them had been the more
shocked.

'But surely it's entailed,' she had protested.

'The title goes to the next male in line,' Freddy had
agreed. 'But there's no legally enforceable entail on
the house. I *had* thought of endowing it for a charity
but most of them are awash with great expensive prop-
erties they don't really want and then, after you moved
here, Honor, and David arrived and the two of you…'
He had paused and looked at Father Ignatius, who he
had insisted was to be privy to what he wanted to say.

'I know the house will be safe in yours and David's
hands, Honor,' he had said quietly and simply.

Instinctively she had looked at David, who had returned her gaze before reaching for her hand, knowing
immediately that she wanted him to respond for both
of them.

'It's a very big decision to make Freddy,' David had
pointed out gently. 'And a very generous one…'

'It's not generous—not really,' Freddy had objected. 'Place costs a damn fortune to run—not that it
will be coming to you without something to support

itself. I've been lucky with my investments and the place is becoming more self-financing and once we get this wedding thing off the ground... Take on Fitz-burgh Place and you can grow as many herbs as you wish,' he had told Honor temptingly.

Later that night when they had discussed his offer in bed, tears had filled Honor's eyes as she admitted to David how surprised she had been and how touched.

'He might not show it but he loves that house so much. To feel that he can entrust it to us is such...'

'I know what you mean,' David had agreed gruffly. In the darkness they had hugged each other tightly.

'It won't be easy,' Honor had acknowledged. 'Run-ning a place like that...making it pay...'

'But the prospect of doing so excites you,' David had teased her before adding with gentle warning, 'Don't forget that people change their minds. Hope-fully Freddy will have a lot of years left to run Fitz-burgh Place himself and in that time he could make other decisions, other choices....'

'You mean like your father with Queensmead?' Honor had guessed immediately, shaking her head.

'No. Freddy would never do that.'

Even so they had both agreed that for the time being they would keep Freddy's proposition to themselves.

'You're not interested, then,' Freddy had barked gruffly at them both before they had left.

'Of course we are,' they had confirmed together. 'But we want to give you time to think things through properly,' Honor had told him gently, her hand on his arm as she smiled at him.

'Think I'm a senile old fool who doesn't know his own mind—is that it?' he had grumbled.

'You? No way!' David had laughed. 'But it *is* a big decision to make.'

'*My* decision has already been made. Can't think of anyone better fitted for the job of taking over the place, nor anyone I'd rather hand it over to when the time comes. Know you'll both do the right thing by it…and by me.'

'Oh, Freddy,' Honor had whispered emotionally as she leaned forward to kiss his cheek.

'No. No.'

In his nightmare Max drew out his protest from tortured lungs as he saw the knife slicing through the air towards Maddy and their child.

'Max…Max… What's wrong?' Maddy asked in alarm, reaching out to switch on the bedside light as Max's cry woke her from her own sleep.

Awake now, Max felt the sick sweat of his nightmare chilling on his bare body.

'I'm sorry. Did I wake you?' he apologised to her. 'I must have been dreaming.'

Maddy watched him in concern. Something was wrong but she had no idea what it was. When she had been told by the hospital that so long as she was careful they felt confident that her pregnancy would now proceed normally and that neither she nor the baby were at any risk, she had expected Max to share her relieved joy, but instead he had seemed preoccupied and almost distant.

She had tried to talk to him, to find out what was wrong, but he had refused to admit that anything *was* wrong.

'Max,' she began tentatively. 'If something's worrying you…'

'It was a bad dream—that's all.' Max could hear the defensive tension in his own voice. 'Go back to sleep, Maddy,' he told her in a more gentle voice.

He was already reaching out to switch off the bedside lamp, turning away from her as he lay down again. Maddy studied the silky back of his head in silent anguish. Something *was* wrong. She knew it instinctively. She longed for Max to turn round and take her in his arms but since her return from hospital he had treated her as though she were as fragile as a piece of delicate china.

Hesitantly she reached out, stroking her fingertips along the exposed line of his shoulder.

Beneath Maddy's gentle touch Max tensed. He longed, ached, to hold Maddy tight, to tell her how he felt and why, but how could he? If he did, she would never feel the same about him again.

Tonight's nightmare wasn't his first and he knew that it wouldn't be his last and that things were bound to get worse once the baby Maddy was carrying was born. How could they not? How could he, Max, look into the face of his new child without feeling guilt?

No matter *what* he did, *how* he tried to analyse his feelings away he knew he could never escape from the knowledge that in his own selfish need for Maddy he would have denied their child life.

Maddy would certainly never forgive him if she knew and he was beginning to fear he would never be able to forgive himself.

When Max showed no reaction to her tentative caress, Maddy quietly withdrew her hand.

Was he perhaps angry because of the disruption this new pregnancy was causing? It had been his decision to continue to work mainly from home until after the birth. Maddy had not asked him to do so, but she knew how much she needed his input into the day-to-day running of their domestic lives at the moment. It was true that he had not shown any signs of being irritated by the demands that were being made on him but she could think of no other reason for the tension she could sense in him.

'Stop worrying,' he instructed her whenever she tried to talk to him about her feelings. But how could she when something was so obviously wrong?

CHAPTER THIRTEEN

DESPITE THE WARMTH inside her car, Olivia shivered violently as she stopped outside David and Honor's house. She had been feeling ill all day, feverish and shivery, her throat sore with a dull persistent headache. There was a particularly virulent strain of flu going round and she prayed that she wasn't about to go down with it.

From where she sat in her car she could see into the sitting room. Her father was seated in a chair, Amelia crouching next to him whilst Alex sat curled up on his knee. He was reading to them and the three of them were so engrossed in what they were doing that they were totally oblivious to her own arrival.

As she watched them and witnessed the closeness between them, a pain seared right through her. Never once during her own childhood could she remember her father reading to *her,* never mind exhibiting the loving closeness he was showing her own daughters.

As she watched, Alex started to laugh and as David bent his head to say something, Amelia reached up and flung her arms round him, hugging him tightly.

A huge lump of pain and anguish ached in Olivia's throat. A mixture of resentment and joy. Resentment on her own behalf and joy on her daughters' that they should so obviously and trustingly be enjoying their grandfather's company—and receiving his love?

No one else would know just how hard she had found it to allow her children to be with her father, how much she had hated having to ask for his help, but there was no denying that they were thriving on the situation. Every day they came home full of what they had done with their grandfather. Every morning they couldn't wait for her to drop them off with him.

Already Honor had become 'Grandma' to them, their faces lighting up when they talked excitedly of the time they spent with the older couple.

Alex in particular was fascinated by the priest who it seemed had a fund of exciting stories to tell them, and their conversation was full of references to Grandma's herbals and Gramps's workshop.

The evening they had come out to the car proudly carrying the cakes they had made for her, Olivia's eyes had filled with tears.

Alex and Amelia were now having a play fight over which of them should sit on David's knee and when he resolved it by reaching out and wrapping an arm around each of them Olivia had to look away.

Never once could she remember him ever being so affectionate and loving with her—because she had not been a child who was *worthy* of being loved?

Bleakly she tried to push the thought away. Now was not the time to allow herself to be re-tormented by what should be vanquished spectres.

'For God's sake, Livvy,' Caspar had accused her in exasperation during one of their rows. 'Forget the past and try living in the present.'

Forget the past! If only she could, but right now she felt like a little girl again; a little girl looking enviously at the happy loving domestic scene from which she was excluded.

As she told herself grimly that she was adding to her own pain, she heard someone rapping on her car window.

Her colour rising, she turned away from the scene which had been engrossing her to find Honor standing at the side of the car smiling at her.

Feeling almost as though she had been caught out in something illicit Olivia opened the door.

'I'm just on my way inside. I've been working in my greenhouse trying to make sure everything is properly protected from the frost,' Honor explained easily. 'Why don't you come in with me?'

Olivia started to refuse but then, for some reason, found that instead of doing so she was actually getting out of the car.

Honor's pregnancy was only just beginning to show. It was hard for Olivia to get her head round the fact that the baby Honor was carrying would be her own half-brother or -sister.

Caspar would have liked more children but she had refused. How could she possibly have another child when she was working full-time?

They had reached the house now and Honor was

pushing open the kitchen door and ushering Olivia inside. Unlike the kitchen of her own childhood, this one smelled warm and welcoming, causing Olivia to suffer a sharp pang of guilt. She had always promised herself that her children would have the kind of childhood, the kind of home life she had been denied; that *they* would come home to a mother who had the time to listen to them…a mother who would cook proper meals for them instead of vaguely telling them to get something out of the fridge.

She did cook, of course, but with one eye on the clock, her thoughts more on the next step in her evening routine than on enjoying the moment.

Honor, she sensed, would enjoy and relish each moment, each pleasure of life as it happened.

'I went to see Ben today,' Honor told her as she removed her outdoor coat. 'He isn't at all well.'

Olivia stiffened. If Honor was going to give her a lecture about Ben then Olivia just didn't want to hear it.

'He's his own worst enemy, of course,' Honor continued, 'and I just wish I could do more to help Maddy with him but…' She paused and looked at Olivia. Honor had told herself that she wasn't going to interfere in David's relationship with his daughter but there was something that she had to say.

'Sadly David is still regarded within his family as someone who isn't to be trusted, which is a shame because—'

'If he's treated like that then perhaps it's because

it's what he deserves,' Olivia cut across her bitterly. 'Grandfather virtually deified Dad—no one else apart from Max ever really mattered to him and Dad.' Olivia stopped, her jaw clenching.

'I know how strongly you feel about the past, Olivia,' Honor conceded, 'but...'

She stopped speaking as the kitchen door was pushed open and Amelia came rushing into the room telling her excitedly, 'Grandma, I got top marks for my spelling today and—' She stopped as she saw Olivia, looking uncertainly from her mother's set face to Honor's gently encouraging one.

Deep down inside her most vulnerable part of herself Olivia felt something crack and splinter—a pain that seemed to radiate out to every single part of her body as she recognised that Amelia, her beloved precious firstborn child, was looking at her with virtually the same look of hesitancy and apprehension with which she had once regarded her own mother. Olivia had seen that look in her daughter's eyes once before, but it hadn't hit home nearly as painfully. Before she could do or say anything, Alex and David were also in the room, Alex still too young to be aware of the adult tension surrounding her, running over to Olivia and beaming up at her.

'Grandad's going to ask Father Christmas to bring me a pony,' she told Olivia excitedly.

'Er...I did say that we would have to ask Mummy about it first,' David interrupted her ruefully.

A pony. Olivia closed her eyes. She could still remember how desperately she had once wanted one but Tania had been horrid. 'A pony. Oh, no, darling, you'll grow up all horsey and horrible…. No…'

As she looked at her father Olivia could see both remorse and concern in his eyes but before she could say anything a spasm of coughing overtook her.

'Are you okay?' Honor asked her.

'I'm fine,' Olivia fibbed brightly, turning away from her to demand sharply, 'Hurry up and get your things please, girls….'

'MUMMY…'

Olivia tensed as she heard the note in Alex's voice. She had just turned into their own drive and her whole body ached for the soothing comfort of a deliciously hot bath.

'Mummy…I wish Daddy would come home.'

Olivia's heart sank.

'Alex, you know what I've told you,' she began.

'Yes,' Alex agreed crossly. 'But *I* want him to come home and so does Amelia.'

Olivia gave a brief look at her elder daughter's downcast head. Why were things always so much harder than you envisaged they would be? She had truly believed that separating from Caspar would help to put an end to her problems and remove the worst source of friction from her life, but instead…

Instead she felt more alone, more bereft, more frightened than she had ever imagined it was possible for her to feel.

'Gramps said…' Alex began and then stopped as
Amelia shot her a murderously silencing look.

Amelia had already warned Alex that there was no
way she was to upset their mother by mentioning the
discussion they had had with their grandfather.

'Why don't you write to your father?' he had suggested to them but Amelia had shaken her head.

'No. We can't. Mummy wouldn't like it,' she had
told him. 'Besides,' she had added hollowly, 'we don't
know where he is.'

She *had* got his mobile number, though, carefully
written down and hidden away inside her old doll's
house. Whenever she felt really bad and lonely about
him not being there she got it out, carefully unfolding
the small piece of paper and reading off the numbers
before just as carefully refolding it and putting it back.

Frowning Olivia demanded sharply, 'Your grandfather said what?'

'He said that Grandma was going to go to hospital
next week so that they could have a look at the baby,'
Amelia told her quickly.

Olivia frowned, making a few mental calculations.
That must be for tests to check on the state of devel-
opment with the foetus—as an older mother Honor
would, of course, be presumed to be more at risk than
a younger woman.

Olivia had undergone similar tests herself, more
routine so far as the hospital was concerned, but she
had been more than relieved to have Caspar with
her—and if *she* had been anxious then no doubt Honor

would be even more so. For the first time Olivia tried to put herself in her stepmother's position. It was obvious how much Honor loved David and how much faith and belief she had in him. Well, Olivia just hoped he wouldn't let her down as he had done virtually everyone else in his family.

Apart from her daughters! A leopard never changed its spots, she reminded herself fiercely as she hurried the girls into the house.

But she couldn't deny the love she had seen in her father's eyes as he looked at his grandchildren. *Her* children!

'HOW IS SHE?' Caspar asked in concern as Molly finally emerged into the hospital's waiting room area.

Tiredly she pushed a hand through her hair, a personal little gesture she only used when she was tired or nervous, as Caspar had discovered. Seeing it now made him want to reach out and tell her not to worry.

'She's okay. At least—' she paused and shook her head '—the crisis is over but Ginna's still on a ventilator and they're not sure which way it will go.' Helplessly she bit her lip and turned aside.

'They can keep her alive but what kind of life…what quality of life will it be for her, Caspar?'

Caspar shook his head. It was impossible for him to answer such a question.

'They still don't know until they run some more tests just how badly affected she is going to be. She's had some kind of brain seizure. They don't know why and they don't even know whether or not she could have some more.

'There's no way I can leave her until I know what's going to happen to her and that could be two or three days. Thanks for bringing me, thanks for everything,' she added fiercely. 'But I guess I'd better say good-bye.... I'm going to have to check into somewhere close by.'

'I'm not leaving you here until you do.'

Molly's head came up, their gazes locking. The air in the waiting room was heavy with pain—and with love.

'You don't have to do this,' Molly whispered, her throat tight.

'Yes, I do,' Caspar contradicted her softly. 'You go back to Ginna if you want to,' he told her. 'I'll go and sort us out some rooms.'

Some rooms... Ten minutes later as he punched the number the hospital secretary had given him into his mobile he had to grit his teeth against the temptation to ask only for one room.

THE MOTEL was only a short distance from the hospital, a clean clinical anonymous place and relatively quiet at this time of the night. The clerk registered them disinterestedly, handing them their keys.

Molly had shaken her head a little over Caspar's insistence on carrying her overnight bag along with his own, desperate to be able to do something for her even if it was only a token gesture.

Their rooms were on opposite sides of the corridor. Caspar waited until Molly had unlocked hers and checked it out before opening the door to his own, fiercely resisting the temptation to cross the space between them. His body ached with tiredness from the drive and its anxiety, coupled with a very different kind of tension.

Once *Olivia* had made him ache like this…need like this…. Olivia… Angrily he pushed the thought of her away. She had no place here in the new life she had forced on him.

The look in Molly's eyes as he had said good-night to her had reminded him of the look in his daughters' when something was frightening them. Without her having to say anything he knew both that she was terrified of losing her sister and terrified of her survival.

Despite his tiredness he knew that he wouldn't be able to sleep. Stripping off his clothes he headed for the shower. He had just put his jeans back on and was drying off his hair when he heard it, a hesitant uncertain tapping on his door.

He reached it in two strides, pulling it open, expelling the hot, hard, aching breath of sharp desire he had inhaled and held as he prayed who his visitor might be.

'Molly!'

White-faced, shaking, she stood frozen in the doorway wrapped in a soft, thick, fleecy robe. Very gently and tenderly he drew her into the room and closed the door. She was looking at him as though she had no idea how, or where she was, or why.

'What is it?' he coaxed her. 'Has the hospital rung?'

She shook her head.

'I was… I was…' He could see her swallow. 'I just wanted to be with you,' she told him huskily, a faint pink colour staining her skin as she looked nervously away from him.

When she started to remove her robe for a moment Caspar was too transfixed to move. Her skin was the colour of soft cream, her naked breasts full with rose-gilded nipples. As she dropped her robe to the floor it made a heavy clunking noise.

'My mobile,' she told him, following his downward gaze. 'Just in case…'

Her eyes darkened, her mouth trembling slightly.

'I shouldn't be doing this,' she said huskily. 'It's against all the ''rules'' and against my own rules, too,' she admitted. 'It's so wrong.'

'No, it isn't,' Caspar corrected her gruffly as he stepped towards her and took hold of her.

'In fact, I can't think of anything that could possibly be more right. Have you *any* idea just how much I've been wanting you like this?' he whispered hotly as he bent his head to kiss her.

His erection was hot and tight, straining against his jeans. Sliding his hands downwards until his fingers entangled in the ridiculous scrap of silk and lace purporting to cover her deliciously curved behind, he pulled her hard against himself, groaning into her hesitantly opening mouth as he felt the sensual weight and femaleness of her against his aroused body. His tongue rubbed against her lips, parting them and sliding, *thrusting,* eagerly inside them. Her mouth was as sweet and hot as he already knew her body would be.

As their mouths meshed, their tongues entangling, then pulling apart to explore further, he waited to feel the sweet savage bite of her teeth against the special sensual place just below his ear, his hands sliding from her buttocks up to her waist and then towards her breasts. Olivia loved it when he touched and stroked them and...

Olivia...

Immediately Caspar froze. Shock and self-disgust filled him. He could feel his erection fading, softening, the heat of his earlier desire obliterated by what he was now feeling. In the distance he could hear a noise. Molly was disentangling herself from him and reaching for her robe.

Well, he couldn't blame her. She had every right to be furious with him and worse.

'My mobile's ringing,' he heard her gasp as she fumbled with her robe.

Her mobile! So she hadn't...she didn't...

He could see her hand trembling as she clasped the phone to her ear. Instinctively he moved to help her on with the robe she was struggling with.

'It's the hospital,' she told him as she ended the call. Ginna has regained consciousness.... I have to go to see her Caspar. I'm so sorry…I didn't…' She looked self-consciously at him and shook her head.

'There isn't anything for you to feel sorry for,' he told her fiercely as she hurried to the door. What the hell was wrong with him? What was he doing thinking about *Olivia* like that when his desire, his longing, his *need* had been for *Molly* and *not* for Olivia…? But thank God Molly herself had not realised what had happened.

'I'm coming with you,' he told her as he opened the door for her. This time she did not demure or protest, saying softly instead, 'Thank you.'

CHAPTER FOURTEEN

'I TAKE IT you aren't au fait with modern technology?' Sara commented flippantly to Nick as he pushed open the door to his cottage and she saw the pile of mail on his mat.

Her flippancy was a desperate grab at something—*anything*—to conceal from him just how nervous she was feeling and how much she was regretting the false bravado which had brought her here. It wasn't that she didn't want Nick—she *did*—but she was now miserably aware that she was masquerading under a false persona and that the feelings she had tried to belittle and dismiss were now showing her their affronted outrage and rebellion.

Her feelings, she recognised, were mercilessly contemptuous about the concept of emotionless sex; and worse, they seemed to have decided that *they* recognised in Nick Crighton everything that they had ever wanted and they were now determined to rush pell-mell into proving to her that there was no way they were going to be prevented from *showing* what they wanted.

'Wrong,' Nick contradicted her as he closed the door on the damp mist. 'I do have someone to come in and sort through my mail, but she's obviously not been for a day or so. I couldn't do my job without technology, but unfortunately the nemesis currently hovering over me is in the shape of big brother Saul—to such an extent that the merest hint I might have received a fax or email from a client is enough to have him put me under lock and key—for my own safety, of course!' Nick grinned when he saw her expression.

'Well, no, it isn't quite as bad as that, but as Saul has pointed out, until my GP has given me a clean bill of health, running the risk of getting myself locked up in some insalubrious foreign gaol is not a good idea.'

'Is that likely to happen?' Sara questioned him.

'Hopefully not, but I suppose it *is* always on the cards. The people who hire my services are hiring me to get my client out of such a situation. But...' He gave a brief careless shrug which showed Sara that he was neither exaggerating nor boasting in an attempt to impress her but simply speaking the truth. 'In some countries there comes a time when negotiation isn't going to get anywhere and a more physical form of action needs to be taken.' He started to frown. The hostage case he'd most recently been asked to take on had fortunately resolved itself as the woman had been released.

'There've been instances—fortunately very few—when my client's health has been so damaged by their incarceration that protracted negotiations could have meant that even if they were freed it might have been too late.

'I had one client…a nineteen-year-old. He was up at Oxford and predicted to get a double first. Unbeknownst to him the person he was travelling with to the Far East had agreed to act as a drugs mule not for money but for a dare. This person was being used as a decoy and of course, he got caught and my client was imprisoned along with him. They'd both been set up so that the real carrier could get through. The country they were caught in has a death penalty for drug smuggling….'

He saw Sara's indrawn breath.

'My client's parents were both distraught and they turned to me as a last resort.'

From the sudden subtle shadowing of his expression Sara knew intuitively that his story did not have a happy ending.

'You—you couldn't help?' she guessed.

'Oh, yes. I got him out and the other man finally got reprieved,' Nick told her. 'But unfortunately my client had been bitten by some insect whilst he was in prison. The wound had not been treated and as a result gangrene had set in and he had to have his leg amputated.

'Oh, hell,' he swore when he saw Sara's expression. 'That was crass of me. I didn't mean to upset you. Saul keeps telling me that I'm getting too old for this kind of work—or rather that it's getting too dangerous for me. He thinks I should give it up and settle for something more mundane.'

'But you don't want to,' Sara guessed, fighting to recover her equilibrium.

'No,' Nick acknowledged. 'Unlike Saul, I'm not the settling-down kind. I'm too restless…there's still too much I want to do…see….'

He was warning her off getting involved with him, Sara recognised; letting her know that there was strictly no future for her with him. But she already knew that—didn't she?

'I'll take your stuff upstairs for you,' Nick was telling her. 'If you want to come up with me I'll show you where everything is.'

Her heart thumping, Sara followed him up the narrow stairs which led off the attractive square hallway. Halfway up the stairs a deep window with a cosy seat looked out across the countryside.

'On a clear day you can see the sea,' Nick informed her as she paused automatically to look out. 'On a day like today, you can't even see the road.'

'Do you live here all the time?' Sara asked him curiously.

'More or less. I'm not as isolated as it may seem. My parents live less than an hour's drive away and the estate to which this cottage originally belonged is only a few miles across the hills.

'I had thought at one time of buying a flat in Chester—but so many members of the family live there that I can always beg a bed for the night when I want to visit.'

They had reached the top of the stairs now. Four closed doors led off it.

Nick pushed one of them open. Cautiously Sara followed him inside it.

'It's a guest room,' Nick told her before she could say anything. 'It's got its own bathroom.

'I'll leave you to make yourself at home while I go down and make us both a drink. Which do you prefer—tea or coffee?'

'Coffee, please,' Sara responded automatically. He was putting down her case, turning to look at her as he did so, not giving her time to conceal the surprise his comment had given her.

'What were you expecting?' he mocked her softly. 'That I was going to throw you on the bed and have my wicked way with you right here and now?'

'Don't be ridiculous,' Sara managed to reply, but she knew that her face was flushing and she prayed that her body language wasn't giving away what she was really thinking—and wanting!

'We've got all weekend, after all,' Nick continued, giving her a wicked smile as he added softly, 'although, of course, if *you* wish to pounce on *me*...'

Refusing to respond, Sara turned her back on him, but she could hear him laughing softly as he left her.

NICK FROWNED as he made his way back downstairs. He had been an almighty fool to ever suggest what he *had* suggested and, as for bringing Sara *here*... Wasn't the very reason he had previously never invited a woman to spend time at the cottage with him simply because he had known what a dangerous, a treacherous swamp of potential disaster he would be letting himself in for if he did? Ah, yes; but *that* had been because he had been afraid that such close intimacy with the woman concerned would lead to boredom and irritation. With *Sara*... With Sara he was fascinated, entranced, driven mad with curiosity and desire, desperate to find some flaw in her which would enable him to step back from her. But instead... Even that unexpected shyness and reserve she had betrayed in the bedroom had idiotically appealed to him. Sharpening his hunting instinct?

In the cottage's well-equipped kitchen he filled the kettle and switched it on. A timer ensured that the place was warm and centrally heated. He might like the cottage's remoteness but Nick was not someone who saw any virtue in depriving himself of civilisation's comforts unless he had to.

IN HER BEDROOM Sara looked uncertainly towards the bathroom. She felt grimy after her journey and would have enjoyed a shower. A quick examination of the bathroom revealed that it had a lock and that her privacy could be assured.

She started to frown. She knew she was inexperienced where 'weekends away for sex' were concerned, but surely it was highly unusual to give one's partner a separate room. Or was that simply a subtle ploy on Nick's part, a deliberate reminder that all they were having was sex and that there was to be no intimacy between them? No intimacy and no preliminaries, either?

'HELLO THERE,' Nick announced cheerfully half an hour later as Sara emerged into the kitchen. 'I'm afraid the coffee's gone cold. I'll make a fresh one.'

'I decided to have a shower,' Sara told him and then blushed. Would he interpret her remark as a hint that she was expecting...that she *wanted*... But to her relief he didn't pick her up on her comment or try to turn it into a sexual innuendo.

'There's quite a good restaurant in St. David's. I could book a table for us there this evening if you like or if you prefer we can eat here. I've brought some stuff with me.'

'Er...I don't mind,' Sara told him awkwardly.

'No?' Nick smiled. 'Well, in that case, we'll have dinner here. A client gave me a case of a particularly good red wine that I haven't touched yet. Will steak be okay for you? I'm afraid I'm no gourmet chef....'

'Steak will be fine,' Sara confirmed.

Nick's eyebrows rose and Sara tensed as he came towards her carrying a mug of coffee.

'You've become unexpectedly docile,' he commented as he put the coffee down on the wooden table next to her. 'If I didn't know better I'd begin to think that you were feeling nervous.'

'Nervous... Of course I'm not....' Sara denied untruthfully.

Perhaps it was something to do with the fact that she had just had a shower herself—she didn't know, but suddenly she felt far too hot and far, far too aware of the tempting sexy scent of Nick's skin, the potential male strength of his body, the sensuality of that just beginning to show through darkness along his jawline, that unwanted fascination possessing her as she watched the way his hand curled round the cup, imagining how it would feel against her skin, her body, how *she* would feel.

'Sara...'

Guiltily she looked up at him and then wished she hadn't as she realised how close to her he was. Her heart was thumping heavily, slow unsteady strokes. For some reason she had started to tremble.

'Mmm...you smell all clean and soapy....'

How had he managed to wrap his arms around her like that without her seeing him move? So tightly in fact, that she had no option but to cling helplessly to him, letting him meld her body to the shape of his own.

'I had a shower,' she murmured incoherently.

'So you said,' Nick agreed softly. 'How disappointing of you. I was hoping you would wait until *I* could share it with you.'

Her heart was lurching around inside her chest like a slingshot being practised by a mere novice.

'I can't... I didn't... Oh... Mmm...' Helplessly her voice faded away as Nick started to drift dangerous little kisses all over her face, his mouth edging closer and closer to her own but in the end *she* was the one who lifted her hand to his jaw to hold him captive as her lips parted against his.

What was it about a certain man…*the* man…that could make a woman feel like this…make her feel that her whole world, her whole life, her whole love, was bound up in the kiss they were sharing, its intimacy so sweet, so piercing, so intense that it was as though in the kiss they were exchanging she had already given herself to him body and soul, flesh and emotions?

Sara could feel her mouth clinging to Nick's as he started to release it. Without a word, one arm still holding her to him, he guided her out of the kitchen towards the stairs.

They paused on the landing where he had told her it was possible to see the sea and as she looked up at him Sara felt as though she were drowning in the depths of Nick's intensely sensual heavy-lidded gaze. Her eyes widened as she saw the spark of fierce desire that suddenly illuminated Nick's as he looked down at her.

'You know that this is sheer reckless madness, don't you?' he told her. His voice was so calm, so controlled, so businesslike and so totally and utterly at odds with the way he was looking at her that Sara was too confused to make any response. And then it was too late because he was kissing her. This time there was no need for *her* to hold his mouth to hers. *This* time *he* was the one holding her in a way that told her that he had no intention of letting her go. Not that she wanted him to. No. She wanted him to hold her like this forever, kiss her like this forever.

They climbed the remaining few stairs still locked together, body to body, mouth to mouth.

On the landing Nick stood still, framing her face as he lifted his mouth from hers.

'This is the time to tell me if you want to change your mind,' he told her soberly.

Sara's eyes widened. He would let her do that *now* even though she could feel and was quite shamelessly relishing knowing just how aroused he was?

This time the liquid melting sensation softening her bones was caused by the intense sweetness of knowing that he would master his own desire for her if she asked him to. Knowing that gave her the courage to tell him huskily, 'No. I don't want to change my mind.'

Beneath his fingers Nick could feel her face start to burn. There was a shyness, a delicacy about her that made him ache all the more for her.

As Nick's silence deepened so did Sara's nervousness. To hide it she turned her head, forgetting for a moment that his hands were still cupping her face but made shockingly aware of their presence when her lips brushed against his skin.

How *could* just the feel of a man's fingers against her mouth make her tremble from head to foot with longing for him?

'Sara…'

The way he was saying her name made her give a

small moan, swiftly silenced as he covered her mouth with his, kissing her with hungry, deep, passionate intimacy.

She was trembling so hard she could only lean helplessly against him as he opened the bedroom door—not to her 'guest' room but to his own bedroom.

Sara had a confused impression of a huge old-fashioned bed, a fireplace stacked with logs, a desk beneath the window and a chair next to it as well as several chests.

Rich heavy curtains hung at the window, the carpet beneath her feet was a plain creamy Hessian, the bed linen an old-fashioned creamy white, a thick, soft, dark throw tossed across the foot of the bed.

The room gave off an almost medieval air, a mixture of the scholarly and the sensual; and something about it touched such a chord of sensitivity and pleasure inside Sara that it was almost as though somehow she had come home to a place that had always been there waiting for her.

A lamp either side of the large bed illuminated the room cloaking it in soft shadows. In a room like this it would be possible to completely blot out the rest of the world and its realities, Sara sensed.

When she shivered, her body reacting to everything that she was feeling, Nick offered quickly, 'If you're cold I can light the fire. I work up here sometimes. That's why I kept it.'

Without waiting for her response he released her and went towards the fire, bending to strike a match and light the kindling. Whilst he crouched over the fire with his back to her Sara greedily absorbed the visual reality of him. After tonight she was never going to be the same person again, she recognised. After tonight...

Nick was getting up and turning round.

'If this was a film or a book I dare say now the awkward practicalities would magically disappear along with our clothes. However, since it isn't... Would you think it very old-fashioned of me if I told you how much I want to undress you and have you undress me? I know that modern manners dictate that we should each remove our own clothing.'

The sound Sara made in her throat was little more than a dry rustle but Nick seemed to have no difficulty in translating what it meant. Dizzily Sara clung to him as he slowly removed her clothes, kissing every inch of revealed flesh, unbuttoning her top and sliding it off her shoulders, kissing her throat and then her collarbone and then all the way down one arm right down to the inside of her wrist.

Already she was breathing as though she had run a marathon, her body weak with a mixture of excitement and pleasure.

She had thought long and painfully about the niceties of what kind of underwear one wore for such an occasion. She was quite definitely not a sexy-underwear sort of person, but she had still rebelled against the practicality of the serviceable neutral flesh-coloured bra and briefs set which she normally favoured which were designed to improve the look of her clothes rather than to highlight the curves of her body. In the end she had opted for a pretty set of lacy chain store bra and briefs which were feminine without looking as though she were trying to be something she wasn't.

But ironically, because of Nick's attitude on their arrival, after her shower she had simply pulled on clean briefs and a clean top; her breasts were firm enough for her not to need to bother with a bra if she didn't want to, and assuming that sex was going to be off the agenda until later in the evening she had not bothered about donning the new lacy pieces.

Now though, the way Nick was looking at her as he removed her top to reveal her completely naked breasts, made her feel as though she were the most seductive, the most desirable, the most sensually wanton woman who had ever lived.

'You're obviously not a fan of topless sunbathing,' Nick murmured as he traced the pale line of her fading tan.

'Er… I…' Sara gave a sharp gasp as Nick bent his head and very slowly but oh so thoroughly, began to caress one bare taut nipple with his lips.

Desire… White-hot lightning sheets of it began to hammer through her body, surge after surge of aching, twisting sanity obliterating need. Sara arched her back, her fingers digging into the flesh of Nick's shoulders. In the mirror over the dressing table Nick caught sight of their reflections. Sara's head thrown back, her body,

naked from the waist up, bathed in the glow of the
fire, her hair tumbling down her back, her whole body
bowing against his arm whilst he knelt in front of her,
their pose so elemental, so pagan and so very, very
right that she stirred every single atavistic need and
desire he had ever felt to life. Never, ever had he felt
so fiercely and so strongly male, so torn between his
desire to conquer and possess and his need to show
tenderness and care, to be as victorious as to be protective.

'Haven't you forgotten something?' he asked Sara
gruffly as his hand covered the tender dampness of the
nipple he had been caressing and he lifted his head to
look at her.

'You're *supposed* to be *undressing* me—remember?' Nick told her softly.

Undressing him… Sara closed her eyes.

'You were distracting me too much,' she told him,
trying to be as sophisticated and relaxed as he was
himself.

'Well then, perhaps I'd better just keep still, hadn't
I?' Nick offered. A little uncertainly Sara looked at
him.

'Come on,' he coaxed. 'It isn't that difficult, is it?
All you've got to do is to unfasten a few buttons…like
this…look….'

As his hands covered hers and lifted them to his
shirt, holding them whilst he deftly unfastened the buttons, Sara wondered if he had any idea just what he

was doing to her, just how weak with wanting him she actually was.

'There. That wasn't hard at all, was it?' he murmured against her mouth as he shrugged himself free of the unfastened shirt.

'Unlike a certain part of my *anatomy*,' he added in rueful self-mocking undertone. 'And if kissing your nipples was so very distracting then perhaps we'd better finish our disrobing before I show you just how much I want to distract you even more,' he teased her sensually.

His body was everything Sara had imagined and more. Oh, so very, very much more. Touching him with wondering hesitant fingers, her eyes wide and dark with all that she was feeling, she was filled with the sharp intensity of her own longing.

To be touched and kissed and aroused by Nick to the point where she was virtually moaning with the intensity of her desire, to imagine him inside her after he finally carried her to the bed, was an experience so far outside even her wildest and most wanton imaginings that she could hardly comprehend what she was actually feeling.

'Shush...shush...just a minute longer,' Nick was soothing her as he laid her on the bed beneath him and kissed her.

'I want you that way so much, Nick...I want *you*.'

Unable to stop himself, Nick responded rawly, 'Like this do you mean?'

The sweet hot tightness of her welcomed him, surprisingly hesitantly at first as though...

Sara held her breath as she felt the tightness of her body softening to accept him. It had been several years.

'You feel like a virgin,' Nick whispered hotly to her, 'All sweet tight hotness....'

'It—it's been a long time,' Sara murmured shakily back. 'And besides...'

As he moved deeper and more strongly inside her, her eyes gave away her shocked pleasure.

'You... You feel...' She stopped. After all, what did she have to compare him *with* apart from her first and her only lover? This magic, their intimacy was uniquely theirs—his—

'I feel what?' Nick demanded as his body reacted to the pleasure of the way they fitted together.

But Sara was beyond being able to make any kind of lucid vocal response. Caught up in the beginnings of the first penetrative orgasm she had experienced, she could only cling to him and cry out her awe and shocked pleasure.

'THE DOCTOR HAS warned me not to get my hopes up too high, but at least she's come out of the coma,' Molly told Caspar, smiling tenderly at him as he took her arm to prevent her from being jostled by the busy crowd in the coffee shop.

'I'm sorry...about...about last night,' she apologised softly.

Caspar closed his eyes. He was the one who ought to be apologising. What the hell had happened? One moment he had been wanting her so badly that he ached from head to foot with his desire for her...the next...

Molly paused and looked down, fiddling with the button on her coat.

'Caspar, I don't want to sound pushy or to presume too much, but we really ought to talk about...about your marriage. You *are* still married,' she reminded him gently, 'and to get involved with a married man—even one as kind and special as you—just isn't something I want to do....'

'Kind!' Caspar grimaced.

'Very kind,' Molly confirmed with a smile, touching him briefly on the arm before saying in a low voice, 'Not many men would have your patience and understanding about...about Ginna. And even if I didn't know from personal experience just how bad the average man can be about handling sickness, just listening to my clients would be enough to warn me. Oh, I'm not saying that men don't care about their families. Of *course* they do, but for a lot of them the reality of a serious illness is so daunting that they either back off from it and their family or simply refuse to acknowledge that it exists.

'Very often their reaction springs from a fear of losing the person they love, of their illness becoming more important to them than their man. Sometimes it springs from feeling that they should have been able to protect the person they love and to keep them safe—that is a very deep-rooted male instinct. It sounds illogical I know, but...' She gave a small shrug whilst Caspar simply bowed his head in silence.

Out of nowhere he had a sharp acid memory of Olivia at the time she had first discovered her mother's eating disorder, her face contorted with pain and shock as she accused him of not understanding. He could still remember how angry with her he had been, terrified that her mother's claims on her might mean that *he* might still lose her to the family she had already told him meant nothing to her. He had been too proud then to acknowledge either his jealousy or his insecurity.

Just as more recently he had been too proud to acknowledge that he was jealous of the fact that she put not just their children but her work, too, before him.

'You are doing this to punish me. Not because you *want* to go to your brother's wedding,' she had screamed at him when he had announced that he was going to Philadelphia with or without her. 'You *know* I can't take time off now....'

'I'm doing it because my brother is getting married,' he had lashed bitingly back.

'Come back,' Molly commanded gently.

Guiltily Caspar focused on her.

UNSEEINGLY, Nick stared across the empty hillside. A sharp wind knifed icily against the exposed tautness of his jaw but he barely registered it.

It was just light, the mists of the previous day having given way to a clear sky and a sharp lemon sun, but he was barely aware of either the sun or the cold.

He had left Sara sleeping in the bed they had shared last night…his bed…. She had, at one point, murmured to him that she would return to the guest room but he had refused to let her go, insisting that she stay where she was—in his bed…his arms. He stiffened, closing his eyes as a shudder of prescient emotion sliced through him. What had happened between them last night had gone way beyond the merely sexual. So now what the hell was he going to do? There was no place in his life for the kind of commitment, the kind of complications that what he was feeling for Sara would bring. No, there was no place in his present life for her and no way he could live without her. But somehow he was going to have to.

After all, *she* had made it plain to him that the last thing she wanted was a permanent relationship with him.

'You're a Crighton,' she had whispered to him last night after the first time they had made love and she had then wept tears of anguish and emotion. He had held her and she had told him what was wrong.

'Whose judgement do you trust more?' Nick had demanded angrily. 'Your stepgrandmother's a—a woman who, by all accounts has the reasoning power of a spoiled two-year-old—or yourself…?'

He had known, of course, that he had said the wrong

thing even before he had seen the anger burning in her eyes.

'What makes you think I see the Crightons any differently from the way Tania does?' she had demanded.

'Do you really need me to answer that?' he had replied rashly. 'And don't bother telling me that what you and I have just experienced…just *shared* is something you've had with a dozen men before me,' he had told her, adding succinctly, 'I've never experienced anything like it before….'

'And because of that you just assume that *I* haven't, either?' Sara had thrown angrily at him.

But in the end she had admitted not just that it had been outside her previous experience but also that her previous experience was limited to just one callow rite-of-passage relationship in her late teens.

'This was supposed to get this ridiculous thing between us totally and completely out of our systems,' she had reminded him and then she had looked at him and he had looked back at her and then… If they were mutually affronted and angered by the way they wanted one another, then they were also mutually unable to stop themselves from giving in to those desires. But for him it went much further than mere physical desire, Nick acknowledged. And for Sara…?

Bleakly he looked back towards the cottage.

WHITE-FACED with anguish and misery, Sara pulled on her clothes with hands that shook betrayingly.

It was no use trying to deceive herself any longer.

There was no way what she had experienced last night and into the early hours of the morning could in any way be described as mere sex. And no way, either, that she could ever allow anyone other than herself to know just what her true feelings for Nick were—and how much she loved him.

He had made it plain to her that he relished his single life; that the kind of commitment she was now craving was *not* part of his plans—with *any* woman. And she was deluding herself if she believed that she could spend much more time with him without completely losing it and betraying how she felt.

No. As she saw it, she now had no choice. If she stayed here with Nick for the rest of the weekend she was terrified that there would come a point when her self-control and self-respect would totally desert her and when she would be reduced to a weeping pleading mess of emotions, begging him to make room in his life for her. The only way she could stop that from happening was to leave now whilst she still could.

Perhaps Nick even already sensed what she felt. That fear increased her resolve—she had to leave—and hope!

She had just finished packing her case when Nick came upstairs. He was carrying a mug of tea—and he was also fully dressed. As he handed her the tea he demanded sharply, 'What are you doing?'

'Packing,' Sara replied as calmly as she could, glad that she had her excuse of putting down the tea to keep her back to him so that he couldn't see her face.

'Packing…now…? We aren't going back until to-morrow….'

'Correction,' Sara told him crisply, '*I'm* going back today…right now, in fact. After all—' she took a deep breath before turning to face him glad of the cloaking shadows of the room as she told him bravely '—we've accomplished what we came here to do.'

Nick stared at her.

'What the hell do you mean?'

'We came here for sex,' Sara reminded him. 'To burn out the *itch* of desire we both felt.'

She could sense her face was starting to burn as he looked at her, but she wasn't going to give in or back down. She daren't.

Nick felt as though he had been engulfed by a huge rolling wave of unimaginable pain.

He wanted to tell her that she was lying…that she felt the same way about him as he did about her. A disorientating sense of shock and disbelief filled him, making it impossible for him to speak, making him *afraid* to speak…afraid of the intensity and savagery of spilling out the pain he was feeling in front of her, like someone mortally wounded spilling out his guts in a mess of raw flesh and blood. What he was experiencing was shocking, agonising, destructive, uncontrollable, uncontainable…

He could see Sara picking up her case and then stepping round him as she headed for the stairs.

Sara wondered if Nick could tell what she was really feeling…if he knew that she was lying…if he was relieved that she was removing from him the necessity of reminding *her* of the facts? Saving them both from the embarrassment of her declaring her love for him and begging him to take pity on her.

Last night he had refused to let her out of his arms even whilst they slept, but Sara wasn't deceived. That was just the male in him and meant nothing.

She wasn't going to cry…not now. There would be plenty of time for tears later.

And yet, right up until she was in her car and driving away, a part of her still hoped that he would say something to stop her…make her stay with him…even if it was only for a few more precious hours.

SARA HAD GONE. Nick stared in disbelief around the empty cottage. Why the *hell* hadn't he stopped her? By doing what? Physically forcing her to stay? *How* could he have done that? He still couldn't fully take on board what she had told him.

He had been so sure…so convinced that she felt the same way as he did. What was the matter with him? He should be pleased…relieved. Now there was nothing, no one, to stand in the way of his plans. Now he was free to do what the hell he wanted with his life!

CHAPTER FIFTEEN

'IS THAT YOU, Grandpa?'

David frowned as he recognised Amelia's anxious voice on the other end of the telephone line. It was nine-thirty in the morning and he and Honor had just finished their breakfast when the phone had started to ring.

'Yes, it is, sweetheart,' he responded.

'Mummy isn't very well,' Amelia told him, her voice starting to wobble betrayingly. 'Me and Alex can't wake her up properly. She won't open her eyes but she keeps asking for our daddy.'

'Don't worry, Amelia,' David tried to reassure her as he sought not to let his own anxiety show in his voice. 'Are you and Alex dressed yet?'

'No,' Amelia answered uncertainly.

'Well, why don't you go and get dressed and by the time you are I'll be there.'

'Olivia isn't well,' he told Honor when he had replaced the receiver.

Quickly he repeated to her what Amelia had told him.

'It sounds as though she's got this flu bug that's

going the rounds,' Honor told him. 'One of the symptoms is very high fever.'

'I told the girls I'd go round,' David added.

'I'll come with you,' Honor offered. 'I've got a draught which is very good for cooling down a fever.'

'Do you think you should come with me?' David demurred. 'The last thing I want is for you to catch it from her, especially with the baby….'

Honor was just about to point out to him that he was just as much at risk from catching it as she was and that if he did he was almost bound to pass the virus on to her but then she stopped.

Perhaps this might be an ideal opportunity for David and Olivia to spend some time together.

'Well, I had semi-promised to help Freddy choose some furniture for the orangery. Permission has finally come through for Fitzburgh Place to be used for civil marriage ceremonies and he wants to get the orangery equipped to hold receptions there. I'd thought a semi-Tuscan theme might be appropriate.'

She stopped and told him gently, 'David, this virus is a particularly bad one. You may need to call a doctor out to Olivia. There have been quite a number of cases where people have had to be hospitalised….'

'Are you saying that you'd prefer me not to go?' David asked her.

Immediately Honor shook her head.

'Certainly not. Olivia is your *daughter* and I *know* how I would feel if it was one of my girls who was

ill—and how I'd feel and what I'd do if *you* tried to
stop me from seeing them. No. Of course you *must* be
there, but I don't want you to think out of loyalty to
me and my "potions" that you can't call in her doctor.'

HALF AN HOUR LATER as Amelia let David into the
house, he could see that both she and Alex had been
crying.

As he hugged them he told them firmly, 'Now, I
want you both to stay downstairs whilst I go and look
at your mummy...just in case the phone rings,' he
improvised when he saw that Amelia was about to
protest.

The curtains were still closed in Olivia's bedroom
and David's heart lurched as he recognised immediately that Olivia was delirious and only semi-
conscious. Her face when he reached out to touch it
was burning hot, the pillow wringing wet, her body
twisting as she moved restlessly beneath the duvet.

Honor had been right to warn him that he might
need to call in a doctor.

The harassed receptionist who eventually answered
his call told him that it would be several hours before
the doctor could get round to visit Olivia.

'Is there anything I can do in the meantime?' David
demanded anxiously. 'She's obviously running a temperature. She's delirious and—'

'You can bathe her skin to try to bring her temperature down,' the receptionist advised him. 'Oh, and make sure she drinks plenty of fluids.'

'Give her four drops of the potion I gave you every half an hour in a glass of water,' Honor told David when he rang her to update her on the situation. 'It should help to break the fever. I've just been listening to the radio and they were saying that the local hospital is having to handle so many cases that they've had to cancel all but the most urgent operations.'

Mentally blessing Honor for calling him back to the house to give him the new Disney video she had bought as a stocking filler for the girls for Christmas, David glanced round the sitting room door to check on what they were doing before heading back upstairs to Olivia.

Both of them were thankfully happily engrossed in their new video.

In the bedroom Olivia was lying still, her eyes wide open.

'Dad,' she queried hoarsely and angrily as she saw him. 'What are *you* doing here?'

'The girls were worried about you,' he answered her honestly. 'They rang me.'

'Worried about *me*…' She broke off as she started to shiver, her hand going to her throat. It felt raw with pain. Her head felt as though it were going to burst open and just as she thought she was so hot that she was about to melt, she suddenly seemed so cold that just to breathe in air hurt her lungs.

'Throat bad?' David sympathised. 'I'll go down and make you a hot drink. You always did suffer with the most vile sore throats when you were a little girl. Your mother wanted you to have your tonsils removed but…'

'But you wouldn't agree,' Olivia finished bitterly for him. 'It would have meant me being off school for three weeks and *you* wanted to go away on a golfing holiday. Yes, I remember.'

'No!' David denied, shocked. 'What on earth gave you that idea? I didn't want you to have the operation because I'd had it myself and I could remember how awful it was. I thought the pain was never going to end and it never stopped me from having sore throats. There was no way I wanted you to be put through that.'

Olivia stared at him.

'No. That's not true,' she denied furiously. 'Mother told me…' She stopped as a fit of coughing seized her.

Immediately David went to pour her a glass of water from the jug he had brought up and placed beside her bed.

'Yuck,' she grimaced after she had taken a sip. 'It tastes bitter.'

'It's got one of Honor's potions in it,' David told her. 'She says it will help bring down your fever.'

'My *fever!* I've got a cold…that's all,' Olivia objected.

'You've got flu,' David corrected her firmly. 'I've called the surgery and the doctor's coming round later.'

'You've done *what?* You had *no* right…I don't want you here….' Olivia began, but her voice started to trail away as the fever returned. She felt so ill that it was impossible for her to continue to speak, to even continue to *think*. All she wanted to do was to lie down and close her eyes. Even the thin grey light seeping into the bedroom hurt her eyes and as for the pain in her head and her body… She couldn't remember ever feeling so ill.

'The girls…' she managed to croak.

'They're fine,' David assured her immediately. Although she was trying to fight it, he could tell that she was slowly losing her hold on consciousness, her breathing laboured and shallow as she finally gave in.

She looked, David reflected sombrely as he watched over her, more like the little girl he remembered than the woman she now was and it made his heart ache to see her looking so frail and vulnerable.

Once he was sure that she was asleep he went back downstairs to check on the girls and make them something to eat.

When he went into the sitting room to call them in for their food Amelia asked him seriously, 'Grandpa, can Grandma do proper magic spells like in Harry Potter?'

David frowned. He had been reading the books to the girls every afternoon after school.

'Grandma Honor is a herbalist,' he tried to explain.

'Is that like being a witch?' Alex and Amelia pressed him.

'We *want* her to be a witch,' Alex interjected excitedly, 'because if she is, then she can—'

'Shush,' Amelia began anxiously, but Alex was in full flood and refused to be deflected.

Thoughtfully David looked from Amelia's guilty face to Alex's defiant and excited one.

'Then she can what?' he questioned calmly.

Ignoring her elder sister's agitation Alex told him eagerly, 'Then she can make a spell that will make our daddy come home.'

David didn't know whether to smile or cry. On balance he suspected that crying might be the more appropriate response.

'You both miss him very much, don't you?' he said gently instead, sitting down with them.

'Yes.'

There was no need for them to answer his question. He could see how they felt in their expressions.

He didn't really know Caspar, his son-in-law, but from what he had heard about him, David had gained the impression that he was considered by the family to be a good and loving father.

'He and Olivia were so much in love,' Jon had told

him, shaking his head in bewilderment. 'I never imagined that they would split up.'

IT WAS LATE in the afternoon before the doctor arrived looking harassed and exhausted.

'Yes, it's the virus,' he confirmed.

'She's got a very bad sore throat,' David informed him.

The doctor frowned. 'Yes, I'll have to give you a prescription for that. She's going to need to stay in bed for the next three or four days,' he grimaced as he told David. 'If she was in her sixties and not her thirties I'd be thinking in terms of trying to find her a hospital bed—not that there are any to be found locally. This thing has struck like the plague. There doesn't seem to be a single household without someone affected by it. If there's anyone available to look after her...her husband...'

'I'm her father. I'll be here,' David informed him quietly.

In the end the regime the doctor had prescribed was very much the same as the one recommended by Honor, as David told her when he telephoned her to update her on what was happening.

'I'll have to stay here tonight,' he said ruefully. 'I can't leave her.'

'Of course you can't,' Honor confirmed robustly. 'In fact, I should be very cross with you if you tried to.'

'The doctor has said it could be three or four days,' David added. He paused then continued, 'There's your hospital appointment coming up.'

Honor took a deep breath. Although she hadn't said so to David she was secretly dreading the test which was one which could reveal whether or not the baby she was carrying was likely to have any abnormalities. As much as she had tried to reassure herself about the health of their baby she was still aware of her age and the risks connected with it. Of course she wanted David there with her when she went to hospital even though, logically, she knew his presence would make no difference whatsoever to the outcome of the tests, the results of which they wouldn't know immediately anyway. But just as much as this child she was now carrying, Livvy was also David's child and now she, too, needed him.

Only when she was sure she had both her emotions and her voice completely under control did she answer as confidently as she could.

'Oh, don't worry about that. You concentrate on Livvy. Right now *she's* the one who needs you, David.'

'Well, if you're sure... I have to admit I don't like the thought of leaving her.'

'I'm perfectly sure,' Honor replied, surreptitiously crossing her fingers behind her back. 'You stay with Livvy.'

'SARA, my dear…what a lovely surprise.'

Sara smiled wanly at her grandfather. Frances had not unnaturally been shocked when Sara had informed her that she was going to have to leave, but nowhere near as shocked as she was when Sara had explained to her who she was and the mistake which had led to her taking the job in the first place.

'I should have told you before,' Sara had admitted, 'But…it was difficult.…'

'I can appreciate that,' Frances had comforted her. 'Conflicting loyalties always are. We shall be very sorry to lose you, Sara.'

'I have to go,' was all Sara had been able to say.

Tania was complaining that Sara's arrival was delaying them from going out to dinner and as she listened to her and witnessed her grandfather's attempts to placate her, for the first time Sara could see why her father was not a big fan of his father-in-law's second wife.

'It's okay, I'm not staying.' She managed to smile at Tania. 'It's just a brief visit.' She took a deep breath. 'I'm going to fly out to join Mum and Dad.'

'Oh, you really are the most lucky girl,' Tania told her enviously. 'I wish I had had your opportunities at your age, Sara dear. Your father is so lucky to have an apartment in such a prestigious place. All those wealthy men… If you play your cards right I'm sure you could end up with a millionaire for a husband.'

Sara closed her eyes swallowing down the nausea

Tania's comments were evoking. The mere thought of any man, any man at all in her life and her bed who wasn't Nick made her skin crawl with horror and her heart ache with a pain so unbearable it made her want to scream that there would *never* be a husband for her now…nor a lover, either…

She knew that both her parents, but especially her father, were against her desire to work for one of the overseas aid agencies.

'It will break your body and your spirit,' her father had already told her brutally. 'Take it from me, Sara, you're far too soft-hearted. Even if you manage to escape going down with some debilitating and potentially life-threatening disease, you've still got to overcome the emotional trauma you're bound to suffer.'

But she had to do something and the only thing she could think of was to lose herself and her pain in the hardest and most gruelling kind of work she could possibly find.

But the reason she was flying out to the Caribbean wasn't simply to persuade her parents to accept her plans for her future. If she stayed at home she wasn't sure she could trust herself not to weaken and get in touch with Nick. Crawl to him…beg him…plead with him to take her back in his arms and back to his bed….

'JENNY, is that you?'

'Caspar.' Jenny's voice betrayed her surprise as she

recognised Olivia's husband's voice. Why on earth was he telephoning *her?*

'I just thought I'd ring to see how Livvy and the girls are,' Caspar told her answering Jenny's unvoiced question.

'They're fine—so far as I know,' Jenny responded cautiously, unable to resist adding, 'why don't you ring Olivia yourself, Caspar. I'm sure—'

'No. No,' Caspar cut her off abruptly, adding, 'and, Jenny, please don't tell Livvy that I rang. I don't want her to think that I'm—'

'...worrying about her?' Jenny supplied gently for him.

'Interfering in her life,' Caspar corrected her firmly.

'Look, I've got to go,' he told her and then, before Jenny could say anything else, he had ended the call.

'Who was that?' Jon asked Jenny, walking into the kitchen just as she was replacing the receiver.

'Caspar,' Jenny told him. 'He rang to ask if Livvy and the girls were all right.'

'Really... You know I can't help thinking how sad it is that those two....' Jon stopped and shook his head, coming over to where Jenny was standing.

'We've been so lucky in our marriage, Jenny. Or rather, I've been so lucky to have you. I hate to think what my life would have been like without you in it.'

He protested as he saw her tears, 'What is it? What's wrong?'

'I don't know,' Jenny admitted weepily. 'It's just

that so much seems to have gone wrong recently and I'd begun to think...to fear...' She stopped.

'You'd begun to fear what?' Jon encouraged her.

'Well, since David came back sometimes I've felt as though you'd rather be with him than with me....'

There, it was out at last, the fear that had been tormenting her.

'How *could* you think that?' Jon asked her in disbelief.

'David *is* your twin brother,' Jenny reminded him.

'And you are my *wife*, my *love*, my best friend, my *soul mate*,' Jon told her emotionally.

'Yes, I love David. Yes, I'm glad that he's come back, and yes, I'm glad that he and I are rediscovering our twinship, but there's no way what I feel for David could ever come anywhere *near* what I feel for *you*...what you mean to me...what our love and our lives together mean to me, Jenny. You are my life and without you...' He stopped and shook his head. 'I knew *something* was wrong but I thought it was because you were concerned about Maddy...because you...'

'I was,' Jenny admitted. 'But I feel so silly admitting to jealousy at my age, Jon, and of your *brother*, but...I've even begun to wonder if perhaps you envy David. There he is, with a new relationship and a new baby on the way....'

At any other time the astonishment on Jon's face would have made her smile.

'*Me* envy *David?*' he protested. 'Oh, Jenny, how could you possibly think *that?* If anything, I've been feeling sorry for him. I know he loves Honor—I can see how happy they are together—and of course I'm pleased for them about the baby, but we've *done* those things, *shared* those experiences.

'I thank God that you and I will never know the guilt that the alienation between himself and Olivia is causing David. That I will *never* suffer the regrets I *know* he suffers. *You* are the most wonderful thing that *ever* happened to me, Jenny, the most precious gift life could ever give me...*you* and our children.'

Such emotional words from a man who was normally so reticent about voicing his feelings told Jenny how genuine and heartfelt they were.

'I've been such an idiot,' she told him ruefully.

'No. I'm the one who's been that,' Jon corrected her. 'For not realising what you were feeling. But now that I do, I intend to ensure that you don't have any more doubts.'

'Jon,' Jenny protested a little breathlessly as he took her in his arms and proceeded to kiss her with very obvious enjoyment. But it was only a token protest and one it seemed her newly masterful husband found relatively easy to ignore.

DAVID WOKE UP with a start, automatically reaching out for Honor, only she wasn't there.... And then he remembered. He was at Olivia's house sleeping in her spare room. Groggily he looked at the luminous dial of his watch. It was four o'clock in the morning. He frowned as he heard something, a noise of some sort...someone crying.

Throwing back the bedclothes he got up and went to the door. The noise was coming from Olivia's room. Quickly he hurried across the landing and pushed open her bedroom door.

Olivia was moving restlessly in her sleep, muttering as she tossed and turned. Anxiously David went over to her. Even before he touched her he could see that the fever was burning through her. She started to cough, a harsh racking sound that made his own chest feel painfully tight. His eyes burned with dry unshed tears for all the times when she was growing up when he had either not been there for her or oblivious to her need.

One of Livvy's hands lay on top of the bedclothes. Very gently David clasped it between his own. Despite her fever it felt cold. Tenderly he started to massage it. How had he managed to be such a blind failure of a father? How had he managed not to see and feel the uniqueness of his children, not to be awed and humbled by their specialness, not to realise the magnitude, the munificence that a child's love for its parent was? That a child *was,* quite literally, a gift of love.

And Olivia *was* his child, just as Jack was...just as this new baby would be. Each of them unique and uniquely loved by him. He had caused Olivia so much pain, done so much harm. Irreparably so? He prayed not.

OLIVIA STARTED to relax as her troubled unhappy dream started to fade and be replaced by something much happier. She was with Caspar. They were walking hand in hand and just being with him filled her with so much love and happiness.

'Caspar…'

David frowned as he heard Olivia saying her husband's name. She was smiling and the restless movement of her body had ceased. He even thought that her temperature might have dropped a little.

'Caspar.'

He felt her hand curl in his own as she repeated her husband's name in a tender little voice, a soft breath of sound that revealed to his paternal ear just what she felt; and then she was opening her eyes, looking at him, her realisation and her disappointment that he wasn't Caspar clouding them before she could conceal her expression.

'Oh, it's you,' she said bleakly, trying to remove her hand from his grip and turning her head away.

Olivia could feel the heat of the salt tears she was furiously trying to suppress. The stark contrast between her dream and her reality was almost too painful for her to bear. What was her dream trying to tell her—that Caspar was far more important to her than she had allowed herself to admit?

Fretfully she moved her head on the pillow.

But their marriage had broken down—irretrievably. They both knew that.

At the side of the bed David was saying ruefully, 'The last time I did this you were six years old and covered in spots.'

Olivia stiffened.

'I had chicken pox,' she told him. 'But you weren't there....'

'Yes, I was, Olivia,' David corrected her quietly.

'You'd gone away somewhere with grandfather,' she insisted.

'I came back,' David checked her. 'Jon rang me and told me—' He stopped.

'Uncle Jon told you what?' Olivia demanded.

David paused before saying reluctantly, 'He told me that you were...crying for me.'

'Me...crying for you?' Olivia's face burned with angry colour. 'Even at six I knew better than to do that. So far as you were concerned I was just a nuisance and I wasn't even the right sex.... You never loved me...never wanted me....'

David closed his eyes. So much of what she was saying was true but... If only he could find a way of getting through to her.

On her bedside table he saw a photograph of Caspar holding Alex—a very tiny baby—with Amelia tucked under his spare arm.

'I can still remember the night you were born,' he

told Olivia quietly. 'Your mother...' His eyes clouded a little. Tiggy, furiously resentful about their move to Cheshire and illogically blaming it on the baby she was carrying had flatly refused to acknowledge that the pain she was having meant that Olivia was about to arrive. They had been due to spend the evening with another couple, a rich financier and his wife who were very much a part of the Cheshire set and Tiggy had been determined not to miss their dinner party.

In the end, though, they had had to. Her waters had broken and she had been forced to admit that they could not possibly atttend.

'Damn this wretched baby,' she had screamed at him in temper David remembered sadly. 'And damn you to hell, too, David Crighton.'

She had refused to allow him to stay in the delivery room with her and David could remember the long agonising wait he had had until he had finally been told that Olivia had been born.

'She's a little bit bruised,' the doctor had told David. 'Mum seemed reluctant to part with her.' He had laughed as though it were a joke, but David knew how shocked he had been when he had seen Olivia's bruised face.

He had wanted to pick her up and hold her, but the nurse had clucked almost disapprovingly making him feel that his presence was an unwelcome intrusion.

'Tiggy what?' Olivia's voice cut sharply and accusingly across his thoughts. 'Tiggy didn't want me any more than you did? I already know that I was an accident.... I'm surprised you didn't suggest that Tiggy had a termination.' She tensed when she saw the anger in his eyes.

'What is it?' she challenged him. 'Did you... Did you?' Olivia was repeating.

'No, I didn't,' he told her sternly, both shocked and saddened at what she was saying, what she must be feeling—must have felt all her life!

'Neither of us *ever* considered that even for a minute, Olivia.'

'But once I was born, you didn't want me—you didn't love me!'

It was a statement and not a question.

David shook his head, unable to explain fully to her just how he had felt.

'I haven't been a good father to you, Livvy, and for that...' David drew in a harsh breath. 'For that I shall never cease to feel guilty. But you are my child...my daughter...and you are very precious to me.'

As she searched his face David held her gaze and his own breath. Olivia didn't know what to think. Somehow just talking to him like this had shifted the whole focus of her own feelings. She couldn't say that she forgave him for her childhood or even that she understood, but somehow her bitterness and sense of pain had softened, loosening its stranglehold of her emotions.... Somehow she felt she could look at the past in a gentler and less harsh light.

'Love doesn't always manifest itself in the way we expect,' David was telling her slowly. 'The girls miss their father,' he informed her almost abruptly, taking a deep breath before he asked her, 'Do you still love him, Livvy?'

Livvy. For the first time since she had grown up, Olivia actually found that she didn't get that familiar rush of resentment and bitterness when he used the shortened form of her name.

'No...I don't know.... Yes,' she acknowledged helplessly when he continued to look at her. Tears filled her eyes.

'But it just wasn't working. Caspar didn't understand how I felt. He was always accusing me of being more concerned about the past and you and Gramps than I was about him and the girls. But that just wasn't true.

'I needed him to understand, to help me, not criticise me.' Her eyes filled with tears and she turned her head away from him, but slowly she found she was telling him about her feelings, her marriage, her fears and her pain and that it seemed the most natural thing in the world to do so.

Just before dawn as she started to drift into an exhausted sleep, David leaned over and kissed her gently.

He ached so with love for her and like any father he ached, too, to put her world to rights for her.

Caspar was only a telephone call away. Surely as

her husband he had every right to know that she was ill…that his daughters missed and wanted him… And that Olivia missed and wanted him, too?

That, David decided, was a decision he could only make once he had actually spoken with his son-in-law.

METHODICALLY, Olivia had stored Caspar's mobile number in her telephone's address book. David had made sure she was asleep before making his call.

CASPAR FROWNED as his mobile started to ring. It was late at night and Molly was in her room sleeping.

When he saw his Cheshire home number flashing up on his mobile, his first feeling was one of such piercing emotional intensity that it caught him off guard but when he heard the voice of an unknown man on the other end of the line that feeling quickly evaporated, his own voice tautly hostile as he responded to his caller's, 'Is that Caspar?' with a terse, 'Yes.'

'I'm David Crighton,' David introduced himself. 'Olivia's father.'

Olivia's *father!* Caspar's tight grip on his mobile relaxed slightly only to tighten up again even more tensely as David informed him, 'I thought I'd better ring and let you know that Olivia isn't too well.'

Not too well— The shock of hearing such news so soon after speaking to Jenny filled Caspar with sharp anxiety.

'What's wrong with her?' Caspar demanded—a moment of unthinkable, unbearable horror seizing him as he rasped, 'Has there been an accident? Is she—'

'It's nothing like that,' David was quick to reassure him. 'She's actually contracted a particularly vicious brand of flu that's going round at the moment and her doctor has decreed that she's got to stay in bed for a few days.'

'Stay in bed—Olivia!' Caspar's voice betrayed both his shock and his cynicism at anyone's ability to make Olivia comply with such a restriction.

David allowed himself to smile a little.

'Well, she wasn't too keen on the idea but to be honest it hasn't been that difficult enforcing it—she's hardly been conscious most of the time, although it looks as though she's over the worst of the fever now....'

As he listened to David's quiet revelations, Caspar was filled with a rush of conflicting emotions. The very thought of Olivia being ill enough to agree to remain in bed was one that upset him far more than he could have imagined. Unwilling to examine what he was feeling too closely, he asked David urgently, 'What about the girls?'

Not even their births had kept Livvy in bed for more than twenty-four hours.

'Oh, I suppose they're with Jon and Jenny,' he added, answering his own question.

'Actually, no, they're here at home with me. They've been asking for you, Caspar. They miss you,'

David told him poignantly before continuing, 'I've moved in for the duration until Olivia is well enough to manage on her own.'

'Livvy has let *you* move in?' Once again Caspar's voice betrayed his feelings.

'Well, she really didn't have much of an alternative,' David confessed, driving home the point he wanted to make by adding gently, 'You see, there wasn't really anyone else. Maddy hasn't been well and has needed Jenny's help, so Livvy didn't actually have anyone else she could turn to.'

David knew that he was being unfair and he could feel in the ensuing silence humming along the telephone line just how Caspar was reacting to what he had said.

'Just how ill is she?' Caspar asked abruptly.

The scenario David was describing to him was so out of character for Olivia that he could feel his anxiety gauge rising with every word David uttered.

'Well, if the hospital hadn't already been full...' David began.

'The hospital!' Olivia was ill enough to be taken into hospital. 'Why the hell have you left it this long to get in touch with me?' Caspar exploded.

'Perhaps because I needed to make sure that Livvy *wanted* me to, first,' David checked him softly.

Caspar stared incredulously across his room.

'Livvy *asked* you to ring me?'

'You're her husband—the father of her children. Is

it really so surprising that she should want you?' David hedged.

Caspar's normally quick intellect was for once subordinate to his emotions so that he didn't pick up on the evasive manner in which David had answered him.

Livvy wanted him. Livvy needed him!

Closing his eyes he told David gruffly, 'I'm out in the middle of nowhere at the moment, but I'll be on the first international flight home I can get...and... David...'

Though he stumbled a little over his use of his father-in-law's Christian name, David himself was too relieved to care.

'Yes,' David responded carefully as he finally allowed the pent-up breath he felt he had been holding for the entire duration of their conversation to leak away in shaky relief. Olivia would never forgive him for this piece of outright manipulation and interference he suspected, but if he hadn't done it he knew *he* would never forgive himself. She was his daughter and her happiness was of paramount importance to him. Far, far more important than Livvy herself could know.

'Thanks,' Caspar told him gruffly.

As he ended the call, Caspar looked towards the closed door of his room. Across the hallway from his room lay Molly's. Was it really only a matter of hours ago that she had warned him that they needed to talk about his marriage and that he... He closed his eyes and squared his shoulders, grimacing as he opened them again. There was no way he could leave without explaining to her, and no way either that he wanted to.

When she opened the door to his knock she looked adorably rumpled and sleepy and he had to fight against taking her in his arms and holding her whilst he told her. *Was* it possible for a man to love two women?

'Can I come in a minute? There's something I have to tell you.'

Molly knew immediately that Caspar's 'something' involved his wife and she had to turn away from him so that he couldn't see the fear in her eyes. She had known him for such a short time and she had known all along that his marriage was far from over as he had tried to claim.

'Olivia's ill,' he told her. 'I—I have to go home...the girls...my daughters...have been asking for me....' he added, unable to look at her as he did so.

As she listened to him, a fierce wild sense of loss invaded Molly but she refused to give in to it. After all, hadn't she known all along that something like this would happen; that all the best men were inevitably already spoken for? Hadn't she known just from the way he said her name that he still loved his Olivia, even though he himself had tried to deny it?

Summoning up all her courage and all her professionalism, she touched him gently on his arm.

'You're doing the right thing,' she assured him. 'A marriage as good as yours deserves a second chance.'

'How do you know that?' Caspar asked her ruefully. Beneath his gruffness was relief and gratitude that she had not reproached him or made things difficult for him, and a sense of sadness and guilt as well.

'I just know.' She smiled.

As she watched him leave, she continued to smile but inside she was already warning Olivia, 'This time I'm letting you have him back, but if you're ever fool enough to let him go a second time I sure as hell won't be so generous.'

CHAPTER SIXTEEN

'YOU LOOK VERY pleased with life this morning,' Maddy told her mother-in-law when Jenny called to see if the younger woman needed any shopping.

'Mmm…' Jenny agreed, soft colour tinging her face as she remembered the special sweetness of the very private and passionate way in which Jon had demonstrated to her just how much he did love her.

'You're looking very well yourself,' she smiled back at Maddy.

'I feel great,' she acknowledged. 'I'm worried about Max, though.' She started to frown.

'He isn't sleeping at all well and—'

'Well, I know he's been concerned about Ben's threats to change his will,' Jenny offered.

'No, I don't think it's that,' Maddy denied. 'We'd both hate to leave this house, of course, but at the end of the day if we had to…'

Jenny's frown matched Maddy's now as she caught the anxious undertone in her voice. The obstetrician might have given Maddy the all clear but Max had made it more than plain to his family that nothing and no one was to cause his wife the slightest degree of concern.

'Have you *asked* Max if anything's wrong?' Jenny queried.

Maddy gave her a rueful look.

'I've tried but Max insists that there *isn't*, but I know there *is*, Jenny. He's been having the most dreadful nightmares night after night *and* they're getting worse, but he simply won't discuss them with me and...' She paused, reluctant to expose to anyone else the way in which Max seemed to be distancing himself from her.

'He has been through a very stressful time recently,' Jenny reminded her. 'I've never seen him react the way he did when you were in hospital, Maddy. We were all relieved, of course, when they were able to bring your blood pressure under control, but for Max the strain must have been unbearable, especially...' Jenny stopped.

'Especially what?' Maddy pressed her determinedly.

Jenny sighed. Jenny was beginning to wish that she had kept silent, but Maddy was looking increasingly distressed and Jenny knew she would have to finish what she had started.

'Max was afraid that he might lose you, Maddy,' Jenny began gently. 'The consultant had explained to him what might potentially happen to you. And—and to the baby if you didn't respond to treatment, and Max....' Jenny bit her lip.

'Max told me that he couldn't endure the thought of losing you and that if it were his decision to make, then to save your life he would have instructed the hospital to terminate your pregnancy—'

As she heard Maddy's shocked gasp, Jenny reminded her quietly, 'Max loves you very much, and we are talking about a situation where he feared that if you hadn't responded to treatment, both yours and the baby's lives would have been lost. However, the consultant told him that you would have had to have been part of that decision had it needed to have been made. Max had wanted to make the decision for you to spare you.'

As Jenny saw her daughter-in-law's face, she sighed guiltily. 'I'm sorry, Maddy, I shouldn't have said anything.'

'No. I'm glad that you did,' Maddy told her truthfully. 'I had no idea. The hospital never said...'

And neither had Max!

Maddy gave a cold shudder and placed her hands protectively over her body. The thought of anyone or anything harming her baby aroused all her fiercely protective maternal instincts.

Half an hour later after Jenny had departed with the supermarket shopping list—although Maddy was fully recovered Max was insistent that she didn't do anything that might overtire her—Maddy made her way to Max's study.

He looked up as she walked in, the immediate pleasure lightening his eyes dimming to wariness.

'Your mother's just been,' Maddy told him quietly.

Walking over to the window and keeping her back to him Maddy continued, 'I told her how worried I've been about you.'

'What on earth for? I've told you I'm fine, Maddy.'

It was strange what knowledge could do. Now, beneath the surface irritation in his voice she could hear quite plainly other and darker emotions.

'No, you're not,' Maddy contradicted him fiercely. 'How could you be when…' She swung round to face him, her eyes brilliant with anger and pain.

'Jenny told me, Max. She told me about what might have happened to our baby.' There was no way that Maddy could bring herself to use the word that had filled her heart with such anguish and rejection.

'What!'

She knew immediately that Max understood what she was trying to say.

'She had no right,' he began furiously. 'There was no need—'

'No *need*?' Maddy's voice shook with emotion. '*You* had chosen my life above our baby's and you say there was no need for *me* to know.'

'Maddy, please try to understand,' Max begged her desperately, leaving his desk to go to her, watching white-faced as she stepped back from him, ignoring the silent appeal of his outstretched hand.

'I couldn't bear the thought of losing you, even though…' He was the one who had to turn away now, as his own feelings overwhelmed him.

'Even though what, Max?' Maddy demanded, her voice was as sharp with pain as his.

'Even though I knew you would hate me for choosing you above the baby,' Max admitted. 'The children we already have need you and I… There's no way I could bear to live without you,' he told her.

'Do you think it's been *easy* for me?' he demanded when she made no response. 'Do you think I haven't suffered, cursed myself in my heart over and over again…hated myself…? In my worst moments I've even imagined that…' He stopped, unable to tell her about the true awfulness of his nightmares.

Max closed his eyes. Having admitted so much he might as well admit the rest.

'And if you want the truth, Maddy, if I had to live through the whole hellish thing again I'd *still* make the same choice. I thought I was strong but I'm not. I'm selfish and weak. *You*'re my *life,* Maddy.

'Don't say any more,' Maddy begged him.

Max waited, tensing his body against the pain of seeing her walk away from him, of knowing that he had destroyed her love for him. But to his astonishment, Maddy was actually walking towards him. When she reached him she lifted her hand to his face, her eyes luminous with emotion as she touched his skin.

It shocked her that he could have borne so much pain without saying anything to her.

She had known, of course, how much he loved her and their children, but the raw naked intensity and depth of the emotion she was now seeing came as a revelation to her.

'I can't bear knowing that I wanted to destroy our child,' he told her emotionally. 'And I don't—can't— blame you if you hate me for it, Maddy.'

'I don't hate you,' Maddy told him softly adding, 'and Max, it wasn't our child you wanted to destroy, it was me you wanted to save!'

As she watched him, Maddy could see from his expression that she hadn't managed to reassure him.

His voice cracking with pain, Max told her, 'I even actually thought…wanted…' He stopped, groaning. Then, covering his face with his hands, he said thickly, 'I wished that this child had never been conceived.' He drew a deep shaky breath. 'And now,' he stopped and then told her harshly, 'it haunts and torments me, Maddy, that somehow he or she will know and that when it is born, it will be born hating me for…for what I contemplated doing.'

'Max!' Maddy's voice rang with shocked compassion. 'No, you mustn't think that.'

'I should have been the one to protect you both and not… But I couldn't bear the thought of losing you,

Maddy, and now I can't bear to think that this child when it is born will believe—'

'Max, stop it!' Maddy commanded him firmly. Wrapping her arms around him and holding him tightly, she whispered to him, 'You're torturing yourself unnecessarily. Look at me,' she demanded.

The unfamiliar note of command in her voice surprised Max into obeying her. The tears had gone from her eyes now and they were clear and calm.

'I promise you, Max, this baby, if it knows anything, will know that it was conceived in love, created out of love...our love for one another and for it.'

'I was so afraid that if you knew what I'd felt...what I would have done...you'd stop loving me,' Max confessed, as the loving reassurance of her words soothed his anguish like cooling healing balm applied to a raw festering wound.

Maddy looked at him steadily, her eyes full of the feelings she wanted him to see.

As she squeezed his hand she told him shakily, 'There is nothing...*nothing* you could do that could stop me loving you now.'

'Maddy...Maddy...'

As she lifted her face for his kiss, Maddy felt the dampness of his tears on her face.

'We're safe now, Max,' she whispered reassuringly to him. 'We're *all* safe, and this baby will love you just as much as I do!'

'BOILED EGG and soldiers,' Olivia giggled as David solemnly put the tray down on the bed beside her.

'Oh, Dad,' she protested whilst David's heart sang at her easy use of the word.

'Now I *know* that I'm an invalid. Do you remember the time I brought breakfast in bed for you and mother?' Her smile shook slightly and she looked away from him. This new relationship they were exploring together reminded her of being a teenager all over again, with all its wobbly uncertainties and self-doubts contrasted with moments of joy and euphoria so intense that they were almost magical.

'How could I forget it?' David mourned with a grin. 'The eggs would have done sterling service as cannon shot and as for the tea...'

Olivia laughed.

'The salt in the timer was wet and it had set, so I was waiting for ages for the salt to run through not realising, and I didn't know you weren't supposed to open the tea bags. Mother was furious with me,' she remembered ruefully.

David watched her but said nothing. Although Olivia wasn't to know it, Tiggy had been on one of her binges the previous night and she had spent most of the night purging herself of the food she had eaten.

'I'd better go and check on the girls,' David told her. 'Otherwise they're going to be late for school. You're out of fresh food so I'll do some shopping on the way back—and no getting out of bed whilst I'm not here,' he warned her mock severely. 'There's no way you're strong enough for that yet.'

Olivia smiled but didn't disagree. She was still feeling ludicrously weak, which must be the reason she was allowing him to take charge and boss her about without objecting. She had to be feeling weak otherwise she would never, as she was doing right now, actually be mentally acknowledging how good it felt to be cosseted and looked after.

Just knowing that he was there somehow made her feel as though a huge weight had been lifted off her shoulders.

'I'll have to ring the office,' she told him. 'I've got a couple of appointments that will have to be cancelled and—'

'When I get back,' David told her and smiled with loving firmness. He was halfway across the bedroom when Olivia suddenly remembered something, calling out urgently, 'Dad…'

'What is it?' David was at her side immediately. 'Aren't you feeling well. What…?'

'No. No, I'm fine, but I've just remembered. Isn't it today you and Honor are supposed to be going to the hospital for her tests?' Olivia asked him.

She saw immediately from his expression that she was right.

'Honor tried to postpone the appointment but unfortunately she couldn't…. She says it's no problem for her to go on her own and she understands that there was no way I could leave you, not the way you were.'

For a moment Olivia was too moved to speak as she absorbed the wonder of what he had said. *She* had been more important to him than either Honor or their baby…. *She* had been the one he had chosen to be with…*her* needs had come first. *She* had come first, but as fast as such thoughts formed, little-girl thoughts that echoed all the pent-up feelings of her past, newer, stronger more mature ones, took their place. She, too, was a mother. She *too* knew that anxiety every woman feels for the health and safety of her unborn child and *she* knew, too, how much Honor must surely really want David to be with her…even more so than a younger mother. Very firmly she shook her head and smiled at her father.

'Dad, I'm fine now,' she told him. She continued insisting wisely, 'And there's no way I could *ever* forgive myself if you weren't with Honor. She needs you to be there—whatever she might have said.' She could see the hesitation and uncertainty in his eyes.

'You must go,' she repeated. 'Please. I want you to.'

As she spoke, Olivia suddenly felt as though she had stepped over an unseen threshold, as though she had overcome an unknown antagonist, as though she had reached out and taken hold of the strong supportive hand she had never even known previously was there waiting to grasp her own. Suddenly she acknowl-

edged she felt secure, loved…shiningly sure of herself
and her place in the world and in her father's love.

'Very well, but remember, no getting out of bed,'
David told her, coming back to her bedside and bending to give her a fierce hug and kiss the top of her
head. His eyes were full of tears. They still had a long
way to go and a lot of problems to solve, David knew
that, but now, for the first time he felt optimistic about
the final outcome.

AS BEN PICKED UP the mail he glowered bad-
temperedly at the front door. He shouldn't have to do
this. Maddy should be here to do it…or Jenny…. They
had no right to leave him on his own. Well, he was
going to make sure that he taught them a lesson. He
was going to change his will and then… He frowned
as he saw a letter addressed to himself. It was thick
and bulky. A little awkwardly and uncertainly he
opened it, leaning against his chair for support as he
did so.

Before she had taken the children to school Maddy
had relit the log fire in his study. She had tried to
persuade him to have one of those newfangled gas log
things but he preferred the real thing. Gas logs! He
snorted as he started to read the letter and then froze,
the gas logs forgotten as a huge wave of icy shock
and fury engulfed his whole body. By the time he had
read and read the letter again he was shaking so much
that he could barely hold it.

Savagely he ripped it up and threw it on the fire. His heart was pounding painfully with a mixture of anger and panic. It was all lies of course, it had to be. He had never... He gasped as out of nowhere a wall of pain suddenly hit him, sweeping him up into a death grip so intense that he couldn't even cry out against it.

It sliced into and through him, tearing at him, clawing and mangling, like a living red-hot fury. He tried to fight it but it wouldn't loosen its grip of him. The familiarity of his study started to darken and fade, he could see a bright light almost too painful for his eyes to endure and then suddenly there *he* was, standing in front of him, laughing as he walked towards him, his hair shining with the light that surrounded him, his eyes unlined and a deep dense blue, his teeth white, his bearing upright. Ben could see tenderness and compassion in his eyes as well as something else he didn't want to see.

'No,' he protested, trying to draw back from his touch.

'Ben, it's me....' the other told him gently.

'Max,' Ben cried out in confusion. 'I don't—'

'No, not Max,' the other corrected him patiently. 'You know who I am, Ben. There's nothing to be afraid of. I've come to take you home.'

'I am home,' Ben started to say but the words froze on the heavy cumbersome weight of the body he could see lying on the floor below him.

'Matthew,' he whispered shakily as his twin waited and watched.

'Yes,' he confirmed…waiting whilst Ben reached for his outstretched hand before saying gently, 'Come. It's time for us to go.'

'Matthew,' Ben repeated, the word sighing through him. 'My brother…'

'WANT TO talk about it?'

Sara tensed as her father walked along the edge of the jetty to where she was sitting hunched, staring out at the blueness of the sea.

'There isn't anything to talk about,' she denied.

Richard Lanyon looked thoughtfully over her down-bent head. She had arrived several days earlier, white-faced and with haunted eyes.

'It's a man,' her mother had pronounced when Sara had flatly refused to say anything to them other than that she had decided to fly out and spend Christmas with them.

'What man?' Richard had demanded, his mouth an ominous line.

'A Crighton man,' Sara's mother had hazarded.

Richard had shaken his head over his wife's female intuition, but now…

'Anything or *anyone,*' he challenged her directly now, watching the way her eyes widened and dark-ened as though she were in physical pain.

'Sara,' he begged her.

But she refused to be drawn, saying only, 'It's no use, Dad. Talking won't do anything. He doesn't...'

Getting up and dusting the sand off her bare tanned legs she told him, 'I love him but he doesn't love me. I'm not a little girl any more,' she reminded him soberly, 'and you can't make the pain go away for me.... I wish you could.'

Sombrely he watched as she walked away—not his little girl any more but a woman.

THEY WERE OVER the worst of the immediacy of the shock of it now, rallying around one another as close families do. David had wanted the funeral to be a quiet family affair but firmly and with authority Jon had overruled him.

'That might be what *we* want, but it's not what Dad would have wanted,' he had told him.

'He liked things to be done with pomp and ceremony. He would think we had done very poorly by him.'

'Mmm...nothing less than a state funeral if it could have been arranged,' Max had agreed and David had conceded that they were right.

It had made his heart ache with love and pride to witness the quiet calm way Jon had automatically taken charge after Jenny had returned to find Ben dead on the floor beside his chair, and he had been more than glad to concede that right to him.

All the family were invited, including the Chester branch.

'You know how competitive Dad always was with them,' Jon had reminded David when David had looked askance at the formal black-edged cards Jon had ordered for the service. 'This is what he would have wanted and we owe him that,' Jon had told his twin gently.

'Mmm… Well, when it's my turn, please remember *I* want something much simpler—a natural woodland DIY burial.'

Jon had laughed chiding him teasingly, 'If you think for one minute *I'm* going to dig a hole big enough for *you…*'

CASPAR SAT forward on the edge of his seat as the taxi turned into the drive. He had asked David not to say anything to Olivia about his return and a little reluctantly the other man had agreed.

'How is she?' he had asked David when he had rung from the airport to say that he had arrived.

'Much better,' David had confirmed. As David spoke to him Caspar had heard in the background the voices of his two daughters and a feeling of aching longing had filled him.

OLIVIA HAD perfectly understood when David had said that he was returning home. She was feeling a lot better although Jon had insisted that she was not to rush back to work. Ben's death had come as a shock to all of them despite the fact that he had been unwell for quite some time.

She heard Ally barking and saw the tail lights of the taxi disappearing but no premonition of who her visitor might be struck her as she went to open the door, so that the shock of seeing Caspar standing there made it impossible for her to hide her emotions from him.

The long flight to Manchester had given Caspar more time than he wanted to think, not just about what he was doing but what he *had* done and what he and Olivia had done—*together* and *apart*—the good and the bad.

He had missed his daughters and he had missed Olivia, too, but it took the fierce jolt of emotion bumping his heart against his ribs as he saw the feelings Olivia didn't have time to hide to make him acknowledge just how strong his love for her still was.

'Caspar…'

No sooner had Olivia done nothing more than gasp his name than Amelia and Alex came rushing into the hallway flinging themselves into their father's arms. As he held them Caspar didn't make any attempt to conceal his tears, hugging them tightly to him as he looked at Olivia over their heads.

It was several hours later before they could finally sit down and talk.

'The girls are asleep,' Caspar told Olivia as he came downstairs.

'They've missed you,' Olivia responded softly.

Caspar gave her a rueful look.

'Have they? Your father seems to have done an excellent job of providing them with a male presence in their lives. All they could talk about was Grandpa.'

'They *are* excited about the fact that they've got another grandfather,' Olivia acknowledged. 'But no grandfather could ever take *your* place in their lives Caspar, or...' Olivia stopped. Now that she was over the shock of him coming home there were things that needed to be said before she could start admitting to him that it wasn't just in the children's eyes and lives that he couldn't be replaced.

'What—what made you decide to come home?' Olivia asked him quietly.

'A lot of things,' Caspar responded. 'You...me... our children...

'Why didn't you ring me and tell me how difficult things were for you, Livvy? Why did I have to learn from your father that you were ill?'

'My father *rang* you?' Olivia demanded. She started to frown. 'Is *that* why you've come home? Because—'

'I came home because this *is* my home. *You* are my home—you and the girls.' Caspar overrode her. 'Your father's telephone call simply gave me the excuse my pride needed. You don't know how many times I've wanted to ring you, how many times I've wished...'

He stopped and shook his head, going towards her as he saw the sparkle of her tears in her eyes.

'Livvy, don't, please,' he groaned, lifting his arms to take hold of her and then letting them drop to his sides again. It was too soon for such intimacies between them, he could sense that from Olivia's expression and yet, it was so damned hard not to be able to short-cut the awkwardness between them by taking her in his arms and *showing* her all the things he wanted to show her.

'If you'd rather I didn't stay here...' he began but Olivia shook her head immediately.

'No, the girls would be devastated if you didn't...' Without looking at him she told him hurriedly, 'I'll make up the spare room bed for you.'

Caspar knew what she was saying.

'If that's what you prefer,' he accepted.

'I—I think we both need time, Caspar. We need to talk, to—'

'It's all right. I understand,' Caspar interrupted her.

'Where did it go wrong for us, Caspar?' Olivia asked him achingly, unable to stop herself.

'I don't know,' Caspar admitted. 'Perhaps we simply didn't value and nourish what we had enough.'

He *had* changed somehow, Olivia recognised; become softer, gentler, as though... A small dark shadow of fear touched her heart. Could another woman be responsible for the change she sensed in him?

He had come back to *her* she reminded herself

firmly. To *her* and to their children, and Caspar wasn't the only one who had changed...discovered... *learned*... The old Olivia she had been would have immediately demanded an answer to her suspicions, immediately challenged and exhumed everything he might say, driven by her fear of losing him and her insecurity. But she was wiser now and stronger, too, and for now it was enough that he was here and that both of them believed they had something worth working together for and building on.

THEY TALKED late into the night about the problems in their marriage and their feelings about their past and their hopes for the future.

'It's late and you look exhausted,' Caspar eventually told Olivia tenderly. 'I keep forgetting that you've been ill.'

'I'm fine now,' Olivia reassured him.

They went upstairs together parting on the landing to go to their separate beds without Caspar making any attempt to kiss her, Olivia noticed.

The whole house felt different now that he was home—warmer, safer...more complete somehow. Or was that more how she felt?

AT FIRST when Olivia woke up alone in the large bed that she and Caspar had bought together she couldn't understand just why she should feel so cocooned in such a state of emotional happiness and then she remembered Caspar had come home. Like a child with a much longed for and still unwrapped present she hugged the knowledge to her sleepily, savouring the sweetness of what was still to come.

In the spare room Caspar, too, was awake. The welcome the girls had given him, the look in Olivia's eyes when she had first seen him, were things to cherish—like those who had given them to him. He was aware of a tremendous sense of protectiveness towards his wife and children, a feeling of being empowered by his love for them. He thought about Olivia sleeping alone in their bedroom. He wanted to go to her but he worried that it would be the wrong thing to do.

Olivia glanced at her bedside clock. It was three o'clock in the morning and she was wide awake and suddenly calmly sure of what she wanted to do.

As she opened the door to the spare room Caspar turned his head to look at her. As she walked towards him he sat up in the bed, reaching out his hand towards her.

'Maybe I'm doing the wrong thing and it's too soon for this,' she told him softly, 'but I've missed you….'

Her body quivered as he placed his hand inside her robe against the bare flesh of her waist. His touch felt both comfortingly familiar and shockingly exciting.

'I've missed you, too,' Caspar responded and realised how much he meant it.

'Perhaps that's been part of the problem,' she suggested. 'That somehow, somewhere we *have* both missed one another and misunderstood one another. I don't want it to be too late for us, Caspar. For us to have lost what we had that was so special...'

His hand was stroking her skin with gentle reassuring movements that made her want to close her eyes and purr with pleasure. As she looked down into his eyes she reached out automatically to trace the line of his jaw. When he turned his head and kissed her fingertips a surge of forgotten sweetly hot desire raced through her. Half afraid of what she was experiencing and wanting, she tried to lighten the intensity of her feelings telling him mundanely, 'My feet are freezing....'

Immediately Caspar released her to flip back the bedcovers, silently inviting her to join him in the bed.

Her cold feet had always been a joke between them, but Olivia had never thought there would come a day when she was glad to have them.

Accepting his invitation, she shrugged off her robe and burrowed down beneath the duvet, closing her eyes in bliss as Caspar took hold of her feet and gently chaffed some warmth back into them whilst she snuggled up to him.

'I thought we weren't going to do this,' Caspar teased her tenderly as he wrapped his arms around the welcoming warmth of her body and gently kissed her.

'Mmm... Well, if you're not sure we should...' Olivia responded huskily.

As he brushed his lips against hers, Caspar smiled.

He had never felt more sure of wanting anything or anyone than he felt right now.

'*Now* it feels like I've come home,' he whispered softly to her as he drew her even closer.

It was like recapturing the magic of their early days together, Caspar recognised as he luxuriated in Olivia's response to him and his own fierce desire for her. Their hunger for one another took them both off guard, keeping the intensity of their lovemaking at the kind of peak Caspar had thought was in their past.

It was almost dawn when Olivia finally fell asleep in his arms, her mouth still curled in the smile she had given him when he had told her how much he loved her.

'Hurry up, you two, otherwise you're going to be late for school....'

Over Amelia's and Alex's heads, Caspar and Olivia exchanged rueful looks. Both of them knew how close *they* had come to oversleeping this morning *and* why!

There were still things they needed to discuss—they both knew that—but lying in each other's arms they had made themselves and one another a vow that from now on their lives together would come first.

'I could work part-time,' Olivia had suggested hesitantly as they lay entwined together, their bodies heavy with satisfaction.

'You don't have to do that for me, Livvy,' Caspar had protested.

'It wouldn't be for you,' Olivia had corrected him. 'It would be for *us*, for *all* of us…you, me, the girls and whatever other children we might have.'

'Other children?' Caspar had demanded bemused.

'Mmm… Two more, perhaps,' Olivia had told him dreamily. 'Well, three is an awkward number and if we have them close together… It would be nice to have boys this time as well, although I don't really mind.'

These last few days at home with her father had given her time to think not just about the past but about the future as well. She was sure now just what she wanted from life for herself and, more importantly, what she wanted for those close to her, the children they already had and those she hoped she and Caspar would have.

'Have you thought about how we're going to finance this extended family?' Caspar had demanded ruefully.

Reaching up to wrap her arms around him and kiss him Olivia had told him happily, 'Oh, we'll find a way.'

As he had held her, Caspar could have sworn he almost saw a small dark shadow melt away and that he was seeing Olivia as he had always dreamed she could be, free of the pain of the past, free to share his love. Now as he waited for Amelia and Alex to gather their school things together he thanked fate for ensuring that he could meet the love, the second chance

Olivia was offering him, openly and honestly without any hidden secrets between them and equally silently he thanked Molly as well.

As she handed the girls their coats Olivia put on her own, too.

'I'm coming with you,' she told Caspar with a warm smile.

'*Now* we're like a *proper* family,' Alex beamed as they all left the house together.

A proper family! As she tucked her hand through Caspar's arm, Olivia thought how good those words sounded.

BEN'S FUNERAL CORTEGE made its solemn way towards the church. It had been agreed that none of the younger children of the family should be at the grave side and Olivia had given Jenny a look of liquid love and gratitude when the older woman had asked her if she would mind staying at Queensmead with all the little ones.

'Thank you for that,' Olivia had told Jenny gratefully. 'I don't think I could have borne to be there, Jenny. It would have felt too hypocritical. I can't grieve for him—not really, and...'

She had stopped speaking, shaking her head, knowing that Jenny understood.

Jack, seated inside one of the cars, tensed and leaned closer to the window as they drove through Haslewich. He knew it was unlikely that he *would* see

Annalise. She would be at school, but still his heart hammered against his ribs. He had tried to ring her several times but she had never answered either his calls or his letters. He ached with the pain of losing her and with the pain of wanting her.

ANNALISE KNEW all about Ben's funeral. His death had been the talk of the town. Unable to concentrate on her schoolwork, she gazed out of the classroom window. Jack would be here at home in Haslewich now. Tears filled her eyes. Angrily she brushed them away. She *wasn't* going to cry over him. He wasn't *worth* it. Not after the way he had lied to her and she was never, ever going to fall in love with or trust a man again. Never...

BEN'S HALF-BROTHER, Saul and Nick Crighton's father, Hugh, read Ben's will. There were bequests to all of Ben's grandchildren and Jon mentally gave a small prayer of thanks as he remembered the furious battle he had had with his father to ensure that Olivia was included along with his own daughters.

Louise and Katie would not have minded a single jot if they had not inherited anything but Olivia would have taken it as yet another rejection which in effect it would have been.

There was a bequest to Ruth, Ben's sister, of some family archives and she flashed Jon a brief rueful look and shook her head as though chiding him. There were various other small bequests, but the bulk of his estate Ben had left to his eldest son David…with the exception of Queensmead, which he had willed to his grandson Max.

Jon could almost feel the collective sigh of relief from the assembled listeners as this last bequest was read out, but instead of looking relieved Max was frowning and standing up, holding up his hand in a request for silence before beginning, 'I'm sure it's no secret to most of you here that prior to his death Ben had made it plain that he no longer wanted to leave Queensmead to me. I was, after all, only his second choice. In reality he wanted Queensmead to go to his elder son and I'm afraid that I infuriated and antagonised him so much towards the end of his life that he had decided to leave Queensmead to charity—any charity rather than to allow me to have it. The fact that he died before he could make any such arrangements does not alter my view that he *wished* to make them and I believe that it would be morally wrong of me to accept his bequest under such circumstances.

'However, my wife Maddy loves this house.' His voice dropped, his eyes shadowing. 'In the circumstances, what I would propose to do is to have Queensmead independently valued and provided I can afford to do so, buy it and pass the sale money over to Ben's estate.'

He stopped as David stood up and walked over to him telling him firmly, 'Thank you, Max. We all appreciate your honesty, but when it comes to moral obligations—' he gave Max a brief smile '—all of us here know just how much my father was morally obliged to Maddy and everything that she did for him.'

As everyone started to murmur their assent and nod their heads, David's smile widened.

'What Max says about my father's desire to change his will, though, is quite correct and therefore…I think the fairest and most just course of action would be—' he paused and looked first at Max and then at Jon '—would be for the deeds of Queensmead to be transferred into Maddy's name and the house and its contents to be handed into her safe keeping.'

For a moment there was silence and then someone—David didn't know who—started to clap and within seconds the whole room was clapping and cheering. And Max, who was standing less than three feet away from him, looked at him with his heart in his eyes as they filled with unashamed tears.

Beside him Jon was thumping him on the back and declaring with delight, 'David that was a decision worthy of Solomon,' whilst Jack was watching him with pride and love.

'A decision worthy of Solomon indeed,' Honor agreed lovingly later when he described the scene to her.

David returned her smile as he drew her closer to him. They had heard the previous day that as far as this test could indicate, their baby was healthy and sound.

NICK PUT DOWN the glass of wine he was holding without tasting it. Nothing in life had any taste for him any more...without Sara. He woke up at night reaching for her, *aching* for her, and the wound that had supposedly been healing so well had developed a secondary infection which had caused his doctor to frown and make worried comments about the efficiency of his immunity system.

A heavy-duty course of antibiotics had routed out the infection but nothing could remove the pain from his heart.

'If she matters so much to you, why the hell don't you do something about it?'

Nick tensed as Saul confronted him.

'You don't know what you're talking about,' he told his brother rudely.

Saul refused to take offence.

'You don't think so?' he countered. 'I've been there before you, Nick,' Saul told him.

'You don't understand,' Nick told him bitterly.

'I understand that you're sick with love and too much of a coward or a fool to do anything about it,' Saul returned with gritty asperity.

Saul knew he was taking a dangerous risk, but Nick was his brother and he couldn't simply stand to one

side and watch him suffer out of some idiotic stubborn
pride.

Saul saw from the hot flash of anger illuminating
Nick's eyes that he had hit a nerve. He watched him
anxiously as he turned on his heel and walked away.

'Any luck?' Tullah asked her husband as she came
over to join him.

'Well, I wouldn't call it luck exactly,' Saul confessed, 'but I certainly hit something.'

'Do you think Bobbie's right and it's that girl who
was working at the restaurant?'

'Oh, I wasn't foolhardy enough to ask him *that*
question,' Saul laughed. 'He's got a pretty mean right.'
He rubbed his jaw reminiscently thinking of their
fights as young boys as he spoke, and Tullah shook
her head disapprovingly.

IT RAINED unceasingly the whole drive down to
Bournemouth and Nick arrived two hours later than
he had expected and in a foul temper, cursing both his
brother's and his own folly.

It had been Olivia who had given him the name and
address of Sara's grandfather, raising her eyebrows a
little when he explained who he was trying to contact
and raising them even higher when he was forced to
admit why.

'Tania's stepgranddaughter was here in Haslewich?'
she had exclaimed, wrinkling her forehead. 'But...'

'Livvy, please don't ask,' Nick had begged her.

'And don't tell anyone else why I was here, either....
Please...' he had demanded abruptly.

Tania proved every bit as silly and selfish as Nick
had expected, alternately pouting and flirting whilst
she complained about her daughter and son.

'Livvy hasn't been very well,' Nick couldn't resist
informing her.

'Not well?' Sara's grandfather had frowned. 'What
exactly's been wrong?'

'A very bad bout of flu,' Nick had told them.

'Flu? Oh that's something that's catching,' Tania
had protested. 'My poor chest is so weak. My doctor
has warned me that I must take every precaution not
to expose myself to that kind of virus.'

Nick had smiled thinly without offering any comment. His feelings for Sara were making him feel savage with pain and he ached to tell Tania what he
thought of her and the way she had poisoned Sara's
mind against Crighton men.

At first Sara's grandfather was reluctant to tell him
where Sara was but, in the end, he relented.

It wasn't long to Christmas and every available
flight to the Caribbean was fully booked, but Nick was
determined he was going to get there even if it meant
disguising himself as luxury goods and flying out
freight.

In the end he didn't have to go to quite such lengths.
An impassioned call to an old client calling in a favour

bought him a grossly overpriced seat on a private jet belonging to a friend of the friend.

To his surprise when he finally cleared customs at the airport, there was a man waiting for him carrying a card with his name on it.

Frowning Nick approached him. He was tall and grey-haired, sharp-eyed and hostile as he refused to shake Nick's hand.

He introduced himself tersely, 'Richard Lanyon, Sara's father.'

Nick froze. Compared with this formidable-looking man in his immaculate tropical whites, he felt jet-lagged and grubby and at a decided disadvantage.

'Sara's grandfather rang to warn us that you were on your way,' he explained. 'What do you want with my daughter, Crighton?'

For a moment Nick was tempted not to reply but he had come too far—endured too much.

'What does any man want with the woman he loves?' he responded equally brusquely.

Richard Lanyon was frowning.

'You *love* her? According to Sara...' He stopped.

'According to Sara, what?' Nick challenged him grimly.

'I think that's something you'd better ask Sara herself,' the older man was telling him. He was smiling at Nick now, placing his hand on Nick's arm as he guided him through the milling throng around the airport.

'Sara's been spending the day with some friends of ours on their yacht. Her mother's got a room prepared for you. I hope you are ready for the questions she's going to ask you.' He was smiling broadly at Nick now, so that some of Nick's own tension began to evaporate—but only some!

In the end, Sara's mother didn't ask him anything, simply smiling at him as she showed him to a blissfully cool room, insisting that he was to make himself at home before saying softly, 'Ah, yes…now I understand….'

SARA HAD REFUSED the offer of a lift home from the harbour. It was only a shortish walk through the town and along the beach and at this time of the evening the air was just beginning to feel pleasantly cool. Carrying her deck shoes she let the sand melt through her toes, her body felt physically tired but nothing could ease her ceaseless, constant mental agonising over Nick.

Richard had told Nick that Sara would probably walk home along the beach but he had almost given her up when he finally saw her. She was walking languidly towards him, her head bowed as she looked out to sea so that she hadn't seen him. Levering himself away from the bleached driftwood on which he had been sitting waiting, Nick set out towards her.

Sara sensed rather than saw his presence, tensing as she saw the shape of a man coming towards her out of the gathering shadows, her heart leaping like a salmon making its final desperate bid to seek home as her brain accepted what her eyes were trying to tell her.

'Nick...? Nick...!'

She had barely finished saying his name before she was in his arms clinging ecstatically to him as he kissed her, returning his kiss with tiny keening noises of pleasure as her mouth opened beneath his. They kissed with the frantic desperation only known to lovers who had feared they had lost one another, stroking, touching, murmuring their joy and disbelief over and over again.

'What are you *doing* here? Why...?' Sara began when she could finally speak coherently.

'I couldn't bear to be without you,' Nick told her truthfully. 'Even if you didn't want my love I had to come.'

'Your *love*? But it was just sex,' Sara whispered.

Nick closed his eyes and shuddered.

'Please don't tell me that,' he begged her passionately. 'Sara, there's no way what we shared could *ever* be just sex. Take it from me. Let me show you, prove it to you. Let me...' He stopped as he felt her start to tremble.

'I'm sorry,' he began to apologise hoarsely, 'I shouldn't—'

'No. No...you mustn't stop,' Sara protested. 'Oh, Nick, don't you know how much I've longed to hear

you say that? How often I've hated myself for fanta-
sizing that you were saying it…for behaving like a
besotted teenager? Oh, Nick, Nick…' she cried as she
clung to him.

'Your parents are waiting for us,' he protested as
she unfastened his shirt and slid her hands inside it,
splaying them across his naked chest, her own rising
and falling with sharp excitement as she touched him.

'*I* can't wait,' she told him boldly. 'I've already
waited too long. Oh, Nick…' His name was wrenched
from her lips as she moved enticingly against him and
felt his immediate response. There were problems
ahead of them that they would have to find a way to
solve, especially with his work, but somehow they
would find a way.

'Your parents have invited me to stay with them,'
Nick told her thickly. 'But right now I wish I'd booked
a hotel room.'

'Who needs a room?' Sara whispered wickedly to
him, 'When there's a perfectly good boat empty right
there.'

Looking over his shoulder Nick saw the boat she
meant tied up at a small jetty.

'We can't,' he protested, but Sara's eyes were full
of mischief and so very, very much more.

'Mmm…this is nice,' Sara murmured half an hour later
as they lay naked in one another's arms enjoying the

gentle movement of the boat as it rocked with the current.

'As nice as this,' Nick teased her as he moved very deliberately against her.

'No, not as nice as that,' Sara whispered back, her voice changing and becoming soft and husky with desire.

'Oh, Nick, I can hardly bear to think of how awful it would have been if you hadn't come to find me.'

'Don't think about it,' Nick commanded her masterfully. 'Don't think about anything apart from us,' he whispered sensually. 'And this…' As he kissed her mouth and then her naked breasts, Sara sighed her pleasure into the still, night air.

IN THEIR APARTMENT Sara's father frowned as he glanced at his watch.

'Surely Nick must have caught up with Sara by now?'

'Yes, dear, I'm sure he has,' his wife agreed with a small rueful smile that caused him to check and then shake his head as she laughed tenderly at him.

EPILOGUE

'ARE YOU SURE this is what you want? There's still time to change your mind, you know,' Max told Maddy as they stood together.

'I'm sure,' Maddy confirmed serenely as she smiled up at him and handed him the securely wrapped bundle that was their son of a few months and watched the love illuminate his face as he held him. She already knew there was a very strong tie between this baby and Max. Right from the moment of his birth he had bonded with Max and he, in turn, adored his son. It was as though the baby knew somehow just how much Max had needed the reassurance of his love.

Behind them in the congregation David was sitting proudly with his own family, Honor and Olivia exchanging mutually understanding and rueful looks as David, Amelia and Alex fought over who was to hold Honor and David's ten-day-old daughter.

It was too soon for Olivia to tell Honor that she hoped she would soon be announcing an addition to her own family, but as Caspar quietly reminded his daughters that it was their grandfather's turn to hold the baby, Olivia squeezed his hand. Tenderly Caspar turned to smile at her.

So often these last few weeks he had felt as though he were seeing a completely new Olivia, an Olivia who had stepped so joyously out of the shadows of her own unhappiness that it caught at his heart sometimes to recognise just how sad she had been.

It had been at her suggestion that they had made arrangements to spend the summer with Caspar's family.

'You're definitely sure?' Max checked with Maddy again as the vicar came towards them.

'Positive.' She laughed.

As he took the baby from them and the service began Max held his breath only expelling it properly once the baby's name had been pronounced.

'Benjamin Matthew Crighton.'

Benjamin *Matthew!* Max's eyes had widened when Maddy had told him shortly after the birth what she wanted their son to be called.

'Ben's name?' he had questioned uncertainly.

'Ben's name and his brother's,' Maddy had agreed.

And now as the vicar formally named their son she could almost feel the wave of peace and love that rippled through the old church. It had been Leo who had casually told her about the two little boys he had thought he had seen playing in Grandfather Ben's study.

'They were wearing funny clothes,' Leo had told her, 'like in a photograph.'

Maddy had simply said calmly that if he saw them again he must tell her.

But when she mentioned the matter to Honor, Honor had sighed and she had asked her quietly, 'Have you seen them, too?'

Honor had shaken her head.

'No. But I thought I heard them when you and I were clearing away Ben's things.'

Without saying anything to Max, Maddy had carefully cleaned her way through the whole house, talking to Ben as she did so, reassuring him that his memory and his home were safe.

'They've gone,' Honor had told her positively the next time she had visited.

'Poor Ben,' Maddy had sighed sadly. 'He was always so very alone and so very sad.'

'He isn't sad any more,' Honor had offered gently.

Maddy smiled as she received her son back from the vicar. The names she had given him were her gift to Queensmead for all of its gifts to her...a gift of love for a gift of love.

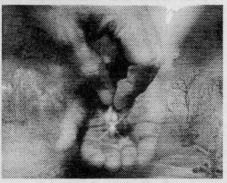